UNDER
CONTRACT

UNDER CONTRACT

A Lauren Vellequette Mystery

Jennifer L. Jordan

CLOVER VALLEY PRESS, LLC
DULUTH, MINNESOTA

Book 2 in the Lauren Vellequette Mystery Series

Clover Valley Press, LLC
6286 Homestead Rd.
Duluth, MN 55804-9621
USA

Cover design by Stacie Smith-Whaley, i.e. design

Author photo by Ginny Rutherford Photography

Printed in the United States of America on acid-free paper. Sustainable Forestry Initiative® (SFI®) Certified Sourcing.

Library of Congress Control Number: 2016938929

Print Edition ISBN: 978-0-9973643-0-9
Digital Edition ISBN: 978-0-9973643-1-6

Books by Jennifer L. Jordan

Lauren Vellequette Mystery Series

Under Contract

Killed in Escrow

Kristin Ashe Mystery Series

If No One's Looking

Selective Memory

Disorderly Attachments

Unbearable Losses

Commitment to Die

Existing Solutions

A Safe Place to Sleep

There was something spectacular about the fire, almost spiritual.

I watched as streams of water arced toward the flames, colliding at the intersection of beauty and tragedy.

I never imagined violence could feel so pleasurable, all but sensual.

I could have stayed for days.

Unfortunately, a shout from Dennis McBride brought me back to attention.

I turned, and he glared at me. "Meet me in my office at eight o'clock. You're getting a partner."

Partner.

I did not like the sound of that word.

What the hell had gone wrong?

CHAPTER 1

Eleven days earlier, Dennis McBride had hired me, on a Friday morning in the second week of September.

"Two houses gone. Do you mind?" He removed his sweatshirt, loosened his belt, and whipped down his zipper before I could reply. "I have a meeting with investors after we're finished here."

I steadfastly maintained eye contact.

He continued in a calmer voice. "Try to ignore the mess. The wife and I are between houses. We sold one in Cherry Hills, had to be out by the end of August, and we can't get into the new house until next week. Everything we own is in semi containers, and we're camped out at the Marriott. My Audi's so full of crap, I can barely squeeze in to drive. How's that for a sorry tale!"

He gestured at the clutter that had spilled into his work environment.

The corporate offices for McBride Homes were located on the seventh floor of a mid-rise in the Denver Tech Center, off I-25 and Belleview Avenue. Dennis held down the southwest corner, and beyond two walls of floor to ceiling windows, he had a panoramic view of the Rocky Mountains, all the way to Pikes Peak.

The décor inside wasn't shabby either. The suburban office had wool carpet, cherry paneled wainscoting, crown molding, heavily textured walls in butter yellow, ceiling medallions, and antique iron sconces and light fixtures. The writing desk, hutch, bookshelf, filing cabinets, and banker's chair, all in cherry, added to the rich look.

Too bad disorder suffocated the design.

A duffel bag, tennis racket, golf clubs, shoes, umbrellas, and pull cart were tangled together in a corner by the door, while balls, bats, mitts, and baseball memorabilia were clumped on the couch. A fireproof safe sat on top of the desk, crumpling blueprints below it, and clothes were strewn across the room.

I tendered a faint smile. "Couldn't you move into one of your company's houses temporarily?"

Dennis yanked plastic wrapping off a lavender, long-sleeve shirt. "I don't have a vacant one. I don't break ground without a contract."

"That's good news, that the homes are selling," I said brightly.

"Tell my wife. She has room service and housekeeping, but can't stop complaining about the hotel closet. It's not big enough for her, not by a football field. Who knew? I've barely had time to get to know her, much less measure her wardrobe. Usually, when we're together, she isn't wearing much," he said, with a randy chuckle.

"You haven't been married long?"

He twisted his wedding ring, a titanium band with blue topaz and diamonds. "What's today? Friday. That makes it six days."

"Congratulations."

Dennis shook his head, mystified. "Damned if I know how it happened. I broke off a relationship in February. Marla and I met in March. I proposed in June. We tied the knot in September. I'm scared to think about what's next."

He was in no hurry to put on his shirt, all the while daring me to look away, which I did, happily.

Too much chest hair, too early in the morning.

A blonde-gray mat on the pecs of an offensive lineman who hadn't played in thirty years—not a pretty sight. He had the same color hair on his head, and he'd brushed it up and back, to where it fell just below the ears. His square head and jaw were proportional to his large frame, and a broken nose added to the hardy look. A distinctive birthmark covered his right cheekbone.

I had to look at something other than my client's half-naked body.

For the time being, I chose the mounted warthog head near my feet. Out of the corner of my eye, it seemed as if the animal's body were stowed below the carpet, a less unsettling visual than muscle turned to flab.

"Is this your first marriage?"

"One and only. Make yourself comfortable wherever you can."

I chose the only vacant flat surface that would bear weight and sat, awkwardly. "What do you want me to do?"

"I want you to find out who's trying to ruin me."

"The police don't have any suspects?" I said, picking up a thread of conversation we'd begun on the phone the previous day.

"My houses burned to the ground, and they're treating me like a suspect. I almost forgot to offer, you want something to drink?"

"What do you have?"

"You're sitting on it," he said, gesturing toward the red and white plastic cooler.

I opened the top of my "chair" to a stash of hard liquor, all at room temperature, no ice. "I'll pass. How about you?"

"Better not. I don't want the investors to smell booze on my breath."

I replaced the lid and repositioned myself. "You have to admit, two fires in three months is suspicious."

Dennis put on his shirt, buttoned it, and rolled up the sleeves. "Damn right it is. That's why I know someone's out to get me. One fire's bad luck. Two has to be intentional."

"Or worse luck."

"No chance. The first investigation, at Landry, everyone was nice and friendly. This time, at Southfield, they won't tell me anything, other than the cause of the fire is undetermined. A friend of mine who went through an arson investigation warned me that they'll be digging into my financials and interviewing anyone they can. Neighbors, partners, employees. I'd be a fool to sit by while they tear into my business and personal life."

"You made the right move, calling me."

"Why would anyone think I set those fires? How does losing two properties under contract benefit me?"

I pulled a notepad from my purse and began to scribble. "The fire at Southfield happened when?"

"Two nights ago. At dusk."

"And the one at Landry?"

He sauntered over to the revolving rack next to his wastebasket and selected a dark blue tie, which he knotted expertly. "About three months ago, on June 11. Two weeks before the house was supposed to close."

"Have you considered hiring a security guard? I could make a recommendation."

"What kind of image would that portray? I sell people on the idea of family-based communities. I can't have armed goons running around the neighborhood."

"They don't have to be armed, and usually they don't run unless they're chasing someone," I said evenly.

"Forget it," he said, in an end-of-discussion tone.

I sighed. "Okay. Let's start with details about the first fire, the one at Landry. Tell me everything you know."

Dennis sat, leaned back, and balanced his bare feet on the desk. "We were building one of our standard, two-story models in the Northwest Neighborhood at Landry. We're calling the collection Hunter's Field. At completion, we'll have seventy single-family homes. Price range, midfours."

"What day of the week did the house catch fire?"

He laced his fingers and put his hands behind his head. "Sunday. One of my workers dropped by the job site around noon to pick up tools for a 'honey-do' project. He saw flames and called 911. Fire trucks came in five minutes, but the structure was a total loss."

"What's the exact address?"

"1125 Trinidad Street."

I shifted uncomfortably on the cooler. Good thing I hadn't worn a short skirt, or I would have had impressions from the lid's bubbles on my thighs. My cropped-length, soft seersucker pants provided at least a little protection. "I'll go by the site after I leave here."

"Feel free, but there's not much to look at."

"What's the name of the worker who discovered the fire?"

"Glenn Warner."

"Do you have any reason to suspect him?"

"None. He's one of my best foremen. I've known him twenty years."

"Did fire investigators label the Landry fire suspicious?"

"Not at the time. They chalked it up to oily rags and sawdust left behind by a crew from Stan's Flooring Company, which ticked me off. Have you seen how much sawdust comes from hardwood floor installation? Bags and bags. Glenn told them not to toss anything into our Dumpsters because of the fire hazard. They were supposed to dispose of sawdust and rags off-site. So much for that plan. They admitted they left them in the house over the weekend. By Sunday, they caught fire."

"Did you agree with investigators, that the fire at Landry was accidental?"

Dennis sat upright. "At the time, I did. I've seen fires like that before, but someone always smelled something and caught them before they could do any damage. It's a miracle there aren't more fires at construction sites, with all the flammables and combustibles. You have to watch what you're doing, but I can't seem to drill that into my employees, much less subcontractors. They get sloppy, cut corners, you know how it is."

"Did the fire set off an alarm inside the house?"

"No. The hardwired system wasn't connected."

"Two weeks before closing?" I said, unable to contain my surprise. "What about battery backups in the detectors?"

"We hadn't installed them. We do now."

"Was the hardwood floor treatment finished at the time of the fire?"

"Just about. Stan's had installed the floors, stained them, and applied two coats of polyurethane. A spark from an electric outlet may have ignited wood dust, or the oily rags spontaneously combusted. Investigators couldn't say for sure."

"Had you hired Stan's before?"

"We've used them for years."

"Are you still using them?"

"For the time being. They do good work, on time, and they have a clean showroom where my buyers can make selections."

"Did Stan's lose equipment?"

"Quite a bit of it."

"Have they bought new equipment?"

"I don't know," he said irritably. "They have rotating crews. I can't tell who uses what."

"Could you find out?"

"I could get Glenn to look into it." He rummaged around on his desk until he located a Blackberry.

"Nothing struck you as unusual at the time of the Landry fire? Nothing before or after?"

5

Dennis propped his elbow on the desk, inserted his chin into his right hand, and stared ahead thoughtfully. After a moment, he spoke loudly. "Come to think of it, Glenn did mention something about cardboard."

I felt a surge. "Cardboard?"

"The Dumpster should have been full of it, from cabinets and appliances our guys unpacked on Friday. On Sunday, there was no cardboard in the trash."

"Maybe someone moved the cardboard into the house and used it as fuel for the fire."

Dennis emitted a snort of derision. "More likely, some bum took it for his shelter. They trespass on my property all the time."

I returned to my notes, slightly deflated. "Who had a contract on the Landry house?"

"Barry Christensen. Stand-up guy."

"Could Barry have torched the house to get out of the contract?"

Dennis shook his head. "Never happen. He loves Hunter's Field and Landry. We moved him into a house down the street. A contract fell through, and we had one available. Everything worked out."

"Has the insurance company settled with you on the first fire?"

"Not yet, but we're close."

"At fair value?"

His lips tightened. "It'll do. You know how it goes. They say a number. I say a number. We both piss and moan. Eventually we arrive at a figure."

"Okay, let's talk about the house in Southfield. What's the exact address of that one?"

"3022 Visalia Street."

"How far along was it when it burned?"

"We were finishing up plumbing, electric, and HVAC. Drywall installation was scheduled for next week."

"Who legally owns it?"

"McBride Homes until we turn over title, but we have a purchase agreement with Fritz Jubera. Now there's a piece of work. He tried to make a custom home out of one of our standard models. Sixty-two change orders. We moved walls, doors, windows, electric. I don't know what I got myself into."

"Why did you agree to the customization?"

"Do you know the markup on changes?" he said, flashing a greedy smile. "But the hassle . . . "

Dennis retrieved a baseball from underneath a pile of papers on his desk. "Tell me about it! This guy's a real know-it-all. He's insulted every one of my employees who's had contact with him, cussed them out for no reason. My salesgirls won't deal with him anymore. They cry every time they see his Hummer pull up to the model home. He's threatened me with lawsuits on three occasions, over minor glitches. I offered to let him out of his contract. Full refund of earnest money, option deposits, change order deposits, the works. Full escrow back, every cent. I've never done that in my life."

I stretched my neck, trying to earn relief for my sloping shoulders. "Fritz refused?"

Dennis nodded grimly, tossing the ball from hand to hand. "He estimates he has $30,000 in appreciation waiting for him at closing. I can't stand the son of a bitch. I was looking forward to his closing on September 21. I couldn't wait to get rid of him."

"It wouldn't have ended there. The closing's the middle of the relationship with a builder, not the end."

"You're probably right. Jubera would have had a twenty-page punch list and sued me if I didn't fix every little problem. I can't stand the thought of that jerk living in one of my properties. I'd almost rather have it burn to the ground than turn it over to him."

"Legally, you don't have to rebuild?"

Dennis set the ball on his desk with a decisive smack. "Not for him. In the purchase agreement, we promise substantial completion of the property six months after the start of framing. If it's delayed past that, either party can terminate the contract. I'm sending Fritz a notice of termination this week."

"You can't complete the house within the six-month time frame?"

He smiled slyly. "I can, but I won't. This is my chance to get rid of the jackass."

"Could Fritz Jubera have set fire to the Southfield house?"

Dennis McBride didn't hesitate. "To spite me? Damn right."

"Do you have any other people who hate you?"

He bellowed with laughter. "I couldn't begin to name them all."

"Try," I said pleasantly. "Any ex-employees?"

He stared at me as if I were brain-dead. "This is the construction trade. We fire as many people as we hire."

"Could I look over the employment records of every employee you've fired in the last six months?"

"Be my guest. I'll have my human resources gal make copies."

"Meanwhile, let's compile a list of other people who might wish you harm."

"How much time do you have?" he said, almost proudly.

Two minutes later, I had the names of nineteen people who had ongoing feuds with Dennis McBride.

Those were the ones he could remember off the top of his head, but he promised more.

"Do you have any suggestions about where to begin?" I said, disconcerted by the volume.

He came around the desk, leaned over me, and flicked at the first name on the page. "Daphne Cartwright."

I looked up. "Any particular reason Daphne—"

Dennis McBride spoke over my words. "She thinks I tried to kill her family."

CHAPTER 2

When people ask what I do for a living, I have a hard time answering. For the past eighteen months, I've straddled two worlds, hiring out as a residential real estate broker and as a private investigator.

With twenty-plus years of experience, I can complete the real estate work with one arm tied behind my back. After a twelve week community college course, a brief apprenticeship, and sixteen cases, let's just say I'm gaining confidence as a private investigator.

Sometimes I have to pinch myself to prove that I'm leading this life at all.

The transition hasn't been an easy one.

It took surviving my own death scare to figure out what I wanted to do with my life.

Without giving career options much conscious thought, I fell into the world of real estate after dropping out of college. I began in a six-agent office as a secretary and followed the natural path of obtaining my license and building a client base. The next fifteen years passed in a blur, as I earned listings, accrued commissions, invested in properties, amassed a fortune . . . and lost myself.

By my midthirties, I felt a disquieting sense of, "Is this all there is?"

One day, a doctor answered with, "No, there could be less."

He diagnosed me with breast cancer and ordered a double mastectomy and rounds of chemotherapy.

That was six years ago.

I spent four years crawling back from the disfigurement and drugs, only to have my parents die of cancer in the same year. Non-Hodgkin's lymphoma took my mother, lung cancer felled my father, and in the year that followed their deaths, everyone I came into contact with was the worse for it.

One day, I caught myself snapping at a girl at the deli when she put Swiss cheese instead of provolone on my sandwich. I apologized at once and, in that moment, felt something shift.

The next day, I signed up for the P.I. course.

I graduated with high praise from the SOB instructor and apprenticed with him for six months before branching out on my own.

Today, with the assistance of a part-time employee, I work out of a three-room suite in a four-story 1970s building at Colorado Boulevard and Mexico Avenue. Nothing spiffy, by any means. I rarely look out the narrow slits that pass for windows and don't dare open them because of highway noise. I'm not too fond of the fluorescent lighting, low ceiling beams with popcorn texture, white walls bordering on gray, or gray carpet bordering on brown, but I have ample parking and a month-to-month lease that's never risen above $500.

At last I have a job I love, and it doesn't hurt that contacts from my years in real estate feed my fledgling detective agency.

In fact, I'd met Dennis McBride once before, in passing. About two years earlier, one of my clients had purchased a McBride Home in Golden. He and Dennis stayed in touch through rounds of golf, and when Dennis mentioned the arsons, the client recommended my services.

That led to this, and here I was, the proud recipient of a $5,000 retainer check from McBride Homes.

As I walked out of the lobby of Dennis McBride's office building and into the blinding midmorning sun, I felt uncommonly contented.

Blue sky, not a cloud in sight, an expected high of seventy degrees in September—what could be better?

I took a seat near the fountain on the plaza, removed my jacket, loosened my sandals, adjusted the straps on my tan tank top, leaned back, and closed my eyes.

After a full minute of reflection, I straightened and reached into my purse for my notebook.

In block letters at the top of a fresh page, I wrote: First impressions.

Below that, I began to jot as fast as I could.

Something seemed off with Dennis McBride.

For reasons I couldn't articulate, I didn't trust him.

When had my apprehension begun?

Sometime before the laundry list of enemies surfaced.

Why had he hired me, anyway?

To stay one step ahead of arson investigators. But what if he was the arsonist?

Assuming the Landry fire was an accident, what if he'd used it as inspiration and set fire to the Southfield house?

He'd said it: He'd rather see 3022 Visalia Street burn to the ground than turn it over to Fritz Jubera.

Not the kind of candor I cared to hear on a first appointment.

If Dennis McBride were guilty, I'd have to turn him in to the authorities. That would be bad for business, but good for the soul.

What was the matter with me?

I was getting way ahead of myself, imagining clients as felons when I could cross that bridge when I came to it, if I came to it at all.

For now, I was anxious to get to the Landry site.

●●●

The Landry neighborhood had it all.

Ask any real estate agent.

All types of residences were sprinkled across the 1,866-acre former Air Force base. They sold in the $100,000s, the $200,000s, the $300,000s, the $400,000s, the $500,000s, and up to and above the $1 million mark. There was something for everyone: apartments, condos, duplexes, triplexes, townhomes, lofts, single-family homes, patio homes, and custom homes. Eighty-nine percent of the decommissioned base lay within Denver, while the other slice belonged to Aurora.

Who would have thought that Landry could blossom into such a vibrant, desirable place to live?

Probably not the soldiers who were once stationed at the base.

The first troops arrived in 1938, and the last departed in 1994. In between, Landry functioned as an Army post, an Air Force base, and a technical training and military readiness facility. For a time, after World War II, President Eisenhower treated Landry as his second home, a summer White House of sorts.

To date, the Landry Redevelopment Authority had spent $555 million and ten years preparing the base for reuse. They'd removed barbed wire, demolished 291 Air Force buildings, recycled five hundred thousand tons of concrete and runways, and laid thirty-four miles of new roads.

City planners were enraptured.

The redevelopment fit with their plans to contain Denver's outward sprawl. In a five-year period, Denver's urbanized area had spread 66 percent, while its population had grown only 15 percent. That had to be curbed. Yet, seemingly, nothing could slow down people's desire for amenities found only in new construction.

What a coup—to recapture a piece of land within existing city limits that could be developed without disrupting greenfields. Everyone had high hopes that the urban-infill neighborhood would become a model for the nation. At full build-out in five years, an estimated ten thousand residents and hundreds of businesses would occupy the land.

There was just one problem.

The land was far from pristine.

Sixty-five acres had served as a municipal trash landfill. The military had used another section of the base as a fire training zone, where soldiers placed waste materials and fuel on discarded aircraft and set them on fire. Bullets and fragments still remained in the outdoor firing range, spoiling the soil with lead. Below ground, steel and concrete storage tanks had held petroleum products, waste oils, and solvents. Ranging in size from 500 gallons to 126,000 gallons, forty-eight had been removed, but no one knew for certain how many remained.

And the list went on.

The redevelopment authority had identified eleven ground-water plumes contaminated with trichloroethylene (TCE), a cleaning solvent used to degrease metal parts. One extended an estimated three miles and held seventy gallons of TCE. When indoor air quality problems were found at an apartment complex on 11th Avenue, the Air Force installed depressurization units to release contaminants from the shallow soils beneath the building.

Government officials assured residents that these were merely precautionary measures. There was no acute risk, but they were unsure of the chronic risk, a mantra they would repeat often.

Enough with the negative, though.

Apparently, not everyone was concerned about pollution.

Landry home appreciation had averaged 11.5 percent per year, and property in Landry sold in thirty days, with multiple offers, versus ninety days for the rest of Denver and six months for the suburbs.

There were valid reasons for the rising prices and demand.

Landry was located near two major interstates, twenty minutes from downtown. It had one of the best public libraries in the state, two community colleges, a Town Center with shops and restaurants, an ice arena, an air and space museum, a community pool, a rec center, a golf course, and tree-lined boulevards and parkways.

Who could ask for anything more?

Daphne Cartwright could.

She wanted someone to take responsibility for the asbestos in the yard of her McBride Home.

•••

The trip to 1125 Trinidad Street, the site of the first fire, would have to wait for a few minutes.

I decided to pay a visit to Daphne Cartwright first.

Dennis McBride had given me her home address, and when I turned onto her street in the Hunter's Field subdivision in Landry, I didn't need to squint for house numbers.

The Cartwright home, at 1406 Rosemary Street, would have stood out on any block.

The house was ordinary enough, a two-story California contemporary covered in river rock and stucco. It would have been indistinguishable from neighboring homes, except for the yard, filled with signs.

Take a deep breath—while you can.

What's more important—economic development or my baby's health?

Something for everyone at Landry—ask about asbestos.

13

I parked in front of the house, walked up the concrete sidewalk, and threaded my way past a jogging stroller and wading pool before making it to the front door.

With slight apprehension, I rang the doorbell.

Three rings and four knocks later, I gave up and left one of my business cards tucked into the doorjamb.

On the back of it, I wrote a brief note explaining the point of my visit and asking Daphne to call at her earliest convenience.

That completed, I moved on to my next task.

I hurried down the Cartwright driveway, hopped in my Subaru Outback, and steered toward Trinidad Street.

Two blocks east, three blocks south, and I arrived at the site of the June 11 "accidental" fire.

Unfortunately, I was a few months too late.

At 1125 Trinidad, I found nothing but an empty lot surrounded by temporary chain-link fencing.

To be accurate, the lot wasn't entirely empty.

A two-car driveway led to nowhere, a rock pathway meandered around the side of the grounds, and a basement foundation awaited a rebuild.

The house next door, to the north, had siding stained black from the heat of the fire and a roof pockmarked from embers. The house to the south didn't seem to have sustained any damage, and families appeared to have moved into both properties, as evidenced by toys in the yards and cars in the driveways.

I thought a peculiar chemical smell hung in the air, but maybe that was my imagination.

At any rate, I made a smattering of notes and headed back to the office.

CHAPTER 3

Four hours later, Sasha Fuller stood in front of my desk, silent.

"Yes?" I said, without looking up.

"Can I have an advance on my paycheck?"

"I just paid you yesterday," I said, in what I hoped was a reasonable tone. "Nice try, though."

"I need more money."

I sighed and stopped reading.

I'd learned long ago that as soon as Sasha planted herself, there was no moving her until she got what she wanted. We'd met three months earlier when I spoke at one of her high school classes. The topic was real estate as a career, but I'd strayed into private investigation.

The same afternoon, Sasha arrived on my office doorstep—with blue and yellow hair—and volunteered to work as an unpaid intern. The position, at her insistence, soon turned into a ten-dollar-per-hour gig, and in her first thirty days of employment, she asked for a raise, pressed for her own cases, demanded paid holidays, campaigned for a new office, pushed for a company car, and begged for a credit card.

I'd lectured her repeatedly about her appearance, hired a clothing consultant, and sprung for a new wardrobe, all to no avail. Three weeks into her senior year at Central High, nothing could keep her from expressing herself in the most bizarre fashions, most of which highlighted the scar on her left leg.

Today's outfit consisted of a white linen skirt decorated in peace-sign appliqués, a black turtleneck, and military boots. The look matched her hair, now shiny black with patches of white, and her makeup, ghostly white with black lipstick and eyeliner. Time and again, I'd told Sasha that she was marring her natural beauty, especially with the nose and tongue jewelry, but she ignored me. It seemed as if she didn't want anyone to notice her high cheekbones, startling green eyes, or tall, perfectly proportioned figure.

I often wondered how I'd survived without her, and I knew she felt the same about me. I'd rescued her from evangelists—foster parents she referred to as the witch and the warden—and set her up in a studio apartment next to my one-bedroom unit. The arrangement had begun a few months back, and so far, so good. I hadn't drilled through the wall to install surveillance equipment, and I hoped she'd afforded me the same respect.

"What do you need money for?"

"Stuff."

"What kind of stuff?"

"Just stuff."

"You're not going to tell me what?"

She shook her head.

"You need to learn to budget, to stretch your money out so that it lasts two weeks, not two days."

"Does that mean you're not going to give me any money?"

"Not today," I said evenly. "You'll get more money in thirteen days."

After she huffed out of my office, I resumed my study of fire.

•••

Everything I knew firsthand about fire I'd learned during an arson investigation I'd conducted with the SOB private eye instructor.

An insurance company had hired the SOB to investigate a warehouse fire near the Stock Show Complex at I-70 and Washington Street, and in the end, we'd cleared the owner of the building but had brought charges against the tenants.

The Smiths (actually their real names) owned a gift basket company, and they'd filled the warehouse with baskets, ribbons, labels, packing materials, and goodies. Coffees and teas, nuts and chocolates, dried fruits and cheeses were stocked from floor to ceiling when the Smiths lost their biggest account.

Overnight, they had too much stock and not enough customers, when lo and behold, the building caught fire.

The Smiths claimed more than $100,000 in inventory losses, which they backed up with receipts.

The insurance company was days away from settling when the SOB and I discovered the allegedly burned items in a warehouse off I-70 and Havana Street. The breakthrough came after a routine interview with a receptionist at a nearby business who remembered a rental truck parked outside the Smiths' business a week before the fire. That led to us tailing the Smiths from their home in Aurora to their new base of operations, where a few days later they confessed to the police.

I never did hear whether they went to prison or escaped with probation and restitution.

In either case, the Smiths learned a hard lesson about the cycles of business, and I learned enough about fire to know what had sparked suspicion in the first place: the use of liquid accelerants. The giveaway was the pattern of the fire, which showed extreme damage from puddles of liquid and finger-like burn marks from spatter. In their haste to find a solution to their troubles, the Smiths had ignored a basic truth of fire.

While no two fires are the same, fire has its own language.

As fire burns, the color of flames and smoke tell a tale. After the fire is extinguished, burn patterns and debris reveal where the fire began, what caused it, and sometimes even who or what was responsible.

Fire always follows the path of least resistance, thriving as long as fuel supply, oxygen, heat, and chemical reactions remain present. It spreads through conduction, convection, and radiation, with upward burning at a rate of sixty-five miles per hour.

Blazes have different phases, with the time and intensity of each depending on the source of ignition and available fuel. From incipient to emergent smoldering to open flames can take seconds or days. However, once free flames appear, flashover typically follows closely, on average in just eight minutes in residential settings. When fire consumes a structure, floors collapse in fifteen minutes, and walls buckle in twenty-eight minutes.

Most fires are accidental: the cigarette on the mattress, the unattended candle, the oven mitt next to the stove, the overflowing dryer lint trap.

17

However, some fires are incendiary, purposefully set for financial gain, revenge, vandalism, heroism, thrill seeking, pyromania, or cover-up.

Sad but true, most arsonists are never caught.

Almost half the fire departments in the U.S. are staffed by volunteers, trained in fire suppression, not investigation. Their goal is to save lives, save burning structures, and save surrounding structures, in that order. Even in metropolitan areas, trained arson investigators have their work cut out for them. Firefighters have to move debris to search for sparks or embers that could reignite, and overhaul wreaks havoc on an investigation. Disturbing the crime scene creates a new tableau, a false override of the fire's true voice, making it tricky to determine the original progression. Adding to the difficulty, fiber and fingerprint evidence are hard to come by or nonexistent, which means investigators have to rely on eyewitnesses who, more often than not, are undependable.

However, there is always at least one reliable witness to every fire.

The fire itself.

•••

I was keen to visit 3022 Visalia Street, the location of the Southfield fire, while the scene was still intact, but that wouldn't be possible anytime soon.

Dennis McBride had informed me that the property was off limits until the Metro Fire Bureau released it. He promised he'd call before backhoes moved in for overhaul and salvage, which left me free to honor my Friday night commitment with Rollie Austin.

Rollie and I had met fifteen months earlier, at an open house I hosted in the Hilltop neighborhood. She didn't buy that house, or the hundred others I'd shown her since, but I tolerated the outings in exchange for mentoring, because she was CEO of Austin Investigations, one of the oldest and most successful detective agencies in Denver. Bear in mind, these boasts came straight from her, but she did have at least fifty investigators on staff and gross revenues in the millions. I relied on her input, as well as the gadgets and manpower she occasionally lent. In exchange, I showed her properties that caught her fancy or mine, and not a week went by when one of us hadn't found the house of her dreams, a fantasy we shared until we opened the front door. Our next home tour was scheduled for Monday afternoon, a condo in Congress Park that I'd chosen.

Tonight wasn't about real estate, though. It was about pool, Rollie's favorite game.

I left the office around six and drove to Hustlers, a dive bar on South Federal Boulevard.

After parking next to a row of Harleys, I walked through the scratched glass door, past the pinball machines and dartboards, to the back room, where I located Rollie, hunched over the green felt.

I knew from experience she wouldn't acknowledge me until she'd drained every ball, so I strolled to the bar and ordered a Coke and nachos.

By the time I returned, Rollie had pocketed a fifty-dollar bill from her opponent, a man with a belly-length beard.

A true Southern belle, Rollie was built like a drag queen, wore more makeup than a Mary Kay rep, and could have starred in every episode of "What Not to Wear." Tonight's ensemble was tame: tight red jeans with rhinestones, scoop-neck clingy shirt, black leather vest, and three-inch, open-toe heels.

She hugged me, and we chatted for a few minutes while she polished her custom-made pool cue.

"I'm giving serious consideration to a run," Rollie said, racking up the balls.

"For office? Good for you."

"For Ms. America."

I looked at her critically. "Aren't you too old?"

She reared back and broke the balls, a neat motion that sent two into corner pockets. "Sugar, you're going to make me say it. For Ms. Senior America."

"Aren't you too young?" I said, playing along with the well-worn fib that she was forty-five, a birthday she'd celebrated twenty times.

"That's the only hitch," she drawled, "revealing that I've reached the 'age of elegance,' the rather large six-oh."

"It would be a fitting title to accompany the tiara you've been known to wear."

"Wouldn't it just, and what a yummy excuse for a trip to Las Vegas, home to this year's competition." Rollie straightened up after sinking three balls and massaged her tailbone. "Lordy, I'm getting too old for pool. I've got a bone spur on my right shoulder, stress fractures on my left foot, and low-back pain. I don't know how much longer I'll be able to play competitively."

"You've still got it." I swung back and hit the white ball, which missed everything except the corner pocket.

She squawked. "Honey, control the cue ball. How many times have I told you?"

Her penetrating stare made me so nervous that, on my next shot, I bounced a ball off the table.

Rollie hid her face in embarrassment, as I murmured thanks to the man at the next table who fetched the ball.

"When do you have to decide?"

"In the next few days. I don't know what to do. There's so much preparation, what with the evening attire and accessories and talent competition. It could be a hoot, but what if I win? I'd be obliged to travel and promote a message. What would my message be?"

"Timeless aging."

A faraway look clouded her eyes. "I'd have the audience and the judges in the palm of my hand if I played the guitar and sang 'The Rose.'" She snapped back to attention. "I'll need a voice lift."

My voice rose three octaves. "A what?"

"An itsy-bitsy surgery to bring my vocal cords closer together. One teeny injection of fat or collagen can alter the voice pitch. Isn't modern medicine wonderful?"

"Are you crazy? What's the point?"

"To match my voice to my youthful looks. Don't move your body until the ball comes to a complete stop!"

I twitched. I couldn't help it. "It already does."

"You wouldn't lie to me, about my looks?"

"Never," I lied. I broke my concentration to tip the bartender for delivering dinner. When I resumed play, I purposefully knocked a ball into a hole.

The move caught Rollie's notice. "That's it, pocket balls. It's all about the balls. Plan three moves ahead."

"I'm just trying to keep the balls on the table."

She flashed her big-teeth smile. "What if pageant rules forbid a voice lift? I'll have to check, but that's neither here nor there," she said hurriedly. "I'm more nervous about summing up my philosophy of life in thirty seconds or less."

"That's about half a second per year. I'll do it for you." I cleared my throat. "Rollie Austin's philosophy. Live rich. Fast cars, strong men, top-shelf liquor. Live fully. Never repeat yourself. Never cry in full makeup. Never dye your own hair. Never travel without a small firearm. Never wear out a pair of shoes. Never stop at yellows."

Her eyes welled up. "Aren't you a peach? Would you mind terribly saying it again, slowly? Or would you be a dear and write it out for me?"

"Sure," I said, sitting down with my nachos after she swept the table on her next turn. I poked at the tortilla chips, beans, guacamole, sour cream, cheese, and black olives. "Before I forget, could I ask a work-related question?"

"Any time."

"I have this arson case I'm working for a builder."

She sat next to me and primped her Marilyn Monroe wig, a temporary fix for her most recent strawberry-blonde rinse, which had turned out to include more strawberry than blonde. "Tell me more."

"Someone set fire to two of his houses under construction, and he's given me a list of nineteen people who hate him. How am I supposed to track down all those people without racking up a huge bill? Where do I start?"

"Start with emotion."

I wrapped a string of cheese around my finger. "Not finances?"

"Rage," Rollie said with certainty, stealing one of my chips. "Follow the rage."

CHAPTER 4

Rage could wait.

At least a few more hours.

I woke up Saturday morning to a message on my cell phone from Daphne Cartwright, the incensed Landry home owner.

She agreed to meet to discuss her dispute with Dennis McBride, but she didn't have time available until midafternoon.

No problem.

I needed the morning hours to gather background research for a new case, this one involving a strange episode that had taken place in the lower reaches of downtown.

I dressed and left my apartment by nine, a cinnamon raisin bagel with cream cheese in one hand, a bottle of orange juice in the other.

Fifteen minutes later, I parked my car in a surface lot at the corner of 14th and Market, only blocks from where Denver's first residents had set up camp.

In 1858, prospectors had found a sprinkling of gold along the banks of Cherry Creek and the South Platte River, and when word of the discovery spread, thousands flocked to the confluence of the two rivers. They lived in teepees, lean-tos, tents, and log cabins as they staked claims and sought their fortunes. Unfortunately, the amount of gold in Cherry Creek and the South Platte didn't prove to be commercially productive, and the stampede headed for the mountains west of Denver, where eventually the rush would net billions of dollars in ore.

As it happened, however, not all of the early adventurers stayed in the Rockies. Some couldn't tolerate digging underground or sloshing in streams.

Others preferred the more hospitable climate of the plains, opting for twenty-nine inches of snow per winter rather than the thirty feet that fell on the other side of the Continental Divide. Many drifted back to Denver, developing it into a major hub of commerce and trade.

The next great rush of speculation came almost 150 years later when a commercial and industrial area in lower downtown emerged as the hottest spot to live, work, and play. Lofts, office buildings, trendy restaurants, upscale bars, and popular nightclubs sprouted, replacing fleabag hotels, seedy bars, poolrooms, and missions.

How did this happen? I still shook my head over the transformation from skid row to highly desirable, mixed-use neighborhood.

The seeds for conversion began in 1988, when the City and County of Denver formed the Lower Downtown Historic District, a twenty-nine-block area that included turn-of-the-century brick warehouses and industrial buildings, as well as Union Station and the Oxford Hotel.

Strictly speaking, LoDo's boundaries extended from 14th Street to 20th Street, Market Street to Wynkoop Street, but the area broadened, depending on who did the hyping. Real estate agents couldn't help but lump the Central Park Valley and Ballpark neighborhoods in with LoDo, oftentimes adding sections of downtown and Larimer Square.

Larimer Square, which shared an alley with LoDo, was the Mile High City's oldest and most historic block, and most of the original buildings between 14th Street and 15th Street were still intact. The block laid claim to Denver's first bank, bookstore, photographer, dry goods store, post office, theater, and speakeasy. Today, boutiques, galleries, fine shops, and restaurants graced the charming block, and yet Larimer Square's real estate prices hadn't kept pace with LoDo's.

From LoDo's historic designation onward, loft prices had skyrocketed, from an average of $60 per square foot in 1989 to $140 in 1994, and the most remarkable changes and highest rates of appreciation came in the following five years, after Coors Field opened. The baseball stadium had helped propel prices to the current, mind-boggling mark of $400 per square foot and above.

The mad dash, I'm mortified to say, I missed completely, even though I was there for every minute of it, watching in disbelief.

I should have known better.

Speculation always comes in waves, and with each wave, prices rise.

Under normal circumstances, I would categorize myself as a risk taker, but with LoDo, nothing felt normal.

I could understand the appeal of commuting to work by foot or strolling to an evening at the symphony, but I kept thinking the area was overpriced.

At per-square-foot prices of $60, $140, and especially $400, I sat on the sidelines.

I watched as amateur real estate investors converted small warehouses. I watched as heavyweight local developers built out large warehouses. I watched as national companies erected massive buildings on vacant lots.

Through it all, I couldn't shake the feeling that the area wasn't desirable, not for private residences, and I'd never helped anyone buy or sell in LoDo.

A recent series of "wilding" incidents had confirmed my worst fears.

Three weeks earlier, a gang of teens had terrorized LoDo with rioting, fighting, and vandalism. In the middle of the melee, an officer had grabbed a video camera from a fleeing suspect, and local news stations had replayed footage from the tape until the inflammatory images became commonplace.

Each rerun caused another decline in business, and the ripple effect had touched everyone who made a living directly or indirectly from LoDo's trade. Bar, restaurant, and nightclub owners and employees, as well as suppliers, valets, deejays, and musicians were suffering, and that's what brought me to LoDo on a Saturday morning.

Roxanne Archuletta, president of LoDo Business Interests, a loose association of proprietors, had hired me to look into the episodes, and we'd scheduled a meeting for Monday at noon.

Before our appointment, I wanted a better sense of the area. To get it, I crisscrossed LoDo on foot.

I began on Market at 14th Street and headed north, turning west at 20th Street and returning to 14th Street on Blake Street. I repeated the pattern on Wazee Street and Wynkoop Street.

Most of the buildings I passed were four stories or less, many with historic plaques on the brick fronts. As I walked, I absorbed the sounds of the city: a church bell chiming, a jackhammer pounding, a garbage truck hoisting a Dumpster, a Vespa whizzing by, an industrial air conditioner wheezing, a delivery truck running over street grates.

Beyond 18th Street, a cacophony of sports bars joined the mix. As young couples, dressed in T-shirts and shorts, filtered through the open doors of bars to join college clubs gathered to watch football games, noise from TV coverage blared. I could hear play-by-play coming out of one establishment from half a block away. From other venues, jazz or rock blasted from loudspeakers mounted under awnings.

I took note of all of this before ten o'clock in the morning.

I also observed the sights of steam rising from manhole covers, a gardener watering street-side planters, an empty city bus rolling by, a homeless man waking up, a woman hosing down a parking lot, a tourist snapping pictures of the skyline. And trash.

Trash everywhere. Plastic cups and straws, beer bottles and broken glass, tubes of lip gloss and empty pill vials, club wristbands and bar marketing cards, cigarette packs and butts.

Men wearing purple shirts with gold lettering that declared, "Downtown Denver, Safe, Clean, & Vibrant" tried their best to sweep the streets, but they had a long way to go. I encountered three teams of them, stabbing litter, filling plastic bags, and loading the rubbish onto six-wheeler ATVs.

Good luck to them.

Their undertaking would begin anew in twenty-four hours, no doubt.

In the course of my trek, I went by hair salons, art galleries, coffee shops, spas, framing stores, historic hotels, artist studios, tanning salons, banks, real estate offices, cafes, and architectural firms.

The bright side of LoDo.

I noticed sushi restaurants outnumbered all of the Mexican, Italian, American, Indian, and Mongolian eateries combined, and of course I saw bar after bar, nightclub after nightclub.

Too many to count, and I gave up after twenty.

I stopped twice for coffee drinks, which I savored as I walked, but the perfect weather—blue sky, full sun, and no breeze—called for a picnic.

I sat at a table on the 16th Street Mall and ate fish tacos. For dessert, I purchased a double-chocolate brownie and iced mocha, which I enjoyed as I strolled along the bike path next to Cherry Creek.

My conclusion after the LoDo walking tour: During the day, the area seemed innocent enough.

In twelve hours, I would return again to find the truth.

•••

Driving out of LoDo, I called Daphne Cartwright to let her know I was on my way.

As advertised, Landry was a hop, skip, and a jump from downtown, an easy twenty-minute commute. Of course, that was in the middle of a Saturday afternoon, without rush hour traffic, bad weather, or accident delays.

At the Cartwright home, I parked on the street behind a silver Volvo S40 sedan.

I knew from county records that Daphne and Eric Cartwright had purchased the 2,600-square-foot house three years earlier for $388,000. Give me two weeks, and I'd have it under contract for $515,000, more if I could pull out those damn yard signs.

A new one had appeared: Liar McBride, President of McBride Homes.

On my stop the previous day, when no one had answered the door, I'd taken the liberty of peeking in the front windows, a real estate agent habit I'd never tried to break.

What I'd seen of the interior was meticulous. A grand, marble entryway with curved stairway and wrought iron balusters, wide-plank red oak floors, and an impressive collection of English Country antiques. To the right of the front door was a living room, which clearly no one used; to the left was a home office.

Builders, by nature, were copycats, and I'd toured enough models to guess at the configuration of the rest of the house. The back of the main floor would lay out in an open plan, complete with a great room with gas fireplace and built-in entertainment center, a kitchen with stainless steel appliances, custom cabinetry, and slab granite counters, a dining room with coffered ceiling and French doors to the backyard, and a powder room with pedestal sink. Upstairs would be three bedrooms and baths, including a master suite with double-sided fireplace, an enormous closet with built-ins, and a bath with double-headed shower and whirlpool tub. The basement would be finished with a guest bedroom and three-quarter bath and a rec room with a wet bar and another built-in entertainment center.

That was my guess, and it had to stay a guess.

After Daphne Cartwright answered the door, she whisked me into her office without so much as a pause in the foyer, and within minutes of my arrival, she'd expunged all of the pleasing effects of my caffeinated drinks.

"I cannot tell you how tired I am of dealing with initials. The LRA, the EPA, the CDPHE, the RAB, the USAF. Why hasn't Landry's cleanup been privatized? The military has no expertise in environmental cleanup."

"I'm sorry, I don't—"

"The Landry Redevelopment Authority, the U.S. Environmental Protection Agency, the Colorado Department of Health and Environment, the Restoration Advisory Board, the U.S. Air Force. They're all involved in a bureaucratic tangle. My life is consumed with this fight. I suppose I should be grateful. On a base in Connecticut, the Navy dumped sulfuric acid, torpedo fuel, waste oil, and incinerator ash."

I raised an eyebrow, a sympathetic signal.

Daphne shook her hands and arms, as if they'd gone numb. "But I don't feel especially grateful. Before civic leaders and developers conspired to develop Landry, they should have done their homework. The military is notorious for its history of pollution and disregard of state and federal environmental laws. Why didn't anyone do a more thorough investigation? Why did they take the Air Force's word for what went on in fifty-six years of active base operation? They should have examined aerial photography from every time period, tested the subsurface infrastructure, and interviewed former soldiers at the base. They could have treated the groundwater and cleaned up contaminated soil before families moved in, but did they?"

I didn't try to answer.

I was never quick enough.

Daphne Cartwright must have been accustomed to holding conversations with herself, because my comments, when I managed to squeeze them in, only startled her.

Her daughter, across from me, said nothing.

The three of us were in a ten-foot-square room, but it felt considerably smaller.

An L-shaped office suite overwhelmed the space, with its expanse of desktop, drawers, and filing cabinets consuming two walls. Add to that stacks of files, magazines, and papers everywhere, towering at precarious angles, and there was hardly room for occupants.

The three-year-old and I were seated at a miniature plastic table in the corner. She was hunched over, intent on drawing a flower. I fidgeted on my chair, twelve inches off the ground, with my knees almost touching my chin.

Mother and daughter looked alike, with straight, wispy, blonde hair, light almost to the point of white, washed-out complexions, gaunt faces, bulging green eyes, and anorexic builds. They both wore red jumpers, white turtlenecks, and black Crocs.

Daphne continued, in an outraged tone. "Greedy developers like Dennis McBride wanted to move as quickly as they could. Rush to install infrastructure, rush to sell property, rush to build houses, rush to lease commercial space. No one considered the threats to my family in the rush to reuse and redevelop. They cared about nothing but the almighty dollar. The Redevelopment Authority claims that land is developed and sold only after state and environmental regulators give approval, only after the land is found to be suitable for transfer and reuse. Is that true?"

I shrugged helplessly.

"Of course it's not. My yard was full of asbestos. Why? Because Dennis McBride built my home on top of an old hospital complex and steam plant. When the Air Force had no further need for them, it tore them down and bulldozed them under, never bothering to remove debris. Asbestos from utility pipes, exterior siding, insulation, tiles, and pipe wrapping was all around me. Whoops!"

"Mm," I muttered, not sure how much more diatribe I could absorb.

"Do you know how I found out about the problem? Two years ago, my baby was crawling on our newly landscaped yard, when workers showed up to remove our sod, trees, and flowers. They wore protective suits, elbow-length gloves, safety boots, and full-face masks with respirators," she said, her cheeks flush. "They fenced off a fifteen-foot radius around my yard, and they hung signs that said, 'Danger—Asbestos Kills.' They covered sections with plastic, monitored the air, and hauled away the dirt. They used all of these precautions, when moments earlier, we thought we were safe. They won't get away with this," Daphne said darkly.

I spoke without inflection. "Do you really believe you were at risk?"

"I most certainly do. No one can say what the lowest level of exposure is to put my family at risk for mesothelioma, and I don't intend to find out. There's a fight between what the Air Force deems acceptable and what the CDPHE considers safe. The military has a long and well-documented legacy of pollution. It acts cavalierly, as if it has blanket immunity. The EPA won't stand up to the military, and this administration has seen fit to do nothing but dodge environmental regulations. The Pentagon wants to reduce the $4 billion a year it spends on environmental cleanup, but that's less than 1 percent of the overall defense budget. Who's more powerful? The White House and the Department of Defense or the EPA? The Air Force still owns a twenty-two-acre lot down the street, and it won't clean it up until it's conducted its own risk assessment. When will that be? Twenty-two acres, that's the size of the World Trade Center redevelopment in New York City, and it sits in my neighborhood, contaminated."

Daphne threw up her hands in frustration. "Emma, are you ready to say 'hi' to Lauren yet?"

The little girl shook her head gravely, unaffected by my beguiling smile.

"I find it ironic that the Air Force created the pollution, and yet demands final say in how it will be cleaned up, in direct violation of environmental regulations. It claims scientific studies on asbestos are flawed and it needs to be a steward of taxpayer money, but who is the steward of our health? The military is supposed to be held to the same environmental rules as private industry, but we know it's not. It's all documented, the way the military flaunts the law. I've reviewed thousands of pages of federal records," Daphne said, gesturing maniacally at the stacks of files on her desk.

"I don't know how you do it," I said softly.

"Who else will?" she snapped. "Who else will fight for my family? The CDPHE has staged three work stoppages in the last three years because the Air Force withheld payment. The latest was in April, over a $100,000 bill, a pittance in the $82 million project. Can you believe the gall? The CDPHE and the Air Force bicker among themselves, while my family suffers. Someone will pay for this mistake. A jury will see to that. The awards could be in the tens of millions."

I grimaced. "You're planning to sue?"

She smiled for the first time, her thin lips twisting. "I'll start with the

Department of Defense and the Landry Redevelopment Authority and work my way down to . . . "

Daphne Cartwright paused, waiting for me to fill in the blank, but I wouldn't.

"Dennis McBride," she hissed. "I will destroy him, one way or another."

CHAPTER 5

I let out a long breath. "How can you sue for health problems that may never surface?"

Daphne Cartwright coughed, on cue. "They talk about soil samples that contain less than 1 percent of asbestos by weight, but in the next breath, they designate my yard an asbestos spill. If the military had demolished the buildings in a responsible manner and handled and disposed of the asbestos as required, instead of leaving scraps in place and debris free to spread around, we wouldn't be having this problem. Do you know what asbestos can do to you? Emma, why don't you switch to Play-Doh now. Share with Lauren."

"More or less," I said, reaching for the mound of clay Emma offered reluctantly, not one specific color but a mash of discards.

"Inhaling airborne asbestos is like breathing in long, sharp, tiny fibers. They slice the lining of your lungs, building up over time, scarring, and eventually suffocating you. If you develop mesothelioma, the cancer caused by exposure to asbestos, it doesn't respond to chemotherapy or radiation. You die within a year."

Daphne touched her chest for emphasis. "What does 1 percent mean? That's a number they pulled out of thin air. It sounds good, but millions of weightless fibers could be in every handful of dirt. They claim to have analyzed twenty-four thousand soil samples at Landry, and they say that 93 percent show no asbestos. What about the other 7 percent? They remove six to twenty-four inches of soil, send 'No Further Action' letters, and expect us to feel safe again? Scientists can't say for sure whether exposure to a small amount of asbestos is safe, and we won't know for twenty to fifty years, not until the disease appears, will we? Other Landry residents should be up in arms, but they're too complacent. Congress is considering eliminating asbestos litigation and replacing it with a $140 billion asbestos trust fund. But guess what?"

Daphne paused until I tore my attention away from the stick figure I was molding and dutifully said, "What?"

"It's only for victims of industrial asbestos-related disease. They want to pay the medical bills for asbestos workers but not for victims with non-occupational or environmental exposures. Where would that leave us? Everyone in Landry should be afraid of what's out there, including the joggers who run on open land and the children who play in dirt yards or undeveloped fields. No one on my street appreciates the threat to our health. They all think the situation's been resolved. Fortunately, I have allies in other areas."

"Such as?"

"Montana and California."

"Concerning Landry?"

"Yours isn't very pretty," Emma interrupted, the first words she'd spoken since I entered the house.

I gave the child a hard look but didn't respond in kind to the blob she'd made.

"Concerning asbestos. Hundreds have died in Libby, Montana, from asbestos released by mining vermiculite. It's the worst environmental health disaster in EPA history. There have been two hundred cancer deaths and two thousand cases of lung abnormalities. Twenty percent of the population is ill," Daphne said in a gasp. "In northern California, in El Dorado Hills, they're building roads, homes, and schools on top of land that's full of naturally occurring asbestos. They dynamited through veins to build a high-end subdivision outside of Sacramento. They've had to pour concrete over lots, ball fields, and a running track. I feel for those families. I really do. Natural asbestos fibers are every bit as deadly as commercial ones. We're in this fight together."

A fist came crashing down on my Play-Doh figure.

I jumped and almost toppled out of my plastic chair.

Daphne waved a finger at her daughter. "Emma, you're not supposed to ruin other people's things. Tell Lauren you're sorry."

"Sorry," she mumbled, not at all sincerely.

"Where was I? Oh yes, I'm also corresponding with neighborhood activists across the country. The media portrays Landry as an example of a successful military base redevelopment. I'm telling the other side of the story to anyone who will listen, and it's not easy. Dennis McBride has some nerve, sending you to my doorstep. He's the one who took out a restraining order on me, and I'm the one receiving death threats."

"Death threats?"

Daphne nodded primly. "By phone. By e-mail. In postings on blogs."

I looked at her skeptically. "You really think Dennis is behind them?"

"I do."

"Want to play mall?"

"Not now, Emma. Lauren's busy with Mommy."

"What's mall?"

"She lays all her Barbie clothes on the couch, and you pick outfits and dress the dolls."

I would have preferred to slam my hand in a car door. "Maybe later," I said noncommittally.

"Now!" the toddler insisted, with a deep scowl.

Her mother shot her a look.

I addressed Daphne. "How do the neighbors feel about your yard signs?"

"They object, but I told the home owners association board that if they try to enforce the rule about signage, I'll file formal complaints about every infraction in Hunter's Field. The Westerphals' garage light that was installed improperly. The Redmanns' gazebo that's out of compliance. The Greiners' outdoor stereo speakers that weren't approved. The Quintaras's RV that's parked for more than three consecutive days. I have a ten-page list I can pull out."

I rubbed my forehead. "Don't you ever get tired of the fight?"

"By the end of every day. But I have a duty to safeguard my family, and I have a right to protect the value of my investment. I should be allowed to enjoy the neighborhood I was promised."

"I'm hungry," Emma said.

"You just ate. Remember, you had Cheerios and toast before Lauren came. With strawberry jam."

"But I'm hungry," she whined.

"You can go to the refrigerator and take out some grapes."

"I want a hot dog."

"Grapes or nothing," Daphne replied firmly. "How many?"

"Five hundred."

"Eight. One for each finger, but no thumbs."

Emma left the room, arms outstretched, digits spread wide.

"I can appreciate that everything hasn't worked out like you thought it would, but it hasn't for Dennis McBride either," I said peaceably. "He's suffered, too."

"Not enough."

"What would you consider enough? He's lost dozens of contracts and spent nearly $3 million that may not be reimbursed by the Air Force. He's not the only one to blame. Ten other builders in Landry have had issues with asbestos cleanup."

"But they didn't sell me my home, did they?" Daphne said, in a frighteningly sweet tone.

"Other home owners have been more patient," I replied pointedly.

"They shouldn't be. They should demand the eight hundred acres of parks and open space that were featured in the McBride brochure. When will we get those? No one can say. The money's been set aside, but the Denver Parks and Recreation department won't move forward until they're assured the cleanup is complete. This is supposed to be a community, not a hodgepodge of homes."

"If you're so unhappy, why don't you move? Dennis offered to buy you out, at appraised value plus 10 percent. That's a fair deal."

"And let him bring in some other unsuspecting family? Not on my life. I'm not a quitter. I'll see this through to the end. Dennis McBride knew about the contamination in my yard, and he should have disclosed it."

"He didn't know," I said wearily, "or he never would have built here. He could go bankrupt waiting for payment from the Air Force."

"I hope he does. If that doesn't destroy him, maybe these fires will."

I rose, my knees creaking. "You really hate Dennis McBride, don't you?"

"More than you'll ever know," Daphne Cartwright said, with satisfaction. "I live on the hatred. If I didn't, I'd tell you who set his house on fire in June."

36

•••

She tried to hold out, but in less than three minutes, I broke Daphne Cartwright.

I started by appealing to her civic duty, explaining that another fire had been set at Southfield, and the arsonist might strike again at Landry.

She didn't bat an eye.

I impressed upon her that the next fire could be fatal.

She remained unmoved.

I threatened police involvement and a subpoena.

That did nothing.

Only the mention of a $10,000 reward for information leading to the arrest and prosecution of the arsonist grabbed her. A complete fabrication, but it did the trick.

I left her house with something, but not much.

I didn't have an actual name, because Daphne had never met the accused.

Nor did I have a physical description, because she'd made it a point never to look at him.

However, she had described his mode of transportation.

He traveled by bike, a red, one-speed, men's model with a small trailer attached to the back. He covered the homemade wagon with a blue tarp, secured by bungee cords, and in a pink plastic basket affixed to the handlebars, he carried a little dog, a black and white terrier mix.

It was a start.

There couldn't be that many homeless men pedaling through Landry with a dog. Most vagrants congregated around downtown shelters and popular begging corners near the Capitol.

The homeless man had set the fire, Daphne assured me.

And if it wasn't him, maybe it was the boy she'd seen in his company.

Proof?

She had none, but I elected to follow her leads.

I drove two laps around Landry with no sightings and left after an hour.

I had other things to worry about.

•••

I'd always found Saturday nights vaguely depressing.

Even when I was younger and in intimate relationships with attractive women, this slice of the week disturbed me.

Probably because it never lived up to its billing.

I held on to the belief that other people's weekend nights were full of dancing and drinking, friends and lovers, revelry and sex, while most of mine had been quite ordinary.

Maybe this one would prove to be the exception.

At 11 p.m., I parked my car in a lot near the Tivoli Center, a few blocks south of LoDo, and as soon as I hit the streets, I was struck by a harrowing truth.

I was old.

When had this occurred?

It seemed like only yesterday that bartenders had carded me. I'd successfully negotiated the transition from miss to ma'am. What the hell was this?

I felt like a dinosaur.

I didn't need a mirror to know that I'd lost an inch from my five-feet-nine, that my trim figure held the extra ten pounds I'd lost so many times, that reddish-brown dye covered a mass of gray, or that my blue eyes had faded with sorrow.

I saw all of this every morning, but I tried to concede my attributes.

I was proud of my implant-filled smile, unlined skin, perfect posture, and long limbs.

Still, on this night, none of those seemed enough.

I fretted as I walked toward the epicenter of LoDo.

Was it the clothes?

No little red dress and stilettos for me, although truth be told, I'd never dressed like that, not even in my twenties and thirties. On this mild night, I was clad for escape. I'd chosen nylon sweats, a "Race for the Cure" T-shirt, a safari jacket, and running shoes.

Leaving the apartment, I'd thought the outfit made me look athletic, but one sideways glance at my reflection in a store window, and I changed the adjective to frumpy.

When had I become so old?

Or when had club-goers become so young?

On the first block, I passed two crying girls, multiple groups of young men, a gaggle of bridesmaids exiting a limo, and a couple arguing in Spanish.

Five more blocks, and I had to endure jeers, requests for money, and offers of drugs. Nothing I couldn't handle.

On the last leg of the journey, I took in three interesting sights: an athletic woman carrying her boyfriend on her back; a girl hanging out the window of a moving Lexus, her legs dangling inside the car; and a woman in a strapless dress walking in a jagged line, carrying her heels, and whistling "Silent Night."

All curious, but when I arrived at the corner of 18th Street and Market Street at 11:30 p.m., I was surprised by how quiet the area seemed.

That soon changed.

At midnight, cops arrived in force. With an impressive efficiency, they erected barricades and closed down streets. In no time, a four-block-square section, from Market Street to Blake Street, 18th Street to 20th Street, was cordoned off, with cop cars parked in intersections, lights flashing.

As I wandered through the area, I counted at least fifty officers. There had been rumors the police presence had increased tenfold since the wilding incident, but district commanders refused to release numbers. Looking around, I guessed the estimates were conservative, if anything. Evidently, the chief of police meant business with his "zero tolerance" posture.

By 1 a.m., LoDo was almost unrecognizable as one of the most coveted residential addresses in the city. Think military zone. Helicopters circled overhead, while Gang Unit and SWAT officers, decked in tactical gear with assault rifles, patrolled the streets.

The noise level rose—a mix of jazz, hip-hop, rock, funk, and salsa—every time club doors opened and cliques stumbled into the street, talking, laughing, and crying.

At 2 a.m., on the stroke of the hour, all hell broke loose in the touted tourism and entertainment district.

I watched from the perimeter of the pen.

Crowds of people disgorged into the streets at once, staggering and yelling, and the police kicked into gear. Through megaphones, they instructed packs to disperse. On the other side of the barricades, where cars were locked in a jam, officers knocked on windows and told drivers to keep moving, though they had nowhere to go. The cops shouted out threats of arrest for loitering and took cans of pepper spray the size of small fire extinguishers out of holsters.

In minutes, the sidewalks were jam-packed, and the surrounding streets were in gridlock. Car horns blared, whether in anger or celebration, it was impossible to tell. In the middle of the block, a skirmish broke out, and while half the people ran away, the other half ran toward it. In seconds, the police had the crowd under control again, with three young men and a woman on the ground in handcuffs.

Soon, the smell of urine and vomit blended with pepper spray and wafted around me.

I stopped breathing through my nose, regretting that I hadn't come more prepared. The burrito vendor on the corner knew the drill. He squished a water-soaked bandana against his nose and kept right on selling, trading foil-wrapped "sober-up" packages for dollar bills.

I'd seen enough, but the walk out was much more of a challenge than the walk in.

I passed random pools of vomit and blood and had trouble navigating the clogged streets and sidewalks. As mobs pressed from all sides, my anxiety rose. I felt like I was the only sober, unarmed person within a one-mile radius, which did nothing to quell my fear.

At the corner of 15th Street and Market Street, I watched a police officer approach a carload of young black men as he swept the lot on the northwest corner. In a courteous but authoritative tone, the cop told the driver of the Ford Taurus to move on. I heard the kid explain that they were waiting for a friend who'd been separated from their group. The officer told him he had five minutes, but seconds later, a second officer approached and told him time was up.

When the driver uttered a few words of protest, the cop sprayed Mace toward the car, hitting all of its occupants with a wide sweep. The four boys crawled out, spitting, choking, coughing, and gagging.

At the red-eyed driver, the cop shouted, "You want some more?"

When the boy rose to his feet, blindly flailing, the officer put the kid in an arm lock, wrestled him to the ground, bent his right leg back, and handcuffed his hands to his leg.

I watched all of this from across the street, but when the cop pulled his gun, my role changed from observer to participant.

I ran as fast as I could, shouting, "What did the kid do?"

The cop glanced my way, took in my forty-something, female physique, and dismissed me. "Stay out of this."

"Let him go."

"You are a serious pain in my ass," he said impassively.

I came within feet of him and the boy. "I want your badge number. This is a Federal civil rights violation."

"Are you trying to tell me how to do my job?"

"What did he do?"

"I could charge him with disturbing the peace and disobeying a lawful order."

"Try it, and I'll be a witness when he presses charges for assault, battery, false arrest, malicious prosecution, and abuse of process."

The cop glared at me, and I returned the favor.

He muttered something unintelligible, and I'm sure unflattering, but bent to unlock the handcuffs.

I took the kid by the arm and helped him into the car. "Don't say a word," I whispered.

I gestured for his friends to get into the backseat as the cop yelled, "Get out of here, and take these punks with you."

I had no choice but to chauffeur them. I hopped into the driver's seat, which was in a reclined position on the last setting. I perched on the edge of the bench, started the engine, and drove straight over a curb.

In the background, I could hear shouts of, "Fuck the police," from the crowd that had gathered, but the young men in the car were quiet.

They stayed that way on the five-block drive to my car. As I exited the Buick, they thanked me profusely, and I warned them not to go back for their friend.

Not under any circumstances.

I told them it could cost them their lives if they tried, and I wasn't kidding.

CHAPTER 6

Fortunately, the young men must have believed me, because there was no mention of LoDo on the Sunday morning news.

As I flipped between channels, trying to avoid any semblance of a church service, a devilish thought danced into my head.

Maybe I should drive by Southfield and take a peek at Dennis McBride's burned house. In all likelihood, arson investigators didn't work on Sundays, and I could conduct a preliminary analysis of the scene unfettered.

No, bad idea, if the Metro Fire Bureau hadn't released the scene.

Then again . . .

If I went, I wouldn't get out of the car.

If I did get out, I wouldn't step inside the house.

If I did step inside, I wouldn't disturb anything.

If I did disturb something, I would put it back as I found it.

What could a visit hurt?

Impatience battled with ethics when I heard a knock on the door, and Sasha let herself in before I could get up.

"I'm bored," she said, her chest heaving with an exasperated sigh. She plopped on the couch next to me and put her feet on the coffee table.

I couldn't tell if she was in her pajamas or had changed into the day's outfit. Black leggings, baggy gray gym shorts that stretched past her knees, and a lacy red silk top with spaghetti straps were hard to classify. She'd put on jewelry—a wide silver band on her thumb and handcuff bracelets on both wrists—so maybe she was dressed for the day. I didn't dare ask.

I pulled sections of the Sunday newspaper out from under her rear end and laid them on the table. "Why are you bored?"

Sasha tore off a section of my pecan roll, rubbed it in the melted butter on the plate, plopped it into her mouth, and chased it down with a sip of my coffee. "Eww. This needs more sugar and milk. Because there's nothing to do."

"Get your own cup. How about homework?"

She snorted. "Homework's boring. Plus, I did all of it."

"All of it."

"Most of it. What are you doing today?"

"Nothing much."

"Are you working on one of the cases? Can I help you?" she said eagerly.

"It's Sunday," I said, evasively.

"So . . . you work on Sundays all the time."

"Not today. Why don't you go to the movies with one of your friends?"

"Because I don't have any money."

I reached into my back pocket and pried two twenties from a wad of cash. "Here, go have some fun."

Sasha broke into a huge smile, leaned over to hug me, then scampered off, leaving the front door wide open.

I stood, brushed crumbs from the table into my cupped hand, and carried the dishes into the kitchen.

It wasn't a long walk.

Nothing was in an 800-square-foot apartment, and that's how I preferred it.

After my parents died, I'd decided to downsize.

I sold a $1.1 million townhome in Cherry Creek North and bought the ClockTower, a 16,000-square-foot, three-story, thirty-eight unit apartment building in West Washington Park.

Several years back, a developer friend of mine had transformed the bland, blonde 1960s-era brick building into a work of art. He gave the façade a facelift, including a curved overhang with recessed lighting, and positioned a sculpture of a giant pocket watch in front of the building. He renovated the lobby using brushed steel and black metal and painted the common areas with olive and burnt orange. In the entrance, surrounding the bank of mailboxes, he installed hundreds of timepieces behind shatter-proof glass and placed an authentic, restored, moon-phases grandfather clock from the 1800s. His business plan called for ownership of ten buildings in two years, each with a different theme, but he drastically underestimated the glut of rentals in Denver. Due to his under-capitalization, I bought the building for $1.05 million, after he'd sunk $1.63 million into it, and with the purchase, I inherited the apartment manager. Bess, a no-nonsense woman in her late sixties, collected rents, maintained the building to scrupulous standards, and kicked out tenants at the first signs of trouble.

No headaches, and best of all, I had positive cash flow.

The move wasn't a temporary one.

I didn't have any possessions locked in storage, waiting for me to renew my interest in them. I'd split my belongings between friends' homes, thrift stores, and landfills, and before moving in, I'd renovated the apartment.

Thanks to frequent cleaning and polishing, I had shiny oak floors that extended through the living room and dining room, and in the U-shaped kitchen that opened into the main living area, I had stone countertops and flooring, stainless steel appliances, a double-sink, and recessed lighting.

Throughout the apartment, I made do with very little furniture.

I had my father's drafting board as a substitute for a dining room table, and it held a dozen piles of carefully stacked paperwork. In the living room, I had a black leather couch, a copper coffee table, two matching end tables, and a thirteen-inch television on a glass stand.

I had yet to hang anything on the cream walls, in any room.

•••

It couldn't hurt to take a peek.

One little look.

Obviously, impatience trounced ethics, because soon after Sasha left, I drove straight to the Southfield neighborhood, formerly the site of Southfield International Airport, where I marveled at the transformation.

On February 27, 1995, when the last commercial flight left Southfield, neighbors rejoiced. As a snaking convoy of baggage carts, rental cars, and maintenance vehicles moved through the night to Denver International Airport, nearby residents congratulated themselves for shutting down an airport that had been in continuous operation since 1929.

In large part, noise lawsuits filed by home owners had forced Denver to build DIA, but two other factors also had played a role in the closure:

bad weather and confinement. Southfield's runways had been built too close together, which led to delays whenever visibility was reduced, and the airport had failed in its attempt to expand onto land it owned to the north.

Without knowing the history of the area, today's visitor to Southfield would be hard-pressed to see the former airport, except for one remarkable feature that stood out in the seven square miles of land: the air traffic control tower. It was prominent from as far away as Quebec Street, which is where I turned into the neighborhood.

I hadn't been to Southfield in six months, and I couldn't believe what I saw.

The one thousandth family had moved in recently, and that was just the beginning. In ten years, at full build-out, the 4,700 acres would include twelve thousand homes, three million square feet of retail, ten million square feet of office/industrial space, and 1,116 acres of open space, including a centerpiece eighty-acre park. The nation's largest infill project would serve as home to thirty thousand people and workplace to thirty-five thousand.

The massive amount of completed development already had impacted central Denver's real estate market, and no one could predict accurately what lay ahead. An estimated 90 percent of homebuyers in Southfield were coming from Denver's more established neighborhoods, such as Washington Park, Congress Park, Park Hill, Cheesman Park, and Capitol Hill. In the past, buyers were attracted to these historic neighborhoods for their brick homes, mature landscaping, and proximity to downtown, and they grudgingly accepted the constraints that came with houses built in the late 1800s and early 1900s.

They had few other options. It was rare to find a new custom home in any of Denver's seventy neighborhoods. One came up for sale now and then, but builders tended to sell the mini-mansions for premium prices.

Buyers could hunt for pop-tops, but most seemed hideous in comparison to new construction. An unfortunate product of the mid- to late-1980s, many pop-tops came in strange configurations. Zoning laws, which restricted home heights to prevent light blockage into adjacent yards, virtually guaranteed awkward floor plans and unsightly roof pitches. Renovators crammed bedrooms and bathrooms into attic spaces, shoehorned new kitchens into old kitchens, and converted musty basements into sub-par quarters. While many of central Denver's pop-tops had square footage equivalent to houses in Southfield, the space wasn't located where people wanted it, and the architectural abominations and dated designs couldn't begin to compete with 21st century homes.

In Southfield, builders advertised that their kitchen islands were bigger than kitchens in Washington Park and that their master closets were bigger than master bedrooms in Park Hill.

They weren't far off in their brags. However, I wondered how historians would view this period of architecture and landscape a century from now.

I couldn't support it.

Southfield's land, as it became available for reuse, was sold to developers by lottery, which made for an unsettling medley of apartments, lofts, townhomes, row houses, and duplexes. Even in the single-family clusters, Victorians, Denver squares, California contemporaries, moderns, ranches, and dozens of lesser-known styles stood side by side or across the street from one another. Block by block, site placements varied. Some lots had common area parks instead of private yards. Others had attached garages on the street or detached garages off the alley.

Despite the variety, however, one message came across consistently.

No one wanted to mess with yard work.

Give the residents patches for their dogs, scraps of sod the size of throw rugs or carpet runners, and that seemed to suffice. Surround the mini-turf with river rock or bark, erect black wrought iron fences, and call it a day!

Why, oh why, were people snatching up these homes as quickly as developers could build them?

Maybe Southfield residents favored the sameness and security that couldn't be found in central Denver. Perhaps they enjoyed the aquatic center, the skateboard park, the farmer's market, the in-line skating rink, the dog park, or the trails, creeks, and wetlands woven into the urban design.

More likely, they craved the retail, a conglomeration that rivaled anything in the suburbs. There were box stores, anchor stores, specialty stores, restaurants, and an eighteen-screen movie theater. The Town Center held a heavy concentration of franchises, with Starbucks, Chipotle, Noodles, Curves, and Cold Stone Creamery vying for business next to a dentist, a vet, an optometrist, a chiropractor, and a pharmacist.

In a way, I could understand the appeal.

I felt the pull of retail myself sometimes.

Point of fact, I stopped at Starbucks and picked up a java chip Frappuccino, which I sucked down on the last leg of my drive to the 3000 block of Visalia Street.

Placards throughout Southfield indicated whether properties were available, reserved, sold, or private residences, and none of the McBride homes I saw was available.

Dennis McBride hadn't lied when he said he never built a home without a contract.

I pulled up to his torched house, the one Fritz Jubera had under contract, and parked behind a red Chevy 2500 pickup.

Enjoying one last sip of the Frap, I turned off the engine and studied the charred vestiges of 3022 Visalia Street. Blackened lumber and peels of white weather-resistant wrap were about all that was left.

The arsonist had burned a Bridgeport model, one of three choices Dennis offered in the Vista Village subdivision. Few architectural features were recognizable, but I compared the roof-less skeleton to the brochure Dennis had given me.

Straining, I could make out a bare outline of what might have been.

The Bridgeport was a two-story, rectangular building with a slightly pitched roof. Shutters on the upper floor, a decorative wrought iron balcony, and arched windows and doorways on the main floor broke up an otherwise monolithic design. Its 3,200 square feet included a grand hall and study on opposite sides of a narrow courtyard, a two-car attached garage on the back, four bedrooms, and three baths. Listing price: $525,000, with standard finishes.

Today's price: $100,000, give or take. Market value for the lot, minus the cost of cleanup.

How depressing.

No wonder Dennis McBride was at wit's end.

I climbed out of the car and walked around the perimeter of the building, cautiously stepping through mud, ashes, and debris. At the back of the house, I was about to enter through the remains of the garage when a voice startled me.

"Yo, you're not supposed to be here!"

CHAPTER 7

I looked up to see a man in a firefighter's helmet, denim coveralls, heavy gloves, and rubber-sole boots bearing down on me, hands on his hips.

"Who are you?" I said, my voice breaking.

He pulled up and tore away his dust mask, uncovering a strong chin and handlebar mustache. "Max Spiker, lead arson investigator, Metro Fire Bureau. Who are you?"

"Lauren Vellequette, private investigator, working for McBride Homes. Dennis McBride gave me permission to tour the site."

"I don't care if you're on God's payroll, this is an active crime scene. Did you see the yellow tape?"

"Of course. I had to duck under it," I said jokingly.

Max didn't crack a smile. "Then get on the other side before you disturb something. It's a crime to be standing where you are."

I retreated. "When can I come back?"

He removed his safety glasses and rubbed his eyes. "When I say."

"How will you contact me?"

"I'll send a signal."

After a long pause, I said expectantly, "Yes?"

"The yellow tape will come down."

"Maybe you could use modern technology and call." I moved forward and handed him one of my business cards.

He didn't return the courtesy. "Don't take one step closer. I'm not kidding. You're contaminating my scene."

I backed up and climbed over the yellow tape, which he'd erected five feet beyond the footprint of the house. "Happy now?"

"Ecstatic."

"Can I ask you something?"

Max reached into a side pocket and pulled out a bottle of water. "You just did."

I blew air out of my cheeks. "Something else?"

"Did it again."

"Is it arson?"

He uncapped the bottle and took a long drink. "Bingo."

"How do you know?"

"Thirty years on the job."

"Which tells you . . . ?"

He wiped his mouth with the back of his sleeve, leaving a black mark on his cheek. "Which tells me I work better when no one's badgering me."

"It was probably a professional, right?"

"Wrong. An amateur torch did this one."

"You figured that out because . . . ?"

"Too much liquid, but that's it! No more questions. If you want to learn anything else about fire, watch the Discovery Channel. Catch you later," he said, motioning for me to leave.

I didn't budge. "Could a kid have started the fire?"

"Two-thirds of all fires are started by juveniles. You figure it out."

"How old would he or she have to be?"

"I hope he's at least ten, otherwise I can't charge him with arson." Max Spiker shot me an accusing look. "Something you want to get off your chest?"

"Not at all," I answered, too quickly.

He spit to the side, and his eyes narrowed. "If you have information that's germane to my investigation, I want it now."

"I was just curious," I said, smiling brightly. No need to tell him about Daphne Cartwright's suspicions regarding the young boy she'd seen in the company of the homeless man.

Max Spiker's tone remained gruff. "I've seen fires set by kids as young as three. Most start multiple fires before anyone catches them. If this fire was set by a kid, he's a full-on delinquent, not some first-timer. Kids play with a book of matches or start a trash can fire. Small stuff. Nothing on this scale. I'd love to stay and chat, but you need to clear out and let me do my job."

"One more question . . . please."

"One, and you'll leave?"

"Without delay."

He stepped back inside the house, but called out over his shoulder, "Better make it a good one."

"What does the type of liquid tell you about the fire setter?"

"It tells me he was lucky he got out alive," Max Spiker shouted.

•••

That was enough work for a Sunday in the fall.

I returned to my apartment and enjoyed a two-hour nap and the fourth quarter of the Broncos game. After the game ended, I took Sasha to dinner at Chili's, and we kept our conversation light, topics of her choice—video games, calligraphy, and Japanese anime.

Come Monday morning, though, I was up with the sun, organizing my thoughts and planning the day.

Before my noon appointment in LoDo with Roxanne Archuletta, I needed to follow up on three leads in the arson case.

I dressed for the day in a purple knit sweater, aubergine stretch jeans, and charcoal wool clogs. On the way out the door at eight, I grabbed a black quilted riding jacket, in anticipation of the cold front that was supposed to move in before day's end.

My first stop was Southfield, where I found the McBride construction trailer and introduced myself to Glenn Warner, Dennis McBride's foreman.

Glenn was the one who had discovered the Landry fire and called 911. Over a cup of coffee and four Danishes, all devoured by him, he stepped me through the events of June 11.

On a Sunday morning, after his wife asked him to install a security light on their garage, he drove to 1125 Trinidad Street to grab a hammer drill for the project. Arriving at the house around noon, he saw waist-high flames in the living room and ran to his truck to call 911. He then sprinted from house to house, looking for a fire extinguisher. All of the houses nearby were vacant, still weeks away from closings, and most were locked. He watched as the flames grew and spread. Within five minutes, firefighters arrived, and within fifteen, they quashed the fire, but the structure was a total loss.

In his frantic dash, Glenn hadn't noticed anyone near the house that burned, and nothing struck him as suspicious, except for the missing cardboard. He swore the Dumpster in front of the house was full of empty boxes when he went home on Friday, and he swore the cardboard was missing when he returned on Sunday. He couldn't say for sure whether he saw pieces inside the house. Understandably, all he noticed were flames. In the retelling, three months later, he still seemed rattled. He spoke slowly, and his hands twitched.

When I changed the subject to the hardwood floor installers, Glenn filled me in on what he'd found out about Stan's Flooring Company. The long-established business was thriving, the two men who had worked on the Landry house were above reproach, and the owner of Stan's had replaced the burned equipment before receiving insurance compensation.

No signs of fraud or financial motive there.

On to the next lead.

I popped over to Landry and drove around, looking for a homeless man and a boy.

No man. No boy.

I was beginning to believe Daphne Cartwright might have intentionally misled me.

I could only imagine Dennis McBride's conniption when he saw the bill for the time I'd spent pursuing this worthless lead at ninety dollars per hour.

Better move on.

I pulled into a Peaberry Coffee in the Landry Town Center, ordered a frozen mocha drink, and spread out at a corner table, where I placed my fourth call to Fritz Jubera, the man who had a contract on the Southfield house that had caught fire.

By some small miracle, I reached him instead of his voice mail. He didn't bother to apologize for not returning the three messages I'd left over the weekend. No matter. I asked him a series of questions and came to the conclusion that he wasn't a viable suspect in either arson.

For starters, he didn't seem overly concerned that he wouldn't be moving into a McBride home. He'd put in an offer on new construction in the Hilltop neighborhood, a find, and was set to move in nine days, on the same day as his original closing with Dennis. The swift rebound and fast escrow were marks of a good real estate agent. When I inquired about who had assisted him, Fritz named one of the top brokers in Denver, someone I knew only by reputation. In answer to my final query, he told me he'd been on a month-long African safari in June, which eliminated him as a candidate for the Landry fire.

Must be nice, having that kind of free time to assassinate wild animals.

What a morning!

Three leads and three dead-ends, but that's how investigations often proceeded, which is why I preferred to juggle several cases at once.

•••

Time for a fresh start.

At high noon, I walked through the door of Sports Fanatics, the bar Roxanne Archuletta owned at the corner of 17th and Blake in LoDo.

The place was empty except for a handful of men sitting at the bar, "lifers" by their appearance. They all had glazed looks, fixed on one of five big-screen TVs spread around the long, narrow room, and they diverted their eyes only long enough to glance toward the front door when it opened and to dip into the piles of food in front of them, baskets of fries and mountains of wings.

The room was decorated with sports posters and jerseys that lined exposed brick walls and hung from timbered ceilings. In the dim lighting, on the north wall I could distinguish a collage of dollar bills. On closer inspection, I saw that each had been defaced and left behind by a patron, most prettified with team logos. In the back of the bar, the flooring changed from hardwood to black tile, and there were two pool tables and six dartboards, none of which were in use. Bruce Springsteen's "Born in the USA" played in the background, and I hummed along while I waited for Roxanne Archuletta.

The bartender, Florence, had summoned her using an intercom under the counter.

In a few minutes, a woman wearing a tan T-shirt, khaki cargo pants, and brown high-tops came down the stairs at the side of the room. She gestured toward the dollar bills on the wall. "Guess how many?"

I factored in fifteen-foot ceilings. "Four thousand?"

She did a double take. "Florence told you?"

"Just a guess," I said honestly.

She raised her eyebrows, cast an appraising look, and extended her hand. "I'm impressed. There are 4,193. Roxanne Archuletta."

"Lauren Vellequette."

"What can I get you?" she said, in a surprisingly soft voice. She was tall, with a wide frame, but no fat, at least not on the body parts that were visible to me. For a second, I wondered about the ones I couldn't see, but then blocked the thought. Instinctively, I sat up a little straighter and tried to hold in my belly.

"A Coke would be nice. Diet Coke." I had no idea why I'd added that, because I hadn't drunk a diet soda since high school.

"Done," she said, signaling to Florence, who was slicing limes. "How about lunch? You want a Cobb salad or something?"

I couldn't continue the low-fat ruse. "Is the special still available?"

She smiled and removed mirrored, wraparound sunglasses, revealing the bluest eyes I'd ever seen. "That's what I like, a woman who likes food."

Roxanne Archuletta raised two fingers, and I noticed she wasn't wearing a ring, on either hand.

Florence nodded acknowledgement, and Roxanne and I headed up the stairs and onto a rooftop patio that offered brilliant views of Coors Field in the foreground and the Rocky Mountains in the background. There were fifteen tables, and Roxanne chose a four-top away from the only other diners, six businessmen.

She removed the umbrella and pulled out my chair, then cocked hers at an angle toward mine. When she sat and crossed her legs, her knee was an inch away from touching me. "Like I said on the phone, I appreciate you looking into this wilding episode."

I scooted my chair back a foot. "It's really had an impact?"

She replaced her sunglasses, despite overcast skies. "Unbelievable. Business is down at every bar, restaurant, and nightclub in LoDo, and that's on top of the shitty summer some of us had. I've tried everything to stay even with last year's numbers, but I'm treading water. If it gets any worse, I'll have to dip into my savings account on the wall down there," she said, no humor in her voice.

"I hope it doesn't come to that."

"Opening day for the Rockies, I had my warm fuzzy feeling, and that was the last time I've felt good."

"About the wilding—" I said, after thanking Florence, who had delivered a Diet Coke for me and ice water for Roxanne.

"That goddamn wilding! What can we do about spring rain and summer heat? Nothing. What can we do about the Rockies? Nothing. They'll be in rebuilding mode for ten years, and that's out of our control. But we sure as hell aren't going to sit by and do nothing about roving gangs. If we don't respond, we may as well kiss our businesses good-bye."

I set the straw to the side and took a sip of the soda. "Do other owners in the LoDo Business Interests feel the same?"

"Hell no!" Roxanne said, with a raucous laugh. "We're a ragtag bunch of hardheads, mostly men, who can't agree on anything. Some owners wanted to send out a press release to drum up business. Someone brought up that suggestion at one of our meetings earlier in the summer, when the Rockies were in the tank and it drizzled three weeks in a row. We brought in candidates for a marketing position, but that went nowhere. After the wilding, a few owners volunteered to bring their own firepower to the situation, if you get my drift. I talked the bunch of them into hiring you. You bring us the information, and we'll go from there. We'll probably deal with it privately, rather than take it to the police."

"Non violently?"

"Is there any other way?" Roxanne said, running her hand through shoulder-length black hair that was parted down the middle.

"I came down here Saturday night," I began delicately. "It was quite the experience."

"Did you get Maced?"

"Almost."

"Can you believe it's come to this?"

"If what I saw continues, there won't be any nightlife left to preserve," I said frankly.

"You're telling me. I don't mind cops directing traffic, but what's with the riot gear? I appreciate everything they're doing, but in the back of my mind, I think, if they dress up in riot gear, aren't they asking for a riot? I wish they'd bring back their old plan. Bag meters, keep out cars in a wider radius, use more plainclothes officers, and bring in mounted patrols at let-out. Did you see the barricades and roadblocks?"

I nodded. "I watched the police set them up."

"Those poor owners in the 1900 block of Market Street are the ones who are really suffering. One owner told me he does more than 20 percent of his business for the week in four hours, between midnight and two on Friday and Saturday. That's dropped to practically nothing."

I unfurled my paper napkin and arranged my plasticware. "Was this weekend quieter than most?"

"Better than last, but slower than usual."

"Has it always been so . . . " I groped for the right word, " . . . chaotic?"

"More so every year," Roxanne said, with a cool smile. "When I first opened this place, landlords realized they could get $8 a square foot from art galleries or $25 from bars and clubs. Guess which way the tide turned? After Coors Field opened, a new bar, restaurant, or nightclub popped up every month. You wouldn't believe the money we generate for the city and state in taxes."

"I'm sure it's significant."

"Millions. We're getting blamed for everything, but the truth is, most of the people who cause trouble never step foot in a LoDo establishment. Midnight strikes, and they cruise in looking for trouble. If they don't find any, they start some. They fire shots in the air, posture, steal cell phones from passersby, hassle women. How is it our fault that the area attracts trouble? If they didn't act out around here, the cops would bust them somewhere else. At a neighborhood meeting in the spring, we suggested turning on bright lights at let-out, airstrip wattage, but residents said the glare would disturb their sleep."

"I can understand their point," I said mildly.

"What are we supposed to do?" Roxanne retorted loudly

"I don't know, but—"

"I know exactly what to do, but it'll never happen."

Florence reappeared with two heaping baskets, and we suspended conversation.

I squirted hot mustard on the bratwurst with kraut and seasoned the

German potato salad with pepper.

Without embellishment, Roxanne tucked into her food, fitting a fourth of the brat into her mouth in one bite. Noting my astonishment, she mumbled sheepishly, "I'm used to eating alone."

"Me, too," I said, mouth full. "You have a way to solve the late-night problem?"

She nodded. "Stop serving liquor at two, but extend bar and nightclub hours until four."

I looked at her skeptically. "How would that help? Wouldn't it extend the problems, not eliminate them?"

"I'll tell you what it would eliminate: the 'one final shot' that takes place after we ring out last call. There would be no rush to clear the bars. No need to finish conversations in the street. Less drunk-driving accidents. The plan has merit, but city officials and residents won't give it a chance."

I crunched down on my pickle spear and covered my mouth, self-conscious about the amplified sound. "It does seem counter-intuitive."

Roxanne Archuletta stared at me intently. "Do you know what really goes on in this industry?"

I swallowed hard. "I'm not sure what you're asking."

"Have you ever worked in a bar or club?"

"No."

"I'm going to let you in on a dirty little secret, but you'd better not repeat it."

"I'm listening," I said apprehensively.

Roxanne Archuletta leaned forward. "We've got a huge problem with drunks, and here's why. No one comes in until 11:30, especially in the summer. We offer drink specials before eleven, but that doesn't change anything. Assuming customers show up around 11:30, that gives them two hours to get good and tanked. Believe me, they make the most of their time. Last call shouts out at 1:30 a.m., and the customers panic and pound down as many as they can in fifteen minutes, before we pull up drinks. Fifteen minutes after that, at two o'clock sharp, bouncers and bar staff push everyone out into the streets. We've instructed our employees to shout and shove, because we're afraid of fines from the city if we don't clear the building in time. Think about that," she said, wiping her mouth with a napkin. "The violence begins inside the establishment. We owners have to operate like that, or we risk losing our licenses."

I nodded restlessly. "I see where you're going with this."

"You don't know the half of it," Roxanne said, resignedly. "The doors fly open, and all these people hit the pavement at the same time, where cops yell at them to get in their cars. Suddenly, all the drunks are on the road. We send them back to the suburbs, smashed."

My eyes widened. "I'd never thought about it like that."

"No one has, but they should. We're talking about problems that extend way past a four-block square in LoDo."

"Have you proposed the extended hours plan to anyone in power?"

She squared her shoulders. "To anyone else who will listen. Most of the LoDo Business Interests owners support it, but they're my only allies. Similar plans have worked in other cities, but I can't get anywhere with the neighborhood groups. They all agree they can't live with the status quo, but they won't commit to anything new, and they sure as hell won't fund it. They say, 'It's your problem. Deal with it.' We try to deal with it, and they say, 'Forget it, this is our neighborhood.' Where's the give-and-take? If they have a better idea, bring it on, but they don't."

"I can see your frustration."

"Do you? LoDo gets slammed by the media, but this last-call, let-out shit goes on everywhere. You think for one minute this isn't happening in Cherry Creek North, Aurora, Glendale, Colfax, and at every nightspot in between? They don't have SWAT teams drawing attention to it, but they have the same problems we do. One of my friends owns the Diamond in Cherry Creek, and he called me this morning, gloating."

"Why?"

"His till was up 50 percent over the weekend, which figures, because mine was down 50 percent. It's always stuck in his craw that LoDo siphoned away Cherry Creek's business, little by little. What can I say? People come down here because it's a hip, vibrant scene. Or at least it was before teenagers started beating on each other in the middle of the street. Cherry Creek should send those delinquents a thank you note," Roxanne said sardonically.

I paused, deep in thought. "Business in Cherry Creek went up?"

Roxanne Archuletta nodded. "Every weekend since the wilding."

CHAPTER 8

"**O**h, Lord, no. I can't live in a church."

"It might be peaceful," I said, surveying the 1911 Congregational Church a developer had converted into five condos. Rollie Austin and I had rolled up to the church a few minutes earlier in her mint-green Nissan 350Z convertible with spinning gold rims, and it hadn't escaped my notice that the engine was still running.

"Honey, you have no idea the sins I've committed. You also must be misinformed about who comes to my house for social visits, and otherwise, at ungodly hours."

"God welcomes everyone, anytime," I said serenely, shifting uncomfortably in my seat. I shouldn't have had that towering piece of mud pie. What was I thinking? I'd felt full when Roxanne Archuletta offered, but I couldn't resist. Dessert or prolonging the appointment.

"You know that's not true about God. Some are more welcome than others, and I can promise you, my friends and acquaintances aren't among the righteous ones. I would further speculate that most haven't been inside a house of worship in years. I'd hate for them to break their streaks."

"You love lofts," I said persuasively. "The unit for sale is in the south half of the old nave, and it has a private yard."

She shot me a warning look, but I continued in a tranquil voice. "Storage in the church basement and period oak doors. Adjacent two-car garage and soaring great room. A high vaulted ceiling with four perpendicular tracery stone windows, whatever those are," I said, unable to spot them from my seat and too lazy to climb out. "It's only $579,000 for 2,213 square feet. That's a bargain for Congress Park."

"I wouldn't pay a cent for a square foot of church."

"You'd be within walking distance of the shops on 12th Avenue. Coffee, ice cream, sandwiches, books, hardware, antiques."

Rollie remained motionless, but her eyes flickered.

"There's a master suite on the site of the original altar."

She gave a dismal groan. "You want me sleeping, nuzzling, and nookying where holy men have walked and prayed?"

"When you put it that way . . . " My voice faded. I lowered my head, studied the sheet in my hands, and felt compelled to add one last feature from the listing agent's copy. "According to this, the windows are supposed to bring in the trees and sky."

"Honey!"

"Yes?" I said humbly.

"I don't care if there's a tree growing in the living room and clouds in the kitchen, I will not live here."

"Why didn't you say so?" I smiled weakly, responding to the tight knit in her brow. "Before I forget, Roxanne Archuletta said to tell you 'hi.'"

Rollie softened. "Isn't she a dynamo?"

"Why didn't you take her case?"

She looked away deviously. "Too busy."

"None of your investigators had time?"

"None with your touch, doll."

I stared at her speculatively. "Are you trying to set us up?"

"What if I am?"

"Don't," I said harshly, before editing myself. "Please . . . don't."

"I made the introduction," Rollie said breezily. "After that, you're on your own."

"I can't date a client."

"Says who?"

"Says me."

"You should give it a chance. She liked you."

I blushed. "You know this, how?"

"She called to thank me for the referral. Did you like her?"

"I liked her $2,500 retainer check."

She chuckled. "You said it!"

On to another subject before Rollie could grill me about Roxanne. "I've been meaning to ask, did you decide to compete for Ms. Senior America?"

"I registered," she said, beaming. "But don't tell the boys at the office. I want to surprise them with a win."

"Good for you."

"If you won't go out with Roxanne," she said, pulling an end-around, "how about that lady at Hustlers? Have you called her?"

Plainly, Rollie and I had different definitions of "lady." That's not how I would have classified the woman at the adjacent pool table, the one with bad breath and bad manners who handed me her phone number on a five-dollar bill.

"Not yet," I said vaguely, inclining my head toward the church. "You're sure about this?"

In response, Rollie peeled away from the curb, giving me mild whiplash.

•••

After Rollie dropped me back at the office, I jumped into my car and headed for Landry.

On the way, I stopped at a Starbucks on Colorado Boulevard and used the tainted five-dollar bill to purchase a java chip Frappuccino. Less than twenty-six hours had passed since my last elixir. The times were coming together closer and closer, but I'd worry about that tomorrow.

If I had to endure another search for a homeless man on a bike, I needed a treat.

My perseverance paid off on the first swipe through the Northwest Neighborhood of Landry.

I saw a bike, a trailer, and a man fitting Daphne Cartwright's description of the man who might have set the Landry fire.

The man looked harmless enough, seated on a bench in a park at Trinidad Street and 12th Avenue, a one-acre square with playground equipment and a picnic shelter.

I surprised him by approaching and landing on the bench opposite him. The dog at his feet, a black and white terrier mix, growled but didn't stir.

"I'm just resting, not hurting anyone," the man said, cradling a 40-ouncer.

I smiled reassuringly. "Me, too."

"This is a nice place to sit."

"It looks like it." I pulled my jacket tight and looked at the sky, full of dark clouds. "Something's moving in."

"Maybe." He swiped his hand across his nose.

"At least we're having a normal fall, instead of going straight from summer to winter."

He looked at me with interest. "Were you born in Denver?"

"I was. How about you?"

"In Conifer. I never meet people who were born in Colorado. What a pleasure. Where did you go to high school?"

"I hate to admit it, but Peak High School."

"Why the shame?"

I stirred my Frappuccino. "Everyone was rich and stuck-up. I didn't belong."

"Me neither. I went to Evergreen High but transferred to the Open School, the alternative high school. If you don't mind my asking, how old are you?"

"Forty-two, soon to be forty-three. You?"

"Forty-eight. Something like that."

That surprised me, because I would have pegged Daphne Cartwright's suspect in his early sixties, not late forties. He had greasy gray hair that stuck out in all directions, a bushy salt-and-pepper beard, a long, lined face, and hooded lids that partially hid bloodshot eyes. He sat in a slouch, his legs crossed like a woman's, the right one twitching. At frequent intervals, he took luxurious drags off a cigarette.

"What's your dog's name?"

"Pepper. We found each other under the Speer viaduct. You know what Native Americans call her?" He paused and blinked rapidly. "Soup."

I smiled politely.

"They eat dogs," he explained, with a wide grin. Behind cracked lips, he had a smattering of teeth, and in the top row, most were yellowed stubs, separated by large gaps. "It's a great honor for Natives. Add carrots, onions, and potatoes."

I licked whipped cream from the top of my drink and took a sip.

"You shouldn't say that in front of Pepper. She'll have nightmares."

"She's heard it all. I have an adopted cousin who's a Cheyenne River Sioux. We do outdoor murals together. You'd never know it, but we do okay," he said, his hands moving in circles powerlessly. "He has the talent, and I'm the grunt."

"He sketches and you paint?"

"Something like that. It's good work. I get by." He extended his hand, which trembled. "I'm Richard Leone."

We shook. "Lauren Vellequette."

"Thanks for talking to me."

I tilted my cup, trying to loosen the pieces of chocolate chip at the bottom. "Likewise."

"It's unusual to find someone who is interested and interesting."

"I've had practice," I said modestly. "I've sold real estate for twenty years, and now I'm a private investigator. Both occupations require an intense interest in people."

"A private eye. Uh-oh. Am I in trouble?" Richard said in a guarded tone.

"I hope not." I kept my tone intentionally light. "A builder hired me to investigate the fire at the house on Trinidad Street. Were you around in June?"

He let out a quick pant. "Must have been. I've been living here a while, off and on since winter. I moved from downtown to Southfield and decided to come over here. I like Landry. It's quiet. No crime, no police driving up and down the alleys, no competition."

I sucked loudly through the straw. "You're pretty far away from everything."

"I get by. I'd rather eat from a trash can than go to a shelter and have do-gooders look down on me. And I've never begged. I won't let another man buy my pride for a few coins, no matter how hungry I am. I don't make excuses. I've been wandering most of my life, and I'll tell you, that's by choice."

"Where do you sleep?"

"My main base is a culvert off 11th Avenue, but don't tell anyone."

I returned the wink. "I won't."

"You'll have to come by sometime. Call ahead." Richard laughed uproariously for a full minute. It must have been the booze. After he caught his breath, he added, "I found a cell phone once, but I didn't have anyone to call."

"No one in Conifer?"

"They've all died, the ones I cared about. Not from fire. No one was hurt in that fire on Trinidad Street, were they? It didn't look like it."

I straightened up. "You saw the fire?"

"The tail end. That was my third time by the house."

My pulse quickened. "The third time? You went by the house before the fire began?"

"I might have."

"Might have or did?"

He dropped his gaze. "Did. Twice."

"Can you tell me about it?"

He stared at me a long time before he spoke. "The first time I rode by, it was six-thirty in the morning, or thereabouts. I was on my way to seven o'clock church services. When I passed the house, Pepper barked. I looked back and saw a boy in the garage, carrying a cardboard box. I waved, but he didn't see me."

"Were there flames?"

Richard shook his head. "I would have noticed."

"Or smoke? Did you smell anything?"

"No, ma'am, but I can't smell much."

I moved to the edge of my seat. "When did you go by the house the second time?"

"After church."

"What time was that?"

He touched his watch, a vintage Mickey Mouse model with a silver, expandable band. "According to Mickey, nine straight up."

"Was the boy still there?"

Richard nodded.

"In the garage?"

"No, on the side of the house, peeking in a window."

"Did you approach him?"

"Not this time. I wanted to be with my thoughts from church."

"Would you recognize him if you saw him again?"

"Oh, sure. We used to bump into each other almost every day when I lived at Southfield."

My excitement rose. "You know him? He lives in Southfield? Where?"

"I couldn't say precisely. I was on his street once, but all the houses looked alike. We usually crossed paths at the skateboard park."

"Would you help me find him?"

Richard studied me, before answering cautiously. "Kevin doesn't need trouble. He gets in enough at school. He doesn't have any friends, except me, and I'm not what you would call reliable."

"If you saw him at dawn and at nine o'clock, I'm sure he didn't start the fire," I said hastily. "No one called it in until noon, but Kevin might have seen something."

"If I let you talk to him, he'll be okay?"

"How old is he?"

"Twelve."

"Legally, he's a juvenile," I said, dodging the question about consequences. "If he's a witness, he could be in danger. If he's the fire setter, someone needs to stop him before he hurts himself or someone else."

Richard's eyes widened. "I'll mull it over."

"Putting me in touch with him could only help."

"I mull better with spirits," Richard said, with a sideways grin. He underscored his point by turning his empty bottle upside down.

I used my straw to scoop out the last bit of chips. "Where's the nearest liquor store?"

CHAPTER 9

What a double-crosser, that Richard Leone.

One malt later, and he'd told me nothing more.

Not Kevin's last name.

Not cross streets that might be near the boy's house in Southfield.

Not his known habits or patterns.

One fact had slipped as Richard sipped—Kevin had a red Mohawk—but that might have been a lie.

Maybe there was no boy.

The more I considered Richard's version of events, the more I had misgivings.

What preteen boy would be up at six on a Sunday morning? If he lived in Southfield, what was he doing in Landry, miles away from home? Why would he spend three hours in an almost-completed house at 1125 Trinidad Street? Wouldn't fumes from the hardwood floor treatments have overpowered him? Presuming he hadn't stayed the whole time, why would he have returned? What was in the cardboard box he carried?

Interesting that Richard had brought up the cardboard box, a detail only the arsonist would have known. Maybe he removed the material from the Dumpster and used it as fuel. Was he the guilty one, trying to pin his crime on an innocent kid?

Who knew with Richard Leone?

How could I accurately evaluate someone under the influence?

We all had our vices, but Richard's chicanery put me in a foul mood.

I didn't like bribing alcoholics with alcohol, especially when the ploy failed.

Back at the office, my spirits sank further when I found evidence of deceit in Sasha's trash can.

I swear I wasn't probing. Something smelled funny, and I had to check every receptacle. I didn't find the source of the odor, but I found something rotten.

As I tried to concentrate on the arson case, thoughts of how I would confront Sasha kept interrupting.

I finally gave in and concocted a short script I'd follow when she came to work after school. The main goal was to control my temper.

After a few rehearsals, I felt prepared and could apply my full consideration to Jerry Hess, Dennis McBride's ex-partner.

•••

Jerry Hess, number two on Dennis McBride's list of enemies, right below Daphne Cartwright.

According to my notes, he and Dennis had dissolved a nine-year partnership over noise.

Specifically, noise from jetliners entering and exiting Denver International Airport.

DIA recently had celebrated its ten-year anniversary, claiming its place as one of the premier airports in the world. It ranked number five in the U.S. in volume and number one in efficiency, with the highest percentage of on-time arrivals.

That was the good news.

The bad news was that city planners in Denver and Aurora seemed to have forgotten why taxpayers paid $5.3 billion to build DIA: noise lawsuits.

The airport, twice the size of Manhattan, was comprised of fifty-three miles of flat land, and getting there required a twenty-four-mile, forty-five-minute, fifty-dollar cab ride from downtown.

Thank you, nearby residents, for bitching about Southfield International Airport.

When DIA first opened, everyone complained about the distance, how the airport was miles away from everything.

Now what was happening?

Denver and Aurora were spreading toward it.

Economists predicted that in twenty years, the area surrounding DIA would become an "aerotropolis," an economic hub capable of rivaling downtown and the Denver Tech Center. Experts forecast that 25 percent of the metro area's growth and 30 percent of its job expansion would appear within a few miles of DIA. They were quick to point out that the area already was growing at twice the rate of the metro area.

Over the past decade, development around DIA had unfolded in a well-designed order. Enterprises associated with airport travel were the first to appear: gas stations, rental car centers, parking lots, and hotels. Next came the relocation of businesses connected to airport commerce, such as shipping and cargo firms. Restaurants, retail, and business parks followed, and when toll-road E-470 was completed, the northeastern region was linked to other metro areas.

All well and good, if the development had stopped there.

But it hadn't.

Next came the houses, which was what had led to Jerry Hess and Dennis McBride's breakup.

I'd heard Dennis's version about their joint venture near DIA.

Tomorrow morning, I'd give Jerry Hess a chance to tell his side of the story.

••••

At five o'clock, Sasha walked through the door, dripping with rain.

Her pink Sketchers were waterlogged, her "Teenage Millionaire" black T-shirt clung to her chest, and her torn bleached denim short skirt had darkened with moisture. She wasn't carrying an umbrella or wearing a coat.

I set aside the list of questions I'd prepared for Jerry Hess and waved a wrinkled sheet of paper at her. "What's this?"

She scarcely glanced at it as she set her backpack on top of a filing cabinet, and she took her time shaking out her hair. "What?"

"You know what it is," I said, in a measured tone. "What was it doing in the trash?"

"It fell off my desk."

I inclined my head toward the corner of her office. "Into the can four feet away, after wadding itself up? Sasha!"

"I knew you'd be mad," she said accusingly.

"With $316.35 in non-work related charges on the American Express bill, you were right about that. Didn't I make it clear that the card was for work only?"

"Yeah, but—"

"Didn't I tell you that if you abused the privilege, you—"

"Yeah, but—"

"Is this why you asked me for an advance on your paycheck?"

"Maybe," she said meekly.

"Sasha!"

"Yes, that's why I needed the money," she screamed.

I folded my arms across my chest. "If you were me, what would you do in this situation?"

She clamped her mouth shut.

"Sasha!"

"Take it away," she mumbled.

"Is that what I should do?"

"You could be really nice and give me another chance," she said pleadingly.

"I don't know . . . "

"You can't take it from me," she whimpered. "All my friends have credit cards. What would I do?"

"What are these charges? Are they legitimate?"

She scrunched up her face. "Probably, but I don't know for sure. I got mad at myself for using it so much, and I threw away all the receipts."

"Next time, you need to throw away the card."

"I won't do it again, promise."

"How did you manage to spend $300 in one month?"

"It's easy," she said cheerfully. "Lunches, CDs, clothes, movies. I never had money before. The witch only gave me five dollars a week. I love having my own money."

"But you weren't using your money," I said deliberately. "You were putting charges on the business credit card. At any other company, you'd be fired for that."

"I would?" she said, stunned. "Even if I meant to pay it back?"

"Yes, and what happened to your paycheck? Where did that money go?"

"I had to pay for something."

"What?"

"I broke a stupid windshield," she said, in a rush. "The car wasn't supposed to be there. He was parked in a yellow zone."

I grabbed my head with both hands, to keep it from exploding. "How did you break a windshield?"

"I skipped a pebble. Taylor did it, too."

My voice became eerily quiet. "You threw a rock?"

"It was tiny. We take them out of the neighbor's yard. It's not stealing or anything. They have a million of them."

"Why do you do this?" I said, mutilating the first word of the sentence.

"It's something to do."

"After you broke the windshield, did you get caught, or did you confess?"

"The man was sitting in the car."

"Otherwise, you would have owned up to it?"

She shrugged indolently. "Probably not. He shouldn't have parked there. It's not fair. He made Taylor cry."

"How much did the windshield cost?"

"Six hundred dollars."

I drew in a sharp breath.

"Is that high?" she said, confused.

"Extremely. Did Taylor pay half?"

"No. She doesn't have any money, and she couldn't tell her mom. She's already in big trouble for a cell phone bill. She won't get allowance for five more months."

"I've never heard of Taylor. Who is she?"

"My best friend."

"Since when?"

"Like tenth grade," Sasha huffed. "Can I go now?"

"Go where?"

"Out."

71

I ran my fingers through my hair, tugging on it a little too hard. "You just got here."

"I don't feel like working. My stomach hurts."

"Why haven't I met Taylor?"

Sasha rolled her eyes. "She doesn't like strangers."

"I'm not a stranger. I'm your employer and your . . . guardian."

"Not officially. Not my guardian."

"Unofficially." I took a deep breath. "Why didn't you come to me when this rock incident happened?"

Her shoulders slumped. "I knew you'd be mad."

I softened my tone. "Are you scared to talk to me?"

"No." She looked down. "Sometimes."

"I'm on your side."

Her head jerked up. "Do I have to pay back the money on the card?"

"Not this time. The $600 extortion was punishment enough."

I threw the credit card statement back in the trash and headed toward my office.

Her small cry stopped me. "Thanks, Lauren."

I turned, and the look of naked relief on her face shook me.

I couldn't imagine the punishment Sasha had faced for every mistake in her life, but I knew the major penalties. At ten, she'd witnessed her mother's rape inside the family home. At eleven, she became bedridden with a "mono-like" illness that forced her to drop out of school. At twelve, she tried to kill herself with her father's vodka. At thirteen, she set off sparklers in her bedroom and lost pieces of her left leg in an attempt to stomp out the fire. From the hospital, she went into foster care, where she remained until I moved her into the ClockTower over the summer.

Technically, she was still in foster care, as far as the state of Colorado was concerned. Her foster parents, the Bidwells, were content as long as they continued to receive monthly stipends, and with any luck, the arrangement would continue, unnoticed, until next May, when Sasha turned eighteen and became legally emancipated.

I could only hope we didn't drive each other crazy before then.

•••

The next morning, the first words I heard were, "You're working for a liar."

Not a very nice thing to say to someone after she'd woken up to drizzle, left the house at the crack of dawn, driven to Commerce City on only one coffee, and ruined her Mary Janes cutting through mud.

I was now standing in an unheated construction trailer, leaning against a watercooler.

I should have worn a scarf, but those were still tucked away in a drawer, awaiting the first snowfall. I cinched my blouse tighter before speaking in a controlled tone. "Excuse me?"

"Dennis McBride is a liar. He breaks his word every day. I'm done with him. Why did he send you to me?"

"Dennis made a list of people he's had conflict with, and—"

Jerry Hess interrupted harshly. "Was I number one?"

I shivered. "You were up there."

He rocked on his stationary chair, the only seat in the trailer. "He has some nerve. He leaves behind a trail of exes— ex-partners, ex-employees, ex-friends, ex-business associates, ex-clients, ex-subcontractors, ex-girlfriends— and he takes a swing at me?"

"Ex-girlfriends?" I said casually.

"Check with the last one. She'll tell you the truth about Dennis."

"What's her name?"

Jerry Hess looked at me shrewdly. "He didn't tell you? She's not on the list?"

I blew on my hands. "No."

"Go ask him. Make him say her name out loud."

Jerry Hess's round face was consumed with fury, a familiar emotion judging by the scowl marks permanently etched between his beady eyes. In his fifties, he had a shiny head with tufts of gray hair above the ears, a graying goatee, and a bulbous nose. His navy corduroys, checked blue shirt, and bomber jacket looked as if he'd just purchased them, and his tasseled loafers didn't have a fleck of mud on them.

"Can you tell me why your partnership with Dennis dissolved?"

"Call it a difference of opinion."

"About what?"

"Everything. How to treat people. How to resolve issues. How to communicate. How to work with integrity. Dennis McBride can't make a single statement without including a lie. You know what was the last straw? I heard him telling an investor that his nephew was a professional snowboarder. Dennis doesn't even have a nephew. Why would he lie about that? Because he can't stop himself."

"People show off all the time, for no good reason," I said mildly.

"Do they steal, too?" Jerry sneered. "You wouldn't believe the stories I've heard since we went our separate ways. People can't wait to tell me what an asshole he is. The best one came from a carpenter in Boulder. He told me how he was building a custom home for Dennis, and the job site kept getting hit. Every sub on the project had something stolen. This carpenter was smart. He'd carved his name onto his tools and equipment. Any idea where his chisel turned up? In Dennis's truck."

"It could have been a mistake, a misplacement."

"It wasn't," Jerry said flatly. "The carpenter went to the police, they searched Dennis's garage, and it was full of stolen goods, all taken from his own sites, all from his own guys."

My head throbbed. "How did he avoid prosecution?"

"He bought his way out of it, bribed the tradesmen not to press charges. He weasels out of everything. Take for example how he left me high and dry on our project near DIA. It's a miracle I found outside financing to continue. Dennis decided at the last minute that it was a bad idea to build too close to the airport. Where did that leave me? With my pants around my ankles."

"Where is your DIA project?"

"Between 60th Avenue and Pena Boulevard, east of Tower Road."

"It's my understanding that Dennis was concerned about noise from the airport."

"Who isn't, but what's the fuss?" Jerry said disagreeably. "The key is conscientious home building, full disclosure, and litigation prevention. I'll install triple-pane windows, heavy-duty insulation, and central air. If I disclose to buyers that they'll be living under aircraft flight paths and put an easement on their titles stating that they have no right to sue over aircraft noise, that ought to take care of it."

"What about when DIA expands to its full capacity of twelve runways and has twice as many arrivals and departures? People might sign a document saying they understand there will be noise, but won't it be different when they actually hear the noise?"

Jerry sprang from his chair and rummaged in the top drawer of a filing cabinet near the door. He retrieved a thick file, laid it on the desk, and pawed through architectural drawings, artist renderings, floor plans, site plans, contracts, and work orders. When he came across two photographs, he twisted around, held the photos in front of me, and jabbed at them.

"These are aerial shots of the Dallas-Fort Worth and Kansas City airports. People buy houses within a mile, and they're not suing anyone. At full airport construction, I'll still be outside the FAA noise-limit boundary, two and a half miles from the nearest runway. A little noise now and then doesn't bother people."

"You call roaring jets passing overhead every few minutes a little noise now and then?"

He plunked down on the metal chair. "I wouldn't live there personally, but I'm getting pressure from other developers. They need the residential to spur more commercial. Do you know why I'm building around DIA? Because buyers want to live there. That's what will drive it, demand. I can't control that. If I don't build the $250,000 homes, someone else will."

"But you fault Dennis McBride for pulling out?"

"I fault Dennis for swindling someone every day before lunch. He's building a house for this year's Carnival of Homes. Did he tell you about that? About how he screwed a rancher out of land that had been in his family for four generations?"

"No."

"Six years ago, Dennis stole land near E-470 and Smoky Hill Road and laughed about it. He lowballed Bob Cavanaugh, had him sign a contract he probably didn't understand, then kept putting off the closing because he couldn't come up with the cash. I didn't think that deal would ever get done, with all the acrimony on both sides, but it did somehow. About a month ago, Cavanaugh showed up here, out of the blue, as mad as ever, looking for Dennis."

A new name, Bob Cavanaugh. I made a note. "What did you tell Bob?"

"That I had nothing to do with Dennis anymore."

"Did you give him current contact information for Dennis?"

"Not after I saw the look in his eyes and his loaded rifle."

My forehead creased. "He was that mad?"

"I'd call him determined. Dennis better watch out," Jerry Hess said ominously, "or his Carnival home might catch fire."

CHAPTER 10

Talk about contrast.

I left Jerry Hess's housing development in Commerce City, where homes that looked like cardboard cutouts sold for $150,000, and headed to the Ice House Lofts, a rugged, eight-story building in LoDo, where parking spaces started at $50,000.

In between, I stopped off for an early lunch at the Sushi Den on South Pearl Street.

I treated myself to a lobster roll, marinated tofu salad, and green tea ice cream, but I should have included an aspirin chaser with my two glasses of ice water.

The hour was now two o'clock, and I had a splitting headache, compliments of Allen Billich, a vocal opponent of the LoDo Business Interests group.

At Roxanne Archuletta's behest, I'd made an appointment with the home owners association president to see if he could shed any light on the LoDo wilding incident.

What a blowhard!

As I listened to his monotone monologue, I blinked slowly, attempting to avert a full-on migraine.

"LoDo is the best place to live," Allen gushed. "We're within walking distance of the Denver Center for the Performing Arts, the opera house, the art museum, the history museum, the library, the Paramount Theater, Pepsi Center, Coors Field, Six Flags, and the aquarium. We have some of the finest restaurants in the state, including six steakhouses. We have wonderful retail, with the crown jewel, the Tattered Cover. We're steps away from the banks of two rivers and within easy walking distance of the train station and bus station."

"As if loft owners travel by Greyhound," I said wearily.

Only fifteen minutes had crept by, and already I'd tired of Allen Billich's pitch and disingenuous posturing.

He should talk. After all, he lived in the quietest building in LoDo.

Built in 1895, the red brick warehouse had started life as the Littleton Creamery, a wholesaler of butter, cheese, cream, and dairy supplies. Nearly 85,000 cubic feet of sawdust were used in the initial phase of construction, and by 1916, when the creamery was producing 30,000 pounds of butter a day, an additional 73,000 cubic feet of cork and plaster were added to bolster insulation. Long after the creamery halted operations, the building was used as a cold-storage facility, housing furs from local stores and even an occasional cadaver. By 1979, all activity had ceased in the building. Yet, when developers purchased the property for $1.2 million two years later, three-foot-thick ice remained on the ceiling, and the building took seven weeks to defrost, a testament to its sound construction. The warehouse sat vacant until 1998, when a builder transformed it into the Ice House Lofts, consisting of ninety upper-floor residences and ground-floor commercial space.

Allen Billich had purchased one of the first lofts available, a second-floor, 1,425-square-foot, two-bedroom, two-bath unit for $375,000. His investment was now worth upward of $700,000 and climbing, as the noise level in LoDo rose.

His corner loft was the real deal, with hardwood floors, one-foot by three-foot bearing supports, thirteen-foot ceilings, exposed rafters, and antique timbers. Abundant natural light flowed through large arched windows, reflected off the steel hood above the kitchen island, and bounced to the mezzanine study above the living room. An archway off the living room led to a balcony with an unobstructed view of the mountains.

In keeping with the rich history of the building, Allen had chosen furnishings straight from the Old West. He had a wagon wheel chandelier, antler lamps, Navajo blankets, a turn-of-the-century scale, and a potbelly stove. Bear traps and antique rifles hung from the walls, a bighorn sheep mount rose above the fireplace, and an aluminum buffalo, at 50 percent scale, overwhelmed one side of the room.

Allen took a careful sip of herbal tea and replaced the cup in its saucer. "You couldn't ask for anything more than the lifestyle we have in LoDo."

"How about a quiet night's sleep?"

He pinched a coarse smile. "I'm not sure I understand why Roxanne Archuletta and her group hired you."

"They want to find out who's behind the wilding, and they want to make sure it doesn't happen again. They want the media to move on to another story, and they want the police to back off so that business stops tanking."

Allen adjusted his bolo tie and put his black cowboy boots on the saddle footstool. "A police retreat would be inadvisable."

"You want the police to set up a militarized zone two nights out of seven?"

"If necessary," he said, loudly blowing his nose into a red handkerchief. "I understand their service to this area can't continue forever, but I'm concerned they'll return to their previous levels of patrols."

"Which were?"

"Inadequate, to say the least. Two or three officers on most weekends, sometimes none. I support an increased police presence, and I'm sure most LoDo residents would agree. My firm belief is that the minute the police pull out, problems will increase. I have no objection to extra officers."

I rubbed my eyes. "In SWAT gear?"

He shrugged indifferently. "I'm sure they're trained to use appropriate force, as each confrontation demands. They've averaged forty arrests per weekend since the crackdown. I'd be happier if it were one hundred, and it easily could be five hundred, if you saw the aberrant behavior. We need to send a message that riotous acts will not be tolerated."

"According to Roxanne, most of the arrests have been African-American and Hispanic youth," I said neutrally.

"What's your point?"

I looked at him squarely. "Don't you find that convenient?"

He met my gaze. "Not at all. They're troublemakers."

"Kids with darker skin tones are more likely to make trouble?" I said, my temper firmly in check.

Allen Billich nodded and pursed his puffy lips. Again, he was one to talk. He was as white as they came. The only color on his oblong, chubby face arose from a vertical vein on the side of his head and liver spots on his beak nose. He had hazel eyes and snow-white hair.

"Or maybe young African-Americans and Hispanics are more likely targets for police harassment," I pushed.

"This discussion is pointless," Allen said grouchily. "We home owners intend to protect our property rights, by whatever means necessary."

"Legal means?"

"Of course," he said, insulted. "If we have to pressure the mayor and City Council to safeguard our neighborhood on Friday and Saturday nights, we'll continue to do so."

"Wouldn't Roxanne's plan for extended bar and nightclub hours make more sense in the long run?"

Allen let loose a bitter laugh. "It's a ludicrous proposal. Insanity masquerading as a solution."

"If the bars and nightclubs could stay open until four, but stop serving liquor at two, and no new customers were allowed in, wouldn't that eliminate explosive let-outs?"

He adjusted his rectangular glasses, which matched the gold band on his pinky. "Under Ms. Archuletta's after-hours ordinance, dancing and entertainment would still be permissible."

"Yes, but people could filter out at their leisure, instead of in a mad rush. Snacks, coffee, and soft drinks might sober them up."

"Longer hours," Allen said darkly, "mean more crowds, more noise, and more crime. Plain and simple. Ms. Archuletta and her friends don't want to hear this, but if they'd look at the most recent arrests in LoDo, by hour, they'd detect an interesting pattern—2,555 were made last year, and about one-third of those came between 11 p.m. and 1 a.m. How would 4 a.m. solve that?"

Before I could answer, he scoffed. "It wouldn't, and I've tried to tell her this. We used to have sociable conversations between neighbors and proprietors, but not since Roxanne Archuletta became the spokesperson for LoDo Business Interests. She devised this ridiculous plan, and the tone is quite adversarial. Their clan would need support from LoDo residents before they could take anything to City Council, much less pass it. I can guarantee that will never happen."

"If Roxanne's idea won't work," I said reasonably, "what would you suggest?"

He didn't hesitate. "We need increased security, more street patrols, better lighting, signage about noise and litter ordinances, and trash removal Saturday and Sunday mornings. All paid for by club owners, I might add."

I concealed a yawn. "Why?"

"Home owners shouldn't have to contribute to those services," he said, horizontal lines across his forehead deepening. "They're the responsibility of proprietors, a cost of doing business. I'll rejoice the day that I hear an admission from Roxanne Archuletta that her responsibility extends past opening the doors at two and sending drunken crowds into the streets."

"I don't know how you can expect businesses to pick up the entire tab when, as you pointed out, everyone benefits from the cachet of LoDo. I doubt any loft owners have complained about the value of their real estate tripling in the past fifteen years."

"I wish you luck, although I doubt you'll have any," he said, his face twisting in condescension. He rose, with effort, and the extra hundred pounds that had settled around his midsection spread out in waves. "The only way to stop this is to catch those ruffians in the act."

I interpreted the signal to leave and stood. "Thanks for your time. Regardless of how everything turns out with the wilding, I hope you can resolve these other neighborhood problems."

For an instant, Allen's features softened. "Talk to Saul Eichelberg about the wilding."

I reached for the notebook in my purse, the first occasion I'd had to write anything. "Who's he?"

"The unofficial mayor of LoDo. He and his wife bought a building on Blake Street in the late 1970s. He and I see eye to eye on holding our ground with the bar closing times, but he's more inclined to push for consensus on other issues."

"Where can I find Saul?"

Allen sneezed, without bothering to cover his mouth. "1423 Blake."

"Bless you." I stepped away from the cloud of germs. "And you think he might know something about the kids who were fighting?"

"He ought to," Allen said, dabbing at his nose. "He saw the entire incident."

•••

Sasha was a breath of fresh air at the end of a day spent with Jerry Hess and Allen Billich.

She seemed so innocent and unspoiled, I thought tenderly, until I caught sight of her camouflage pants tucked into knee-high combat boots. At least she'd tempered the effect with a braided Moroccan belt.

I waved as I walked by her desk.

She was on the computer and phone, but acknowledged me with a quick wave.

I went into my office, closed the door, and changed clothes.

I traded a textured jacket, V-neckline blouse, and cotton pants for fuzzy sweats and a rugby shirt. I tossed my brown ankle boots under the desk and removed onyx earrings and a glass bead necklace and placed them on the blotter.

I lay on the couch, in the dark, struggling with the graffiti-like images that flashed in front of my eyes.

After a short period of time, my headache subsided, and I could sit up without feeling nauseous. For good measure, though, I plucked two Bayer from the bottom drawer of my desk and swallowed them dry.

I turned on a desk lamp, opened my laptop, and began to type a progress report on the McBride Homes arson case.

Where did the investigation stand at the end of five days?

I'd eliminated two suspects, Stan's Flooring Company and Fritz Jubera.

If the cause of the Landry fire was accidental, as initially determined by the Metro Fire Bureau, the last workers on the job site certainly were to blame for leaving behind oily rags. However, if someone intentionally set the blaze, which I accepted as fact in light of the subsequent fire at Southfield, that would clear Stan's workers. After my meeting in LoDo, I'd stopped by the company's showroom on 6th Avenue and spoken with the manager. Everything I learned confirmed what Glenn Warner, Dennis McBride's foreman, had conveyed. The folks at Stan's seemed genuinely distressed by the catastrophe, they had high opinions of McBride Homes, and they'd replaced all of the equipment they'd lost in the fire.

Dead end there.

On the drive back to the office, I'd also called Fritz Jubera's real estate agent and verified that, indeed, Fritz had been on a safari in June, making it impossible for him to ignite a fire from another continent.

Another fizzle. Damn.

At some point in every investigation, I had to remind myself that negative answers eventually led to positive outcomes.

This was that time.

Two leads down, a score to go.

I had several viable suspects from the Landry neighborhood: Daphne Cartwright, the asbestos activist; Richard Leone, the vagrant; and Kevin, the boy who might have started the fire at Landry or seen the fire setter.

I could conduct background checks on Daphne and Richard, a task made simple by the generous monthly subscription fees I paid to information firms, and as soon as the concrete dried—the rain had stopped around noon—I could visit the skateboard park in Southfield, allegedly Kevin's favorite hangout.

Good plan.

That brought me back to Dennis McBride's list of enemies.

Jerry Hess was bitter, no surprise, and eager to implicate his ex-partner in all kinds of nefarious doings. He'd also added to the number of people who hated Dennis. An ex-girlfriend he wouldn't name and Bob Cavanaugh, the rancher with the shotgun.

Cripes!

No sooner had I crossed off one suspect than two more appeared.

At this rate, I'd exhaust the $5,000 retainer before the end of the week and have to requisition more.

What to do next?

That was a good question.

The Southfield site held promise, but I couldn't legally intrude.

I'd passed through the neighborhood on my way to lunch at the Sushi Den and cursed at the yellow tape still stretched around the burned house.

I needed to instruct Dennis to lean on authorities to release the scene. If by the end of the week Max Spiker continued to refuse, I'd sneak in when he wasn't there. The arson investigator had to rest sometime. If not on Sunday, then perhaps in the middle of the night.

In the interim, whatever happened to the list of employees Dennis had fired in the last six months? No one from McBride Homes had sent over personnel records.

I'd deal with that, too.

I stopped typing and reached for the phone to call Dennis McBride.

CHAPTER 11

That night, I tossed and turned, visions of arsons and wildings dancing through my head.

Sleep was out of the question.

I focused instead on one of my favorite subjects: pretext, a powerful investigative tool I used in a variety of ways. I posed as someone I wasn't. I told lies. I pretended to represent people I didn't. I created deception. I misrepresented the true purpose of interviews.

I did it all.

As a private investigator, I used pretext every week to obtain otherwise unobtainable information.

In a first-party pretext, I lied to the subject, and in a third-party pretext, I approached someone familiar with the target and lied—to a friend, family member, coworker, acquaintance, or business associate.

Lie, lie, lie, that's all I did.

As long as I didn't lie to myself about lying, I felt comfortable with the levels of deceit required to operate as a detective.

Truthfully?

Maybe a smidge more than comfortable.

From the moment I heard about pretexting, I rejoiced, for it fit me like a skin I'd worn all my life.

I was born to lie.

What did that say about me?

That I was a damn good investigator.

How would I handle this gift for pretext, okay lying, if I ever found a girlfriend again?

Someone like Roxanne Archuletta, perhaps?

Well, I'd cross that bridge when I came to it, and I surprised myself (more than a little) by realizing that I wanted to come to it.

I drifted to sleep with a smile on my lips.

•••

The next morning, Dennis McBride wiped all the cheer from my soul.

"If Jerry Hess touches my Carnival home, I'll kill him," he shouted, unnecessarily.

I sat ten feet from him and wasn't hard of hearing.

The office was in the same state of chaos as on my last visit, but at least Dennis was fully dressed this time. He wore a white, starched shirt, taupe twill trousers, and slip-on leather shoes.

Because the red and white cooler was missing, I'd pushed aside a duffel bag and was making do with six inches of leather couch.

"Calm down," I said softly, concerned by the coloring in his face, a reddish-purple hue.

He flung back his head. "I have my sweat and blood invested in that house."

I answered with a cool smile. "Jerry won't do anything to your Carnival home. He's upset that you pulled out of the project near DIA, but he doesn't seem bent on revenge."

Dennis sat, as if praying, shaking his head in denial, eyes fluttering. "I don't know why. We never intended to do vertical at DIA. We planned on picking up sixty acres, subdividing, and selling it off."

"He claims you did plan to build, but you couldn't come up with your share of the money."

"Not true," he yelled. "Homes and runways don't mix. Jerry's asking for trouble."

"Dennis, please," I said, almost inaudibly. "Jerry's housing development is 2.5 miles away from the end of a proposed runway. The airport might never add it."

"They'll build that runway," Dennis said stoutly. "What if home owners decide to fight airport expansion? I don't need that crap. There's plenty of land around Denver to develop, without asking for trouble. I want to create communities, not sit in depositions with airport lawyers. They can conduct all the noise assessments they want and mark up maps, but people will be miserable."

I consulted my notes. "Jerry's houses will conform to FAA regulations of noise levels. They'll be below the 65-mark designated for residential—"

"That doesn't mean buyers won't complain," he said, silencing me. "Go stand on the ground where he's building. Even without the new runway, the noise is deafening You have to stop talking every time a plane passes. Jerry can do anything he wants with the houses, the best windows and insulation, but people won't be able to sit outside. Why include yards, patios, or decks? No one will use them. I can't have my name attached to a project like that."

I looked at Dennis, somewhat appalled. "Yet, you felt comfortable selling the land to other residential builders."

He shrugged dismissively. "I have to make a living. What exactly did Jerry say about my Carnival home?"

"Only that you'd screwed Bob Cavanaugh out of the land. Jerry told me Bob came looking for you about a month ago, with a loaded rifle."

"Cavanaugh does that all the time," Dennis said, his breathing more controlled. "He's steamed that I paid $2 million for land his great-grandfather bought for $500. He saw the price of the lots I'm offering and blew a gasket. He does the math and comes up with $18 million gross, but he's not figuring in infrastructure, land set aside for open space, sales and marketing costs, those type expenses. He didn't have the expertise to subdivide a homestead. He had to sell to someone. Why not me?"

"Did Bob find you a month ago?"

Dennis cracked his knuckles. "I'm hard to miss. I've had the same office for ten years. Cavanaugh came here after work one day, I poured him a whiskey, and we came to an understanding."

"That involved money?"

"Hell, no. I gave him enough of that already. Naming rights. I told him we'd call the next subdivision Cavanaugh Ranch. That's all he wanted. It's a hassle to change everything in county filings and marketing materials, but what can I say? I'm a nice guy."

I didn't respond to his smarmy smile. "Jerry said this year's Carnival of Homes is near Smoky Hill Road and E-470."

He nodded. "That's the closest major intersection, but Prairie Acres is ten miles to the east. I bought 1,500 acres off Cavanaugh, and I'm selling custom sites. Half I sold to Frontier Homes for semi-customs. The rest are available to the public. I have reservations on eighty, and I should be sold out six months after the Carnival. Lots start at $120,000."

"How much will the houses cost?"

"Most builders are shooting for the midsixes to the mideights."

"And the Carnival homes?"

"We'll have five, on a cul-de-sac, on one-acre lots. They should come in between $1.5 and $2.8 million."

I shifted my weight on the couch and almost fell off. "I've never heard of Prairie Acres. What's out there?"

"Nothing," Dennis said, buoyed. "That's what people love. They're away from civilization, but close enough to commute to the Denver Tech Center or Inverness Business Park. We set aside a large gulch as open space. Wildlife is everywhere. I've seen meadowlarks, owls, foxes, coyotes, eagles. We have design restrictions that cap home heights so that none will top the crests of hills. This is a classy project."

"How far along is your Carnival home?"

"We're finished with framing, roofing, and sheathing, just moved into the dried-in stage, on track for a spring completion." He rubbed his hands greedily. "I can't wait. This one will set me for the next five years. People in the industry still talk about the one we did in '97, in the Pinery, south of Parker. Did you tour it?"

"Er, no," I said, not wanting to admit that I'd never been to a Carnival of Homes. The thought of hundreds of people traipsing through a house at the same time made me claustrophobic.

"That was a once-in-a-lifetime, one-of-a-kind, Old World design. We had a mural in the sunroom, lots of wood, two-story fountain in a copper turret, columns, extra-wide halls, music room, three-story stairway. I lost money on it, but in terms of reputation and marketing, it was worth every penny. I'm still riding the wave."

"How were you chosen to participate?"

"In the Pinery, I submitted a design, and a committee awarded the slot. This time, I coordinated the project. I acquired the land, set up the review team, the works. I'm on the board of the Builders Association of Colorado, which sponsors the Carnival. This is the twentieth anniversary, and we should see one hundred thousand people come through next April. Some people complain that Carnival houses are obscene, but that's what I like about them. All of the builders can show off their talents. It's like having a piece in an art gallery."

"Were you awarded a slot again this year?"

"Sure," Dennis said, with a guileless grin. "In exchange for all my hard work, I had first dibs on the best lot. It can't be beat."

"Is your Carnival house under contract?"

"Nope. Not until it's done. This is the only exception I make."

"Doesn't that make you nervous, building something so expensive on spec?"

"Every year, during the public showings, at least one house goes under contract. I'll wager all the marbles, it'll be mine. Take a look," he said, rising from his chair. He moved a set of golf clubs from in front of the credenza and fumbled through a stack of blueprints. After he retrieved a full-color sketch, he stood over me with it.

I let out a low whistle. "Handsome. How much?"

"Two-point-five million, somewhere in there. Seven thousand square feet, six bedrooms, a guest house, an outdoor pavilion," he said, becoming more animated with every feature. "A two-thousand-bottle wine cellar, black glass his and her showers in the master bath, hidden poker room, library with rolling ladders, butler's pantry, elevator, two-story wall of water. I'm not holding back anything. You'll have to see the sliding glass doors that disappear into the exterior wall of the indoor/outdoor sunroom."

I nodded admiringly. "I've heard about those sunrooms."

"Chances are you've never heard of this," he said, stroking the garage doors on the sketch. "A four-car garage with rotating turnstile. You pull in, park, and it rotates your car. You never have to back out. That was my contribution. I got the idea from a car collector in Los Angeles."

"Clever. Who came up with the French Chateau design for the house?"

"That was my ex-girlfriend's idea. Don't tell my wife, or she'll burn the place down," he said, with an easy chuckle, "The ex loved that Loire Valley, French Renaissance, Louis-whoever period."

"Now that you mention your ex-girlfriend," I said, taking advantage of the opening, "could she have set the fires?"

His smile faded. "Not a chance."

"Are you sure?"

"We're not bringing my ex into this."

I remained expressionless. "What if she—"

"She didn't. She wouldn't set a fire, for fear it might chip her manicure," he said, with an unpleasant undertone. "She's never filled a gas tank in her life. She'd drive ten extra miles for a full-service station, and she didn't like me pumping either. She said I came into the car smelling like gas."

"Jerry Hess was fairly insistent that she might hold a grudge, and if—"

"Drop it," Dennis McBride said calmly, over my words. "We gave each other enough grief when we were together."

CHAPTER 12

I should have been immune, inoculated over the years, but occasionally Denver's outrageous housing prices shocked even me.

I expressed my dismay in quarter-million, half-million, and three-quarter-million-dollar increments. As in, how could anyone pay a quarter-million for an 816-square-foot Tudor in Mayfair? How could someone pay a half-million for a 1,500-square-foot bungalow in Washington Park? How could someone pay three-quarters of a million for a 2,200-square-foot Mediterranean in Congress Park that would have cost a quarter-million fifteen years ago?

Later that afternoon, when Rollie Austin and I pulled up to the curb in the middle of the 2500 block of South Emerson Street, I almost laughed at the audacity of the agent who had priced this property slightly below $400,000.

If someone had asked me two minutes earlier, I'd have said that I'd seen it all in my years of driving up and down the streets of Denver, but I'd never seen anything like this.

Smack in the center of Denver's Harvard Park neighborhood, a middle-class collection of traditional Tudors, ranches, and bungalows, sat Hansel and Gretel's home.

Rollie cackled enough for both of us. "This is a hobbit house, honey."

I consulted the MLS description. "The agent describes it as, 'An English cottage that invites comparison with the famed Cotswold Cottages.' She didn't say anything about asymmetrical design or peeling stucco."

I shook my head slowly as I studied the sloping, uneven slate roof that mimicked the look of thatch, the steep gables, and the massive stone chimney that dominated the side of the house.

"Watch out, or half-sized hobbits might run out the front door," Rollie said, amusing herself. "I may be too tall for this house."

"You want to skip it?"

She giggled. "Never."

We went inside, and Rollie chuckled through the entire tour, while I felt like crying.

Call me cynical, but I didn't see the charm.

The house had low doors and a weird smell emanating from the living room—mildew coated with baby powder. Every room was small, dark, and irregularly shaped. The hardwood floors were warped and stained black, and the narrow stairway, which tilted dangerously, creaked with every step. The upper floor was filled with sloped and cracking walls, but Rollie had fallen under some kind of spell.

She raved about the casement windows with small panes, no two the same, and fawned over the oval window on the front of the house that had been installed vertically. She praised the complex roofline that rolled under and couldn't stop admiring the inglenook fireplace and basket of kindling. She fell in love with the Juliet balcony off the second floor bedroom, from which she insisted on delivering a sonnet in a high-pitched voice.

Despite all these hints, I almost fainted when Rollie Austin said she couldn't live another day without the eyebrow dormer.

I stared at her in horror.

She added, with a wink, "Let's do it! Let's write up a contract."

My mouth fell open. "You're serious?"

"What a lark, why not? How many people can live in a fairy tale?"

"Not many," I muttered. "How much do you want to offer?"

"How long has it been on the market?"

"Since February."

"Tell me again how much they're asking."

"Try $395,000."

"Is that reasonable?"

"It would be hard to pull a comp. The style is so . . . " I paused, before adding diplomatically, "unique."

"Which makes it worth more?"

"Or less, depending on your taste," I said, starting when I realized that

Rollie Austin's apparel matched the style of the house. She'd dressed for the day as if attending a shooting party in the English countryside. She wore a lace skirt, a blouse with layered ruffles, a baroness scarf, a buttery leather belt with brass rose buckle, a velveteen sweater coat, and calf boots.

"What are the property taxes?"

I couldn't stop gawking at her. "Last year, $1,600."

"Bedrooms?"

"Four, with three baths."

"Square footage?"

"The agent says 1,500, with another 1,000 in the basement, but it doesn't seem that big. We should measure."

"Utilities?"

"Average $130 per month."

"When was it built?"

"In 1932."

"It suits me," Rollie said pensively, gazing at her reflection in a tulip mirror in the entryway. "Offer full price, sweetie. I don't want to haggle over a storybook home."

"Are you sure?" I said, floored.

In the previous fifteen months, Rollie and I had evaluated 129 properties.

I knew the precise number because I'd looked it up the day before, in response to Sasha's curiosity. Most of the lofts, condos, townhomes, and houses blurred together, and honestly, I'd lost hope we'd ever find anything.

I leaned against a crooked door frame, slack-jawed.

Rollie applied a fresh coat of flaming red lipstick and adjusted her Fergie-like wig. "Positive. Let's get a drink, sugar. Toast new beginnings."

"I have a better idea," I said, leading her by the arm out the front door. "Let's go to my office and e-mail the listing agent a contract."

"You're a party-killer," she said, affectionately squeezing my cheek.

More like superstitious.

Over my twenty-year real estate career, I'd seen too many deals fall through to risk delay.

Alcohol would have to wait.

•••

We did pause on the way back to the office, but only long enough to purchase three java chip Frappuccinos, one of which we brought back for Sasha.

I filled out the contract, Rollie and I signed everything, and Sasha e-mailed the documents to the Century 21 agent who had the listing.

An hour after Rollie departed, I nursed my drink, still dazed by the turn of events.

A hobbit house. For Rollie Austin. What was the world coming to?

Sasha broke into my thoughts by skipping up to my desk. "Can I have a pizza party tomorrow night? Say yes! Please, Lauren."

"Thursday? On a school night?"

She crossed the room and hugged me. "We won't stay up late. I promise."

"Who do you want to invite?"

"Payday and Jason."

Ray Martinez and Jason Rehm.

I'd met both of these boys and trusted them, although sometimes I had my doubts about Sasha.

In the middle of the summer, Sasha had spotted Ray Martinez on the corner of a check-cashing establishment, waving an arrow to draw customers to the business. She recognized him from one of her classes at Central High, and feeling sorry for him on the sweltering day, she brought him a Slurpee and joined him on the rock parkway until his shift ended. Sasha nicknamed him Payday Ray, which she eventually shortened to Payday. Their relationship hadn't developed beyond friendship, but if the long looks he gave Sasha were any indication, I suspected Payday would have accepted more.

She'd known Jason Rehm since kindergarten, although they'd lost touch between grades six and ten. He stood in as the informal head of our IT department and was a frequent visitor to the office, sometimes by request, usually not. After school and on weekends, Jason worked for Geeks Rx, a small business that offered technical support and repair. When he and Sasha started talking tech, I had to close my door to avoid a headache.

"You can have your party," I agreed. "But only if you wrap it up by nine."

Sasha clapped her hands. "We will. You'll see, because you'll be there."

"What?"

"Pretty please, will you come?"

"You want me at your party?" I said, instantly suspicious. "Why?"

She flashed a disarming smile. "Because I like you."

"Why else?"

"Just because."

I looked at Sasha steadily. Was she up to something? Hard to tell with her. "When do you want me there?"

"Six." Her face contorted into a teasing look. "And will you bring the pizza?"

"Of course," I said, in a pained tone.

"I might invite Taylor, too. If she comes, you have to be nice to her."

My eyes contracted. "When am I not nice?"

"Sometimes you say hurtful things," Sasha said shyly, fidgeting. "Usually when you're mad, but still . . . "

"Don't worry. I won't embarrass you," I said shortly.

"Don't accidentally refer to Taylor as he, either. She hates that."

I let out an exasperated sigh. "Sasha, give me a little credit."

"Taylor looks like a boy, but it's not her fault. She was born intersexual."

I looked at her skeptically. "What?"

"It's hard to explain," she said, flustered. "When Taylor was born, her parts, you know, weren't male or female. Her parents raised her as a boy, but then a doctor changed her to a girl when she was two. She's had a bunch of surgeries, and kids bully her. She doesn't know what she is, but she had to choose. She's taking hormones so she'll look like a normal woman."

I shook my head in confusion. "Is Taylor a boy or a girl?"

"She doesn't know," Sasha repeated loudly, before lowering her voice. "But I told her she's both. Which is cool."

"All right. I'll be there at six."

I spent the next five minutes assuring Sasha that I would be on my best behavior with all of her friends.

•••

"Young lady, there's no good answer," Saul Eichelberg said in a kindly tone that evening, capping off the end of my workday.

Not at all what I wanted to hear about LoDo's late-night problems, and not a revelation I could pass on with any pleasure to Roxanne Archuletta and her LoDo Business Interests group.

But Saul, the unofficial "mayor of LoDo," had a point.

We'd spent thirty minutes chatting on the roof of his loft at 14th and Blake, one of LoDo's original conversions.

After retiring as a New York securities lawyer in 1975, Saul and wife Sheila had relocated to Denver. Initially, they'd considered purchasing a home in Cherry Hills or Hilltop, but ultimately they'd chosen a dilapidated four-story warehouse in the middle of skid row. They'd redeveloped the building into three floors of office space and a 3,500-square-foot residential penthouse, which functioned as their private living quarters.

The loft had the most gorgeous hardwood floors I'd come across, darkened by the footsteps of more than a century's worth of workers, and the walls and posts in the living room and dining room were painted a deep burgundy, which contrasted elegantly with the Eichelbergs' blue metallic furniture. A wrought iron railing separated the study from the common area, and the kitchen, built on a raised platform and accessed by three wide steps, had an open design. By the looks of the cherry cabinets, Viking stove, and concrete countertops and sink, the room had undergone a recent remodeling.

As Saul and I had passed through the living room, I'd smiled at the whimsy of the hand-carved, wooden carousel horse in the corner, the marble column plant stands, and the Coca-Cola cooler that held linens.

Saul had led me out onto a cantilevered deck, from which we'd climbed to the rooftop terrace, where we'd watched the sun set from inside a red-shell, six-seater Vail gondola. Sheila had fallen in love with the ski area reject at an antiques shop in Evergreen and arranged for it to be brought to Denver by flatbed and lifted to the roof by crane. Before his wife's death in the spring, the couple had enjoyed many days and nights behind the glass, in all seasons. I could understand the appeal, as the gondola sheltered us from the slight breeze that swirled among the planters of aspens, geraniums, and tomatoes.

The building had no elevator or lift, and Saul seemed to have profited from the exercise. I pegged him in his early eighties, deriving the age from his tales, not outward appearance. He had a wiry build, with no paunch or stoop, and thinning white hair that he'd combed over to its best advantage. He used glasses for reading only, half-frames chained around his neck.

"There has to be some way to resolve the conflict in LoDo," I pressed.

Saul scratched a sprig of whiskers on his chin. "I wish I could agree, but everyone has a different agenda. For instance, the industrial companies would prefer we'd never moved onto their turf. Gentrification has pushed up their taxes, without bringing benefits. For years, they had the place to themselves, and they got used to blocking alleys and streets as they loaded and unloaded merchandise."

"Their properties have appreciated," I said lightly.

"True enough, but that's akin to telling a farmer his land is worth millions when he just wants to bring a crop to market and feed his family. As another example of discord, the shop owners rely on traffic from restaurants, bars, and nightclubs, but they refuse to hose down vomit and urine. The entertainment businesses rely on the historic district's distinction but won't accept liability for the havoc their patrons wreak. We home owners aren't perfect either. We enjoy the retail and nightlife, but we also crave peace and quiet."

I took a sip of club soda. "It sounds bleak."

"I've felt increased strain since the boom began in the early '90s. From day one, we fought over construction detours and parking congestion. In retrospect, those squabbles seem trivial. We've never achieved peace, and I'm not referring to noise. LoDo has been at a crossroads since my wife and I moved here. Three decades ago, I hoped tensions would die down, but they've escalated. Each stakeholder relies on other factions, but only wants his own interests represented. I used to feel disagreement was healthy, part of what made LoDo unique."

"You don't anymore?"

In the dim light of the rooftop lanterns, Saul released a thin smile. "As we work through our issues, will everyone get everything he wants? Never. Everything he needs? Unlikely. I'm not naïve, I accept that truth. Lately, however, the differences seem insurmountable, the conflict more personal. The tenor of neighborhood meetings has devolved into malice. Everyone claims to be getting nothing he wants or needs."

"Maybe that's why there's stricter zoning in other parts of the city,"

I said, chewing on a sliver of lime. "Once you overlay office, commercial, industrial, residential, and entertainment, it sounds as if you create something more combustible than vibrant."

"I'm afraid that's what it's come down to," Saul said, tipping a rye and ginger to his lips. "If you'd asked me ten years ago, perhaps even five, I would have told you that folding residences, nightclubs, sports bars, and stores into a long-established warehouse district was brilliant. We could give rise to a twenty-four-hour neighborhood teeming with activity. I envisioned LoDo as a cosmopolitan hub with the energy of New York, Boston, or Chicago."

I stretched out my legs. "Past tense?"

"Indeed," he said despondently. "I appreciate the fragile balance, based on mixed uses. Yet, as often as not, I find myself contemplating LoDo's warring factions and strife, not its diversity and character. We share streets, alleys, and sidewalks in an uneasy truce during daylight hours. After sundown, we're under siege. Partygoers enter LoDo and trash it at will. They conduct themselves entirely without manners. I'll never understand why they feel it's acceptable to carouse in the streets, converse at the top of their lungs, and scuffle. Their behavior is deplorable, but turning an historic district into a combat zone isn't the answer."

"You're not a fan of the increased police presence in the last few weeks?"

"I most certainly am not. I'm glad my wife isn't here to experience the captivity. If she—" he began, breaking down midsentence.

I reached across the gondola and covered his hands with mine.

He bowed his head and took a series of deep breaths before resuming. "I never thought I'd say this, because you won't find a more ardent LoDo supporter, but I wish we'd retained more control of what came into our neighborhood as it came in. Look at Larimer Square, our partner to the south. They have the odd problem, but nothing like this."

Saul and I stretched our necks at the sound of an engine backfiring, before he added in explanation, "Not all liquor licenses are equal. We've discovered that the hard way. In Larimer Square, restaurants serve liquor. In LoDo, bars serve food. The distinction seems fine, until you observe the patrons that visit the establishments. Add cabaret or entertainment to the license, and the problems compound."

I sighed heavily. "I see your point."

"No one leaves Rioja, Larimer's darling new restaurant, and empties his bladder against the side of the building. The driving forces behind Larimer Square have effectively controlled their tenant mix."

"It seems as if you've looked at the dilemma from every angle."

"Repeatedly. Ten years ago, I told my wife that LoDo was at an awkward stage, trying to decide what it wanted to be when it grew up. We have our answer."

I released his hands and said, with a sympathetic smile, "A problem child."

"Something along those lines."

I nodded. "Speaking of problem children, Allen Billich at the Ice House Lofts told me you may have witnessed the wilding incident in August."

Saul closed his eyes for a moment. "Regrettably, I did."

"What were you doing out that night?"

"I had an errand to run."

I tore my gaze away from the city lights twinkling in the distance and looked at him curiously. "Really? At 2 a.m.?"

Saul paused, before admitting, with a slight apology, "I often walk around late at night. Since my wife died, I've had terrible insomnia. If I can't sleep because of the noise, I may as well take a stroll and look at pretty girls."

"In skimpy outfits," I said indulgently.

He didn't reply beyond a guilty half-smile.

"What did you see on August 21?"

"A mild ruckus. Kids tussling among themselves."

I straightened up. "That's not how the media portrayed it."

"The news stations have delighted in airing inflammatory snippets, but I'm offering a first-hand account."

"Car windows were shattered. A man had his arm broken."

"The kids didn't mean to harm anyone," Saul said stolidly, avoiding eye contact.

I began to feel uneasy. "Have you made a statement to the police?"

He shook his head, a slight movement. "I don't want to get involved."

"You, the people's mayor of LoDo, won't cooperate with police?"

Saul stiffened and made no comment.

"Why?" I prodded.

At last, with difficulty, he said, "I recognized one of the participants."

CHAPTER 13

E ureka!

My first big break in the LoDo wilding case.

Saul Eichelberg would identify the LoDo wilding participant only as 11-up, a graffiti artist he'd caught tagging a utility box. He claimed 11-up was a good kid who had done little more than observe on the night in question, and despite my cajoling, Saul would say no more.

But he'd said enough.

I had connections.

Sasha's friend Payday was a skilled graffiti artist who knew every other graffiti artist in the Denver metro area. In junior high, Payday had belonged to a "tag-banging crew," which included kids from all ethnic backgrounds who hit high schools in central Denver. They left behind pieces on sidewalks, doors, windows, and fences and competed for territory almost as ruthlessly as their drug-peddling counterparts.

As Payday matured, he favored solitary assaults and came to disdain taggers who hit anything other than garbage bins. He further curbed his illegal pursuits when he began attending evening classes at the Colorado Institute of Art. He had pieces legally displayed on yoga studios, coffeehouses, nightclubs, rec centers, and other urban buildings. He'd also had his art transferred to graffiti clothes, magazines, and websites.

With my permission, Payday had painted a wall in Sasha's studio apartment in his flowing style of letters and graphics. The eight-by-twenty-foot mural, which he completed days before school started, draped around Sasha's Murphy bed. The primary images consisted of floating body parts: a woman's hand, with bright red nails, gripping a waffle iron; a man's teeth, only partially visible below a mustache; an old woman's eye with cataracts; a baby's leg in "feety" pajamas. Payday had left a whiteboard section in the middle of the drawing, where he or Sasha posed questions. At the mural's unveiling, the inquiry stood, "Where does time go when it leaves the moment?"

No one had ever answered that one, but on this night, it was time for me to go home.

•••

Unfortunately, I had one last stop to make before I could turn down the bed covers.

Thanks to a voicemail message that had come in while I was at Saul Eichelberg's loft, I headed to Landry.

The drive took eighteen minutes, and in darkness, I made my way to the park where I'd last seen Richard Leone on Monday afternoon.

I came across him, on the grass, wilting against one of the ornamental lamps that illuminated the grounds.

Pepper, ears back, tail wagging, growled as I approached.

While I tentatively patted the terrier, Richard cocked his head quizzically. "You look familiar. Haven't we met?"

Not a good start.

"Yes," I said patiently. "I'm Lauren Vellequette. I'm a private investigator."

Richard stood to shake my hand, lurched forward, and had to abandon the endeavor. "Good to see you. What brings you to these parts?"

"You called me."

"Did I?" he said, befuddled. He touched the makeshift bandage on his forehead, a patchwork of napkins and duct tape. "I don't remember."

"You said you had information about the fire."

He wiped his clouded eyes. "Which fire?"

"The one at Landry, on Trinidad Street, in June." I hesitated, aggravated. "Maybe it was the one at Southfield, on Visalia Street. You weren't exactly coherent."

With massive exertion, he returned to his seat on the embankment. "I'm sorry. My head's pounding. I can't concentrate. You say I phoned you?"

"Yes!" I said loudly.

He roused himself and licked his lips. "Why?"

"I have no idea."

"Where did I get a phone?"

"Maybe you found another cell phone," I said hotly.

"No, no, I don't think so." He frisked himself. "I must have used the pay phone at 7-Eleven, but why? What did you want?"

I censored a sigh. "I didn't want anything. You called me."

He scratched his head. "How did I get your number?"

"I gave you my business card two days ago. Was it about the boy?"

"It could have been." Richard paused, hunched over, and mumbled, "What boy?"

When he shivered violently, I removed my coral, wool-blend peacoat and handed it to him. He spread it across his legs, ironing it with the sides of his hands.

I knelt down and spoke solemnly. "The boy who might have started the fire at Landry. The one you told me about on Monday. On Sunday, June 11, you saw him on your way to and from church. Does any of this ring a bell?"

Richard's head shot up, his eyes a slit. "What fire? I thought it was a woman."

"What woman? Did a woman start the fire?"

He stared at his Mickey Mouse watch for a full minute. "She's too clean for that. Her hands are never dirty, not like mine. Women always smell good. That's what I like about them."

"Richard!" I snapped. "Are you drunk?"

He tilted his body. "I may be in my cups, but that doesn't affect my reasoning. Not too much. I wouldn't drive in this state, but that's because I no longer own a car," he said, with a girlish giggle. "Nonetheless, I can converse. What would you like to talk about?"

"The boy."

"Who?"

"Kevin."

He bent to examine his fingernails, which were long and dirty. "The one who murdered his father?"

I blew air out of my cheeks. "No! The one who set the fire."

Richard Leone's face crumpled in confusion. His eyes welled up, and he shook off tears. "Isn't he the same one?"

•••

I wrapped up the pointless inquiry and offered Richard a ride to his shelter in the culvert, but he refused.

I left him and Pepper, in the spoon position, huddled under my coat.

I thought about Richard Leone as I drove to my apartment in my toasty Outback, as I lingered in a bubble bath and put on a clean nightgown, as I turned on an electric blanket and snuggled under a down comforter, and as I fell into a fitful sleep.

I thought about him the moment I woke up, hours before the alarm sounded.

This wouldn't do.

I had to stop thinking about him.

I rose and emptied my linen closet of blankets, pillows, and comforters, threw in a parka from the front closet, and grabbed nonperishable items from my kitchen shelves.

I stuffed bags and boxes into the back of my car and headed to Landry, where at dawn's break, I returned to an empty park, covered with autumn's first frost.

I crisscrossed from Quebec Street to Havana Street, Alameda Avenue to 11th Avenue, but found no sign of Richard or Pepper.

At eight o'clock, I abandoned the search and steered toward my office.

•••

The first call of my day came from the agent with the hobbit house listing, and what cursed luck!

The property was gone, under contract, at full asking price. Cash offer, short escrow.

Damn, damn, damn.

I felt like throwing something against the wall.

How could two people want the same house on the same day, after it had spent seven months on the market?

I wouldn't have believed the multiple-offer phenomenon, except that I'd witnessed it too many times in my career.

Sometimes to my advantage.

Today, not.

I reached Rollie Austin on her cell phone and imparted the news, which she accepted stoically.

"We'll just have to keep looking, doll."

By her casual tone, I wondered if she'd had a change of heart overnight. Not that I would have blamed her.

Someone should have burned that crooked house to the ground.

To dull further merciless thoughts, I turned to other people's vengeance and spent the better part of the day working the arson case.

I drove to Dennis McBride's office to pick up the personnel files he'd promised nearly a week earlier. He wasn't around but had left directives with his human resources manager. I signed a confidentiality agreement, and she released, all too happily, a small dolly loaded with cartons of files.

Leaving the Denver Tech Center, I grabbed lunch on the run, a Frappuccino from Starbucks and a stale power bar and blackened banana from the floor of my car.

Back at the office, I couldn't face the work histories of the employees Dennis McBride had fired in the previous six months, which left me no alternative but to sit at the computer and start surfing.

I ran a background check on Richard Leone and turned up nothing, as if he'd dropped off the grid or never existed.

I had more success with Daphne Cartwright. I entered her name and address into an information broker's database and hit a bonanza. In all of the background checks I'd undertaken for the SOB instructor's clients, Rollie Austin's clients, and my own clients, I'd never come across this much litigation. In the past five years alone, Daphne had been involved in nine civil suits.

I printed out the documents and leaned back in my chair to study them.

Daphne had filed suits for wrongful termination, malpractice, workers' comp, sexual harassment, and injuries sustained in a car accident. The last one resulted in a settlement in the low four figures, the rest in dismissals. In the same span, a bank, a credit company, a car rental company, and a nanny had sued her, and all had won judgments.

My inference after a lot of legal reading: Daphne Cartwright was one anger-filled woman.

I'd already known that, but confirmation never hurt.

After the computer searches, I broke for a three-hour nap, only because I'd captured less than ninety minutes' sleep the night before, none consecutive.

Revived by late afternoon, I returned to Landry yet still couldn't locate Richard Leone.

On a whim, I zipped over to Southfield and took a swipe by the skateboard park, hoping to find Kevin, the boy connected to Richard.

Another strikeout.

Why did builders include amenities that no one used?

The early evening weather was cooperative—full sun, sixty degrees, and a mild breeze—except there were no takers in the concrete bowls at the skateboard park. What kept them away? The helmet requirement? The cameras mounted on poles? The ill-conceived design of tabletops, quarter pipes, and rails?

Who knew, but I couldn't find a skateboarder to save my life.

Oh, well.

I switched gears, called Pizza Hut, and ordered food for Sasha's party.

•••

A few minutes before six, I pulled up to the ClockTower and parked in my assigned space.

In the lot, I recognized Payday's 1964 black Ford Falcon, decorated with a white skull and crossbones on the hood, and Jason's company car, a yellow VW Bug with the Geek Rx logo emblazoned on the doors.

I climbed the stairs to the second floor, stopped by my apartment to drop off my purse, and scooted over to Sasha's.

Without knocking, I opened the door and shuddered, something I did every time I went into her apartment.

When she'd moved in two months earlier, I'd approached the task of furnishing and decorating the space as a joint venture, an occasion to bond. However, after hearing "That's too old-lady" one too many times, I wrote Sasha a check for $1,000 and cut her loose. She was on her own to choose paint, bedding, furniture, fixtures, window coverings, wall hangings, and accessories.

She spent hours at design centers, hardware stores, malls, garage sales, fabric outlets, and thrift shops before creating the mishmash she called home.

She must have brought back at least fifty paint chips and a dozen samples before settling on lime walls and a blackberry ceiling. She didn't like it when I called her taste "fruity," but with accent colors of lemon, strawberry, plum, orange, and blueberry, how could she deny it?

The colors she'd chosen stood in stark contrast to the silver and black Payday had used to paint the graffiti mural on the Murphy bed wall and to the current message on the whiteboard, "If it gets any darker, will I disappear?"

Sasha had divided the square room into five functional spaces—galley kitchen, living room, dining room, study, and bedroom—using brick landscaping pavers, which I always seemed to trip over. A raspberry and mango bathroom was separated from the main room by a short hallway.

After I resigned from the project, Sasha explained that she wanted her personal space to resemble her, to explain her true self to everyone who entered.

If she'd succeeded in achieving this goal, God help us all.

Scattered around the room, she had a headless and legless mannequin, a plastic palm tree, a coffin that doubled as a seat and storage bin, a mirror with leaves glued to it, a beaded wall hanging, paper ceiling lanterns, fuzzy pillows with chiffon ribbons, and a birdcage with no occupant.

If this stood as her shout-out to the world, what was the message?

I suppose it didn't matter, because at the grand unveiling, she'd told me the apartment made her feel "happy inside."

That it caused me intestinal distress was of secondary importance.

On this night, I was the last guest to arrive.

Payday and Jason had chosen seats at the picnic table in the dining room, and Taylor was splayed across a chaise lounge in the area designated as the living room. Payday wore his usual outfit of all-black clothes and boots, the only hint of color coming from a Court Jester stocking cap he wore year-round. He had black hair that fell loosely to his shoulders, a fine, thin mustache, and prominent acne on his forehead and chin.

Jason was in his work uniform: a short-sleeved white shirt, pre-knotted clip-on tie, green Dockers, sensible lace-up shoes, and black socks. Rarely making eye contact, he wore mirrored, cop-style sunglasses indoors and outdoors, only removing them upon request. He had short, reddish-brown receding hair, and when he smiled, which was often, he displayed crowded teeth.

Without Sasha's forewarning, I wouldn't have known whether Taylor was a girl or boy. The full-length black velvet cape with reaper's hood, black pants, and short, brown hair spiked with gel certainly didn't shed any light.

Sasha, perched on the end of the lounge chair, for once looked positively normal in a loose-fitting, celery tracksuit with flip-flops.

All four teens looked at me eagerly, my entrance enhanced, I'm sure, by the two pizzas and three liter bottles of soda I clutched precariously.

I deposited the food and drinks on the kitchen counter and shook Taylor's hand, which was cold and clammy. She mumbled that it was nice to meet me, and I told her she had pretty brown eyes, which made her squirm.

After Sasha laid out paper plates, napkins, and cups and announced that dinner was served, everyone plated up from the choices of mushroom and black olive or pepperoni and sausage.

The girls returned to the chaise, and I sat with the boys at the table.

I ate quickly—trying to join in to their conversations when I could, which wasn't often—and then excused myself and went home.

Two hours later, Sasha came through my front door, without knocking.

She crossed the room, leaned down to reach me on the couch, and gave me a lingering hug. "Thanks, Lauren."

I pried her hands from my shoulders. "For what?"

"For being nice to my friends." Sasha clasped her hands together. "I know a secret. Want to hear it?"

"I doubt it," I said, with a weak smile.

"Payday thinks you're smokin' and way-out."

I raised my eyebrows. "Is that good or bad?"

"Good. When you left, he said your body was—"

"I'm going to stop you right there—" I said rapidly.

She cracked a lopsided grin. "He can't believe you don't have wrinkles. His mom has a ton."

My face relaxed. "Did you ask Payday about 11-up, the graffiti artist?"

Sasha slapped her forehead. "I totally forgot. Want me to call him?"

"Not while he's driving. You can let me know tomorrow."

"I'll talk to him before physics, promise."

"Okay," I said, dragging myself up to a seated position. "Don't stay up too late."

Sasha kissed me on the cheek. "I won't."

.

CHAPTER 14

True to her word, Sasha called the next morning.

She relayed that Payday knew 11-up and would try to contact the renegade artist, but he couldn't guarantee anything. Apparently, Payday and the tagger only connected through intricate graffiti marks left on a Dumpster near the corner of 13th Avenue and Pearl Street.

It might take days or weeks for a face-to-face.

I couldn't wait that long.

I moved on to Plan B.

From a copy of the police report Roxanne Archuletta had given me, I extracted the name of the innocent bystander who'd had his arm broken in the fracas, Joseph Verre. I called him, and he agreed to meet later that night, at the Neptune Café, north of downtown.

For the moment, that was about as far as I could take the LoDo wilding case.

In the meantime, cartons of files beckoned.

I made a run to Starbucks and returned with four java chip Frappuccinos, three of which I placed on the top shelf of the refrigerator, where partially-frozen liquids miraculously retained their form.

I plucked a McBride Homes personnel record from the top of the pile and began to read.

Five hours and sixty-seven files later, I had trouble imagining how the company completed any projects on schedule.

They were a sorry lot, these men and women who had been asked to leave in the past six months. The causes of termination varied, but several patterns emerged: intoxication; tardiness or no-shows; fraudulent social security numbers; thefts; violations of health and safety regulations; fights with coworkers or supervisors.

The stories in the records began to blend, and at the end of four Frappuccinos, I'd separated only one man from the pack of involuntary separations.

Josh Mifflin.

He'd had a five-year history of solid reviews, promotions, and pay raises until this spring, when he started showing up late or missing work. His supervisor, Glenn Warner, had responded with warnings, probation, and eventually termination.

Josh's erratic behavior had all the markings of a substance abuse problem, and I wondered why Dennis and Glenn hadn't supported him through counseling and recovery.

I'd soon find out.

I went online, and after spending five minutes on a social security trace, I found Josh Mifflin's current employer.

I called the drywall business and reached an after-hours recording. I made note of the company's Saturday hours and set the alarm on my cell phone to alert me at eight o'clock the next morning.

After that, I headed home to change clothes for an evening out.

•••

Talk about a trip down memory lane.

In my youth, I'd spent too many nights at the Neptune Café, listening to bad poetry, bad comedy, bad music, and bad storytelling. The Neptune's open mic policy led to some unintentionally funny moments, most of which I'd endured through a cloud of French cigarette smoke while on a series of bad dates, eating bad food.

Admittedly, not bad food. Good food that tasted bad, when I would have preferred bad food that tasted good.

I was reminded of the multitude of awful nights, looking for dates, on dates, or breaking up with dates, as I sipped a sour, all-natural lemonade and waited for Joseph Verre to complete his Friday night Swing lesson.

I hadn't stepped foot in the Nep since my early twenties, but it hadn't changed much. It remained a community gathering place, with health food, music, art, and politics as the draws. Its latest manifestation, as an all-ages, full bar, nightclub and restaurant on the fringe of downtown, included a 3,000-square-foot ballroom, where Joseph and ten ladies were learning the Lindy Hop.

I watched for a few minutes before returning to the dining area, where I chose a corner table, and at ten o'clock, Joseph joined me, breathless and sweaty. He insisted on eating before he'd talk about what happened in the early morning hours of August 21, when he was attacked in LoDo.

I struggled through a nut and cheese sandwich on the most dense bread I'd ever swallowed, undoubtedly due to the restrictions outlined on the menu. All breads and pastries were made using only whole grains, natural sweeteners, and cold pressed oils. I quit halfway through the meal, ostensibly to take notes.

Joseph Verre's story unfolded over the next few hours, but I can summarize it in a few paragraphs.

He and a woman he'd met online were on a first date in LoDo the night of the wilding. Reading between the lines, I surmised that Joseph's date would have preferred to end the experiment about five minutes after they met, but he'd kept her occupied until last call by jumping from bar to bar. At last-out, as they exited El Chapultepec, a venerable jazz club on Market Street, fighting broke out, which he described as "the most frightening bedlam."

Acting on "honorable instinct," he fell back on his high school ROTC training and attempted to make a citizen's arrest. When he saw a young man thumping on a car, he reached for the perpetrator. Said thug grabbed Joseph's arm, twisted it, and broke his wrist. Joseph tumbled to the ground and hit his head on something—a newsstand or fire hydrant. He bled profusely, which caused his date to curse plentifully, as splatters hit her best dress and shoes. Livid that he'd tried to play the hero, the woman left him then and there. After giving a statement to the police and declining an ambulance ride, Joseph drove to the nearest emergency room, where doctors X-rayed his wrist and cleaned his head wound.

He hadn't managed to get a good look at anyone and could only describe the participants, inside the car and out, as "angry young African-American men."

To put it kindly, Joseph Verre was a poor prospect as a self-anointed lawman.

A nebbish man, at least three decades removed from his ROTC training, he was a half-foot shorter than me, putting him a few inches over five feet, and he probably weighed less, downward of 150. Unless he was hiding solid muscle beneath brown corduroys and a tan turtleneck, which seemed unlikely, I couldn't picture him subduing a riot.

The cast on his left wrist bore out my suppositions.

He was, however, an effective eyewitness with excellent recall, not of physical traits but of behavior patterns, and he presented a perspective that was at once sensible and mind-boggling.

After replaying events, obsessively and painstakingly, he felt certain that the young men in the car knew the young men in the street. That in itself wasn't earth shattering. The police had pegged the episode as gang rivalry, which would explain the familiarity. Yet, Joseph insisted the groups of teens were friends, not enemies, and that both groups had known the videographer whose camera and tape the police had confiscated.

By accepting Joseph Verre's version—and why wouldn't I when he had a front-row view and no reason to contort the truth—I had to accept a new reality.

The entire LoDo wilding incident had been staged.

CHAPTER 15

Assuming someone had staged the LoDo wilding effectively upended my investigation.

I needed to meet with Roxanne Archuletta as soon as possible.

Minutes after midnight, I disentangled from Joseph Verre, left the Neptune Café, and headed on foot to Sports Fanatics. The police had cordoned off large sections of LoDo, and on the walk I encountered clusters of officers. Inside Roxanne Archuletta's sports bar, I could count the customers on two hands, the rest plainly having fled before let-out. I caught Florence's attention, and she motioned for me to go upstairs, where I found Roxanne in a cramped room near the toilets, pounding numbers into an adding machine.

When she raised her head, her eyes lit up, and our handshake turned into a glancing embrace.

"You look nice," she said, referring to the Shetland wool turtleneck and herringbone tweed pants I'd selected for my return to the Nep.

I blushed uneasily under the compliment. "Thanks."

She didn't look bad herself, but she appeared fatigued, as if she'd worked back-to-back shifts.

"What can I do for you?" She rose, offered me her chair, and switched to a three-legged barstool.

"I came by to give you an update on the wilding incident."

"This late?"

"I couldn't wait," I said, instantly wanting to rephrase. "Are you ready for this?"

Roxanne studied me with an air of quiet amusement. "Lay it on me."

"You won't like it."

"I'm a big girl."

"I'm beginning to think someone staged the wilding incident."

"Son of a bitch!" Roxanne Archuletta shouted, standing. "What the fucking hell!"

I waved at her to calm down. "It's only a theory at this point, but I shouldn't have trouble proving it. I have a lead on one of the young men, possibly the leader. He's a graffiti artist who tags as 11-up."

Roxanne stomped her foot. "Why would he pull a boneheaded stunt like this?"

"Who knows? Maybe he was bored. Maybe he wanted to impress someone. Maybe he had nothing better to do on a Saturday night than start a fight and tape it."

"You're sure it's him?"

"Fairly certain. Do you know Saul Eichelberg?"

"The mayor of LoDo? Sure. Everyone down here knows Saul."

"Saul told me he saw 11-up participating in the wilding, but he wouldn't give me the kid's real name or a physical description. I'm working another angle. My office assistant knows a tagger who knows 11-up. The kid'll set up a meeting, and I'll get to the bottom of this. The way it's looking, though, 11-up encouraged the disturbance."

"Which has cost us hundreds of thousands of dollars," Roxanne said slowly, between clenched teeth. "Maybe millions, if the police don't get the fuck out of here."

"Presuming the wilding wasn't a random act of violence, who benefited from it?"

"Not me." Roxanne ripped the tape from the adding machine and held it up. "I'm not even breaking even. I've had to lay off two bartenders and a cocktail waitress."

"The media," I mused. "They had a story to tease with every night. How about the bars and nightclubs at the periphery of the street closures?"

"I know every one of those owners. They'd never—"

"Hold on, I'm only speculating. We have to consider residents, too."

She looked at me, confounded. "How so? Cops swarmed their lofts."

"Don't you get it?" I said urgently. "The residents would rather have a visible police presence than what they had before the wilding. Allen Billich told me he hopes the cops never leave, and if the incidents continue, they won't."

"And/or business will drop away to nothing, and they'll have their goddamn way."

"That speaks to how miserable they are, if they'd prefer flashing lights, helicopter buzz, and bullhorns. The more I look into this, the more I appreciate what a mess it is. A band of teenagers may have exposed the extremes, but the problems didn't start on August 21. And they won't end when we catch the wilders."

"We didn't pay to find this out," Roxanne said, disheartened.

"I know, but your after-hours ordinance is looking better and better, if for no other reason than there's no better option. I'm not convinced it would work. The residents have legitimate concerns about the new law lengthening the nightlife hours. But what else can you do?"

She smiled wryly. "Maybe I hired those kids."

"Allen Billich suggested as much, but I corrected him. Why would you pay me ninety dollars an hour to investigate?"

Roxanne exploded. "Maybe he's behind the incident. Have you thought about that?"

I kept my tone level. "I have, and he's a legitimate suspect. Allen Billich and anyone else whose life improved after the wilding. Again, who benefits?"

Roxanne stared at me for a full minute, speechless.

"What is it?"

"I just had a crazy thought." She jumped up and began to pace wildly. "This gal came in the other day, Victoria Farino."

"How does this relate?"

"I interviewed her sometime in the summer. Mid-July, maybe."

"For a position here?"

She shook her head. "For LoDo Business Interests. We'd tossed around the idea of hiring a marketing person. She was one of the applicants, my first choice."

"Did you offer her a job?"

"I wish I had. I went to bat for her, but when it came down to it, we didn't have anything to offer. Not all of the members would agree to pay for the position. The owners who were behind it didn't want to chip in for something that benefited everyone, if everyone wouldn't pay. We brought Victoria in for three interviews, and I had to call and tell her that she didn't get the job. She was pretty pissed."

"How pissed?"

"Enough to threaten to sue if we used her marketing ideas. I stroked her ego, told her we loved her work, loved her experience, loved her enthusiasm, but couldn't justify the cost. We'd decided we didn't need the publicity, but I'd keep her resume on file, in case anything changed."

"Which it did," I said, my pulse quickening. "A month later."

"No shit."

"What's Victoria Farino doing for work? Did she mention anything?"

"Second sentence out of her mouth. She's landed a great job, as marketing director for the cock-and-rob."

"Excuse me?"

She smiled irresistibly. "Inside joke. CCNRAB. Cherry Creek North Restaurant and Bar Association."

"If that was the second thing Victoria said, what was the first?"

Roxanne Archuletta took in a deep breath and let it out slowly. "How's business?"

•••

My cell phone dinged at eight o'clock, a scant four hours after I'd fallen into bed.

Blame it on Roxanne Archuletta.

She'd convinced me to join her for a drink, which led to a few more, which led to . . . ?

Honestly, I didn't know what.

I only knew that I hadn't felt this hungover since high school.

What had I done?

I'd damaged brain cells, liver cells, and stomach cells.

My mouth, not quite wet enough to be considered pasty, felt like I'd eaten a pound of cotton balls. My gums hurt, my head spun with the room, and I feared I would throw up if I moved too quickly.

An hour later, coping in slow motion, I fit right in with Richard Leone, who reeked of alcohol, moved unsteadily on his feet, and stared at me through bloodshot, watery eyes.

I'd found him in his usual spot, the park in Landry, digging through the trash.

"Murderer? I called the kid that?" he said, a note of marvel in his voice.

"Yes."

He hiccupped. "When?"

"Wednesday night?"

"You must have left this." Richard tugged at the coral peacoat he'd buttoned crookedly. "Do you need it back?"

"You keep it."

"Thank you for the kindness." Richard squinted. "Was I sober?"

"No."

He extracted a can and crushed it expertly with one boot stomp. "That explains it. Did I offend you?"

"Not especially."

"But I wasted your time?"

"A little." I sat on the grass, which, I discovered belatedly, was damp. Pepper, who had barked at my approach but never stirred from the warm sidewalk, ambled over, settled into my lap, and crossed her front paws.

"Perhaps I can acquit myself." Richard scratched his matted beard with both hands. "You want to know about Kevin Slyford?"

"That's the kid you saw going into the house in Landry, shortly before the fire?" I verified, trying to take notes, but the paper kept moving.

"He is. He killed his daddy, but he's not a murderer."

"Killed accidentally?"

"On purpose, but it wasn't his fault."

I rubbed my head. "Maybe you should start at the beginning."

"Kevin's daddy tried to commit suicide, but the first bullet to his head didn't kill him. The boy had to shoot him again."

I partially covered my sunglasses, alarmed at how bright the sun seemed on a cloudy day. "How do you know?"

"Kevin told me about it."

"When did Kevin's father die?"

"A while back."

"Was he charged with a crime?"

"Must have been, because he lived in an institution until last summer, when his aunt took him in." Richard's head bobbed. "Woman works the night shift, sleeps all day. The boy has too much time on his hands, which is something we have in common. Maybe that's why he likes to set fires."

My eyes narrowed. "You know for a fact that Kevin sets fires? Where?"

Richard shrugged. "In fields, mostly. Or maybe his aunt's shed. I can't remember."

I checked my temper. "Why didn't you tell me this before?"

"Didn't I?" he said vaguely. "It must not have been important."

"It's extremely important," I said, my voice strained. "Kevin could kill himself or someone else."

"He wouldn't do that."

"I should call the police."

"Don't! Kevin didn't set the fire in Landry. I swear! I don't know what I was saying."

Pepper, startled by Richard's agonized cry, let out a low growl. Absent-mindedly, I scratched the dog's ears. "How about the one in Southfield?"

"No, no."

"How can you be certain?"

Richard looked around shiftily. "Kevin wasn't anywhere near the house that day."

"Which house?"

"In Landry."

"Why did you tell me he went into the house with a cardboard box, came out, and stared in the window? You saw him twice, on your way to and from church. Remember?"

Richard's eyes flashed with surprise. "I did?"

"Supposedly," I said admonishingly. "Why would you implicate Kevin Slyford if he wasn't involved?"

Richard grinned stupidly. He leaned toward me, sending a wave of combustible breath. "I must have wanted to keep talking to you."

•••

Richard Leone had lied to me.

In our first meeting, when he reported seeing Kevin Slyford hanging around the house in Landry, the morning of the fire?

Or today, when he denied everything?

I had no idea.

I was tempted to dismiss all of his statements, but I had a gut feeling that truth lay within the lies.

Maybe blankets, comforters, pillows, coats, and food would prompt him to separate the two.

They couldn't hurt.

It felt like a bribe, until I remembered my motivation had been pure three days earlier.

Richard gratefully accepted the donations but declined my offer to drive them to his shelter.

I unloaded the boxes and bags onto the sidewalk, where he assured me they would stay until he could transport them. Taking note of the upper-middle class homes that encircled the park, I didn't doubt his prediction. After strapping a hefty portion of the goods to his trailer and tucking Pepper into the basket on the handlebars, Richard pedaled off at a slow clip, and I pulled a U-turn and headed to Washington Park.

On the way, I had my customary craving for Starbucks, but stopped at 7-Eleven instead and bought a six-pack of Gatorade.

I drank two bottles before arriving at my destination, an address Josh Mifflin's employer had provided in our early morning phone call.

I rang the doorbell, and when no one answered, I entered anyway. I cut through vacant rooms and headed to the basement, where I immediately began to cough.

Over the clang of an air compressor, I shouted to a man as he methodically sprayed texture on the walls of a large rec room. He paused with the gun and said, "Gimme five minutes." Exiting through a humid, white cloud, I almost tripped over the drywall hopper.

I waited on the back porch, shivering in the sixty-degree heat, nursing my third sports drink, and in about ten minutes, Josh Mifflin came out the back door, clutching a Bud Light in one hand and a Snickers in the other.

The screen slammed behind him, and he crouched and removed his mask and goggles. He had a round head, as true as a basketball, with an

121

angelic face and full lips. Speckles covered every inch of his jeans, T-shirt, work boots, baseball cap, and exposed skin. Plaster residue had infiltrated his curly, sandy hair, imitating salon highlights, and he didn't look a day over twenty, which meant he must have gone to work for McBride Homes as a teenager.

We introduced ourselves and debated the finer points of orange peel, knock-off, and popcorn texturing before the discussion soured, climaxing with, "Dennis McBride can suck my cock."

"Do you think that would be wise?" I said placidly.

Josh wiped his brow with the inside of his elbow and held the beer bottle to his forehead. "He doesn't care about anyone but himself. I built for him at Landry. I put money in his pocket. I built for him at Southfield. That didn't matter. At company parties, he talked shit about loyalty and family, but he didn't back it up."

"He fired you in May?" I said, shifting on the concrete steps we shared.

"Dennis ain't got the balls. He made Glenn tell me. Two months after my son died."

"I'm sorry," I said, with deep feeling.

"Three days. That's all God gave us. Why did He give us any days?"

I responded in a quiet tone. "Some things don't make sense, no matter how much faith you have."

"That cocksucker Dennis catches me on my way to the mortuary, to pick out my son's casket. He wants to know when I'm coming back to the job. No sympathy, no nothing. All he says is, 'I didn't know they made coffins that small.'"

Josh Mifflin's grief was tangible, his eyes the giveaway. A dark shade of green, they registered everything a moment too late. I touched his arm lightly.

He chugged the beer. "He didn't come to the funeral. He didn't let my buddies come. It's like it didn't matter to him. He wants me back at work after a week. Every day, at eight, Monday through Friday. How am I gonna do that? My wife's crying. I'm crying. I can't pick up tools when my heart's caved in. I come in when I can, but that's not good enough."

"Did you talk to Dennis about what you were going through?"

Josh offered me a chunk of the candy bar, but I declined. He swallowed a bite, barely chewing. "I asked about me coming in late and working late.

Getting in eight hours when I can, maybe making up time on weekends. That's all I can do. I can't sleep at night, and come morning, all I want to do is close my eyes. I promised I'd give him forty, as soon as I could."

"He turned you down?"

"Flat. He didn't want to help me, or it'd set a bad example for the rest of the crew. He didn't care about my five years on the job or the hard work I gave him every shift. My pops taught me that if a man pays you, you give him the best you got, or you don't take his money. This is the best I got."

"Your new boss understands?"

Josh nodded dismally. "All he asks is that I call him when I don't feel good. We're working it out."

"It's not easy to cope with death," I said haltingly. "Everyone does it differently."

"I'd help you out if it was anyone but Dennis," he said stubbornly.

"I understand."

"He ain't worth it."

"No, but the people who work for McBride Homes are. If more houses burn, your buddies might be unemployed, too."

Josh kneaded the back of his neck. "That ain't right."

"They're good people, I'm sure."

"I told you earlier I didn't know nothing, but maybe I do," Josh said, hesitantly. He stood and stretched, and in his coiled pose, reminded me of an animal about to strike.

"If you feel comfortable sharing . . . "

"You wouldn't tell that cocksucker I helped?"

"You have my word."

After a considered pause, Josh spoke. "Dennis goes around his properties every day, hassling street people. He throws buckets of water on them when they're asleep. Why's he have to do that? They don't hurt nobody. One guy, especially, Dennis liked to mess with him. He used our john in Landry, but he always cleaned up after himself."

"Do you know the man's name?"

"Richard. I can't remember his last name, but he rides a bike with a rig on the back. Makes a big racket. Every time Dennis heard the noise, he'd load up on dirt clods or rocks. As soon as the guy came close, Dennis launched."

The hair on my arms stood on end. "Hitting Richard?"

"Dennis said he aimed for the bike or trailer, but sometimes he nailed him. Why'd he have to do that? The guy was straight up. He started out living in an outbuilding at Southfield, but last I seen, he was hanging around Landry. He's ex-military, served in the Persian Gulf and killed some sheik's son. His mom and dad are missing. Retaliation by the Arabs. They were living in Conifer, and he ain't heard from them in seven years. He's a veteran, and Dennis's got no respect for that."

I shook my head. "You know what? You're better off not working for Dennis McBride," I said candidly.

Josh Mifflin looked at me inquiringly, causing me to wonder if the same applied to me.

CHAPTER 16

I returned to my office, an empty building in the middle of a Saturday afternoon.

Several hours later, I heard, "Cat got your tongue?"

I raised my head to find all six feet of Rollie Austin looming over me. "What?"

"I've been calling your cell phone all afternoon. Whatever you're reading, it must be juicy." She glanced at the papers spread across my desk before leaning in for closer scrutiny. "You're looking peaked."

"I had too much to drink last night."

"With someone sexy, please Lord."

"Roxanne Archuletta," I said with a tiny smile.

"I knew it!" she exclaimed. "It's about time you got some!"

"I don't know what I got," I said truthfully.

She cut in. "You can tell me about it on the way."

"The way where?"

She motioned for me to follow her. "I've found my new home."

My head began to throb in giant booms. "You can't be serious."

"Never more so."

She grabbed my coat, took me by the arm, and led me to her 350Z. From there, she blindfolded me and drove way too fast and way too far, with every bump in the road delivering a fresh blow to my stomach.

Once we came to a stop, she guided me up three steps, and when I flung off the eyeshade, I almost crumpled to the floor.

"No, Rollie," I groaned. "I know you were disappointed about the hobbit house, but please, tell me this is a joke."

A hurt look crossed her face. "This is my dream home. Ask me something about it, like I always ask you."

I walked outside, did a quick appraisal, reentered, and gritted my teeth. "Price?"

"$599,000."

"Bedrooms and bathrooms?"

"One of each."

"Square footage?"

"Approximately 300."

"Okay, this kills me to ask—"

She wiggled a finger, beseeching me to continue.

I took a deep breath. "Miles per gallon?"

Rollie flashed a sweet smile. "Eight."

I held on to a grab bar for support. "No, Rollie! You can't pay this much for a Winnebago."

"It's a Grand Eaglebahn, forty-five foot Class A coach, I'll have you know."

"What appeals to you about this?"

"I love the neighborhood."

I said sourly, "Which neighborhood?"

"Whichever one I choose. If I win Ms. Senior America, I'll travel around the country. If not, I'll settle somewhere in Denver. If I don't like my neighbors, I'll roll down the hill. Ask me more questions."

"I can't think of any."

"I'll tell you everything," she said, giddily. "It comes with a five-hundred-horsepower diesel engine, a two-hundred-gallon tank, independent suspension, and three air conditioning units. The cockpit has leather pilot seats, security cameras, twelve-disc Bose CD player, and built-in GPS navigational system. Look around, what do you see?"

Rollie's enthusiasm had done nothing to defrost my dismay. "Hell on earth?"

"Crown molding, vinyl wallpaper, sculptured wool carpet, imported tile in the entryway, gold bathroom fixtures, and a hardwood slide-out fascia. Look at the wooden blinds and valances, king-sized bed, plasma flat-screen televisions, washer and dryer, rope lighting, and Ralph Lauren fabrics. Is this luxury, or am I dreaming?"

I gagged. "You're in the middle of a nightmare."

She waved her arms and lovingly touched items, an easy accomplishment in the eight-foot wide confines of the RV. "The kitchen is a jewel. Oak cabinets, Corian countertops, built-in microwave, and four-door stainless steel fridge with icemaker. It's everything I've wanted, but never imagined I'd find."

"In an area so compact," I said, somewhat maliciously.

Rollie's smile never faded. "There's a full entertainment center above the dinette and behind an outside flap. I can sit under the stars and watch movies or listen to satellite radio. Isn't the floor plan splendid?" she said, dropping to the sofa bed and patting the cushion next to her.

I dutifully joined her, but I soon slumped over, put my head in my hands, and moaned.

"The flow is magnificent. Living room in front, kitchen and dining room in the middle, toilet, vanity, shower, and bedroom in the back. It sleeps five comfortably."

I raised my head pathetically. "One, if the person snores."

"The use of space is exquisite, and I'm gaga over the aerodynamic shape and custom paint job."

"You like black paint with yellow flames?"

"The spiffy racing stripes make me giggle."

I almost gagged when she accented her point with fresh peals.

"When can you move in?" I said, choking on the words.

"I take delivery in twelve weeks."

I shook my head fiercely. "I can't let you do this, Rollie."

"You don't have a choice, dearie," she said, her delivery lacking warmth. "You can be happy for me or not, but you won't change my mind."

I gestured helplessly at the books, candlesticks, throw pillows, and vase of flowers. "How does all of this not fly around when you drive?"

"I'm looking forward to cutting back on clutter."

"Or it'll end up in your lap on the first descent. I don't see the appeal," I said frankly. "Your makeup alone would fill up the storage space in this rig."

"Why don't you say what you really feel?" she said, her voice brittle.

"I can't condone this," I began softly. "First of all, I've never helped anyone buy a house that moved. Second, this monstrosity will depreciate every day you own it. How will you pay for it?"

"The dealership offers a twenty-year loan."

"What about the price of gas? It could skyrocket."

"I'll take my chances."

"Have you decided where to park it?"

That silenced her.

I could see the doubt in her eyes, but she never articulated it.

On the way back to the office, Rollie and I exchanged less than ten words, and in the parking lot, I climbed out with a hurried good-bye and no hug.

She peeled out, spraying me with gravel, and I drove home and went straight to bed for the night.

•••

When I woke up Sunday morning, my electrolytes had rebalanced to some extent, and I felt capable of walking to Cherry Creek North for my ten o'clock appointment with Victoria Farino, the marketing expert the LoDo Business Interests group had spurned.

In forty-five minutes at a brisk clip, I made it to the neighborhood where I'd once owned an ultra-expensive townhome. I'd purchased the 4,000-square-foot pad for my fortieth birthday, a signal to the world that I'd arrived, and sold it days after my forty-first, an admission that I didn't belong. A mixture of high-end residential and equally high-end commercial, Cherry Creek oozed exclusivity, and while I'd bought my way in, I'd never gained access.

I didn't play golf or tennis. I didn't have my hair and nails done once a week. I didn't drink green apple martinis or cosmopolitans. I didn't drive a BMW or Mercedes. I didn't have a trust fund or favorite charity. I didn't take three hours to dress or spend three hours at lunch. I didn't have a personal trainer or plastic surgeon.

In short, I didn't have the credentials for Cherry Creek North.

Victoria Farino, on the other hand, fit right in.

We met at a pastry shop on 2nd Avenue, and between the time I walked through the door and the time we placed our order at the counter, Victoria had greeted five people, each with more enthusiasm than the previous one. Two she'd seen through the storefront window and chased down the street. As soon as we settled in with coffee and breakfast treats, however, her "bon vivant" attitude disintegrated.

"I'm sure I have no idea what Roxanne Archuletta's talking about. She believes I created the stir in LoDo?"

"Perhaps encouraged it," I said diplomatically.

"In these heels?"

I shrugged, eyeballing the four-inch stilettos that clicked with every step and remained attached to her feet by hazardously thin, faux-stone bands. They complemented a deep purple designer suit, floral scarf, and chandelier diamond earrings but wouldn't have performed well in a riot.

"Do I look like a young African-American person?"

Not even close.

The primary colors in Victoria's complexion came from tan-in-a-can, heavy layers of makeup, permanent lip and eyeliner, frosted lip gloss, and etched eyebrows. She had long blonde hair, the texture of straw, and a mouthful of oversized veneers. A face lift, Botox, and wrinkle filler had done little more than make her look like a woman in her forties trying to look like a woman in her thirties. I tried to calculate how many calories she consumed and how many hours per week she worked out to limit her weight to 120 pounds on a five-foot-seven frame, but I gave up at not many and a lot.

I crossed my arms. "It's interesting that the LoDo wilding incident occurred soon after the LoDo Business Interests group decided not to hire you."

Victoria tapped her French manicured nails on the round table. "As I made clear at the time, they needed a director of marketing, whether they chose me or Suzy-Q. Marketing is a constant, consistent process, not something cyclical or crisis-driven. In lean times as well as prosperous ones, branding, market position, and publicity drive the success of a business or organization. The LoDo business owners may not have shared that opinion, but I certainly didn't retaliate by sending out-of-control black gang members. Why would Roxanne accuse me?"

"She didn't accuse you," I said mildly. "But she felt it odd that you recently stopped by Sports Fanatics, after having parted on uncomfortable terms."

A frozen smile joined her frozen stare. "I came in for a drink. She's a contact I developed, and I make it a point to nurture contacts. They're my equity in this business. You never know when you'll need to call on someone or work side by side."

"Will you admit that you were upset when you found out you didn't get the job?" I pressed.

Her voice rose shrilly. "Of course I was. I'd passed two personality tests and spent four hours in interviews and thirty hours on a proposal."

"Roxanne didn't mention a proposal," I said, a bit chagrined.

"Isn't that special! Between the first and second interview, the hiring committee asked the leading three applicants to submit a marketing plan for LoDo."

"Isn't that fairly standard?"

Her large eyes didn't blink. "An overview, yes, but they wanted a one-, two-, and five-year marketing calendar, two sample press releases, and a demographic study of the 80202 zip code."

She responded to my look of surprise. "It was entirely unprofessional."

I recovered quickly. "Yet you complied."

"What choice did I have if I wanted the job? I would have accepted the news more graciously if a qualified applicant had earned the job, but to hear they didn't have the budget and had wasted my time . . . " Victoria's voice dropped to a whispery level. "Taking everything into account, I believe I showed remarkable restraint."

"Has bar and restaurant business in Cherry Creek North increased since LoDo's troubles began?"

"Oh, yes," she said, with a laugh designed to draw attention. "Every time the media broadcasts a LoDo story, we're blessed with another spike. Police officers harassing patrons as they exit LoDo establishments certainly makes my job easier. Not that I struggled before. Cherry Creek North practically markets itself. We have pedestrian-friendly streets, with very little trash or graffiti. The Cherry Creek shopping district includes more than three hundred trendy shops and restaurants, and no nightclubs, thank you very much. Our bars, for the most part, cater to a more mature, affluent crowd."

"It sounds perfect," I said, with more than a trace of sarcasm. "Why does the CCNRAB need you at all?"

Victoria waved at a woman passing by on the street and cooed at the toy poodle in her purse before tearing her focus back to me. "To disseminate the message, repeatedly and uniformly. I'm here to ensure that Cherry Creek is never far from people's minds. That the image of our shopping and nightlife is positive and aspirational. Few can afford to live here, but anyone can visit and feel like a king or queen for a day. If you doubt my credentials or integrity, I can provide references."

"That won't be necessary," I said hurriedly.

The noise level in the pastry shop had reached a crescendo after the entrance of a family of six, with four girls under the age of ten clamoring to order. I leaned in closer and could smell Victoria's perfume, a musky fragrance that cancelled out the taste of my cherry turnover.

"Did Roxanne happen to share my accomplishments?"

I winced inside. "Not in detail."

"I have a degree in city and regional planning and fifteen years' experience in public relations. As director of community development, I opened Bella Villa in Lakewood four years ago. You're familiar with the project?"

"Somewhat. I have twenty years' experience in residential real estate sales."

"Then you'll appreciate that I transformed an outdoor retail space into an inviting residential and commercial oasis. I coordinated interactive displays, plaza concerts, movie nights, food and wine festivals, and contemporary art shows. Our urban wind farm—my suggestion to break up the monotony of the parking lot—won a national award for ingenuity. When I moved on to my next career opportunity, the 100-acre, $45 million mixed-use development was generating more than $1 million in sales tax revenue."

A man at the next table bumped me with his chair, and I shot him a look before scooting forward. "That's impressive."

"Roxanne Archuletta needed me more than I needed her. It's a shame that I have a non-compete with Cherry Creek, or I'd offer my consulting services. I could correct their little situation in thirty days."

"How?"

Victoria Farino threw back her head, almost colliding with a helmet of hair at the next table. "I'm not falling for that again. If they want my ideas, they can pay for them in two years when my contract expires. I will say this, however. I successfully turned around Alameda Mall. Have you been there recently?"

"No. I'm not a big fan of shopping malls."

"When I took over as marketing manager three years ago, the Montgomery Ward had closed, vacancy rates had soared, and upper management was in denial. They expected merry-go-rounds and pretzel stands to lure shoppers. Maybe in the 1970s, but not in today's competitive environment. Shoppers crave an overall experience, and we had to find new ways to compete for a shrinking pool of dollars. Complacency was the enemy. Without my expertise, Alameda Mall would have gone the way of Cinderella City, Villa Italia, Crossroads Mall, and Westminster Mall. Gone, gone, gone, steep decline," she said, stabbing at the air with her index finger as she recited the fates of four shopping centers in the Denver metro area.

"Mm."

"My bosses at corporate headquarters in Texas didn't know what to make of my forward thinking. I single-handedly pushed through $100 million in renovations. I secured Dillard's as the new anchor, added an indoor miniature golf course, launched a series of concerts, redesigned a children's play center, attached a patio to the food court, and upgraded the tenant mix."

Victoria used a plastic knife to divide her low-carb breakfast bar into tiny pieces, one of which she raised to her lips between the nails of her pinky and thumb. "Everyone said I was unrealistic, but I knew we could persuade shoppers within a five-mile radius to make Alameda Mall their first choice."

"Why did you leave that job?"

"Differences of opinion," she said crisply, before perking up. "My resume also includes significant charitable work. Do you recall the story of Pedro Herrera?"

"The name sounds familiar. Is he the kid from Mexico who needed a life-saving procedure?"

She nodded, and not one of her hairs moved. "A bone-marrow transplant. I raised money on his behalf and represented the family in their dealings with the media."

"How did you meet him?"

"A mutual friend introduced us. Anna Cedra. She owns the most quaint import shop on 32nd Avenue, Cedra's. Have you been there?"

"Er, no."

"You'd love it. She brings in fair trade goods from Central American countries. I used to stop in once a week to see what was new, and last December, she told me about poor Pedro."

I rationed the last of my cold coffee, reluctant to break through the throng for a refill. "What ever happened to Pedro?"

"He died," Victoria said, with no emotion. "But I raised $425,000 for him."

CHAPTER 17

On the long, hot walk back to my apartment, I obsessed about Victoria Farino's reaction to me.

Before I'd had a chance to speak, she'd analyzed my clothes, hair, and makeup (casual, short, and none)—and dismissed me.

It was almost as if she'd heard about me and wasn't impressed.

I hated that.

Did the sentiment influence my impression of her guilt?

Maybe.

Something nagged, but I honestly couldn't visualize the marketing director lowering herself enough to coordinate the LoDo wilding. However, to positively exclude the possibility of Victoria Farino's involvement, I needed a character reference from someone other than her.

On the spur of the moment, I decided to phone Cedra's, and Anna Cedra answered and agreed to meet with me over her lunch hour

•••

I had to hustle to make it to the Highland neighborhood before Anna Cedra's lunch hour ended.

I arrived with fifteen minutes to spare and proceeded to spend most of the afternoon in the import shop, listening to Cedra family history and traipsing after Anna as she performed tasks among the rugs, folk art, musical instruments, shawls, tote bags, and masks.

A heavyset woman in her midfifties, she wore a turquoise jacket, a low-cut lavender blouse, and a hot pink scarf that draped down her chest, only partially covering ample cleavage. She had dark eyes and black and silver hair, cut short and tousled.

All too content to share about herself and her family's escape from El Salvador in the 1970s, she became closemouthed when the subject turned to Victoria Farino.

"Victoria gave my name as a reference?" Anna asked, after she'd returned from assisting a customer.

By Anna's tone, I could tell she wasn't about to give one. "Indirectly."

"That's unfortunate."

"I'm part of a steering committee that's considering hiring Victoria. We're holding a fundraiser for domestic violence, and she's come highly recommended. Could you tell me what happened with Pedro Herrera? In general terms," I said, doggedly.

The pretext worked.

After a moment's consideration, Anna spoke. "One day last December, Julio Herrera came into my shop. His five-year-old son Pedro had leukemia and needed a bone-marrow transplant. Julio was asking businesses in northwest Denver to let him set up jars for donations. Children's Hospital had spent $400,000 on chemotherapy treatments for Pedro, but hospital policy prohibits transplants for families who can't pay. Because Julio and Carmela had entered the country illegally after Pedro was born, he wasn't eligible for Medicaid coverage. The day I met Julio, he had raised $600 for his son."

"How much did he need?"

"Another $314,400."

Anna acknowledged my astonished look with a slight nod. "I know it sounds like a lot, but in my culture, people are central. I couldn't see anything but an anguished father's face. I offered to translate for the family and suggested we contact the media. I called a friend at Channel 9, and they featured Pedro on the ten o'clock news. The next day, calls flooded into my shop. Hundreds of people and businesses offered money, services, and fundraisers, and I couldn't keep up. A friend recommended I contact Victoria."

"Did you hire her?"

"She was generous enough to volunteer her time, and she was a miracle worker. I don't know what I would have done without her. She took charge and set up a system to handle the response. Within the week, we had a dedicated phone line, a trust fund, a website, and a system for tracking commitments."

"Pedro's plight must have touched a lot of people."

"It did. Pedro had been ill for more than a year, and chemotherapy had failed. Yet he had the spirit of a warrior," Anna said, with difficulty. "It was Christmastime, and Victoria knew how to exploit the angles. I give her points for that."

"I vaguely remember this hitting the news, but more for the illegal immigrant issue."

She nodded. "I felt uncomfortable with the politics and diversions, but Victoria insisted the debate would lead to more donations. She was right. By mid-January, the community had given $425,000 in cash, products, and services. It was all we could do to keep up with what was coming in and publicize events. Victoria was expert at handling the media, particularly when it came to controversy."

"Surrounding the family's illegal status?"

"That, too, but I was referring to the hostile response when someone caught Julio buying furniture at Foley's and contacted the media."

"Was it true?" I fiddled with soaps from Costa Rica, while Anna tidied cards from Guatemala.

"Yes. The Herreras hadn't done anything illegal, but it certainly appeared improper. A community had gathered round, with pennies and crumpled dollars, to save a boy's life."

"Not buy a recliner," I said offhandedly.

Anna smiled grimly. "Fortunately, Victoria shifted the focus from furniture back to Pedro. She also suggested the family set up a trust fund for other illegal immigrants, but that didn't necessarily match people's intentions. They were drawn to one child, with a bald head and an ear-to-ear smile," she said sadly. "No one cared about broad social causes."

I spoke softly. "When did Pedro die?"

"In April, two months after the procedure at Children's Hospital." She choked up, but continued with effort. "I feel enriched to have known him."

I allowed an appropriate delay. "Let me tell you the truth," I said, lying. "I have reservations about Victoria Farino, but if I can't come up with something specific, the steering committee will hire her." After another carefully timed pause, I added, "Everything you've told me so far reflects well on her."

"I don't have proof of anything," Anna said, almost powerlessly.

"This isn't anything formal," I replied easily. "Just two women talking."

"I don't trust Victoria."

"Why?"

She took a deep breath. "The first time I lost respect for her was when I found out a hospital in California had offered to perform the transplant at no charge. Victoria never told the Herreras about it."

My eyebrows shot up. "When?"

"In our second week of fundraising. The hospital had opened a state-of-the-art bone-marrow transplant center and needed to perform twenty-five procedures to gain accreditation. The family's citizenship wouldn't have been an issue."

My mouth fell open. "Why would Victoria decline the offer?"

Anna Cedra waved her hands in frustration. "Personally, I feel as if Victoria wanted to keep attention on herself. If Pedro had the transplant in California, the story would die. As it was, the tale began with one boy, but came to encompass an entire society, with emphasis on people of color."

"How did you discover the hospital's offer?"

"In passing, from a woman who runs a leukemia foundation."

"Did you confront Victoria?"

"At the first opportunity, but it was too late. I didn't hear about the offer until the middle of February, the week after Pedro had his transplant in Denver."

"What did Victoria say when you spoke to her?"

"She felt that traveling to another state would have been a hardship on the family."

"But at the time she turned down the offer, you couldn't have had all the money you needed," I said, incredulous.

"We had less than $60,000."

"That was a risky move."

"It was reckless," Anna said, her appall obvious. "Victoria broke down when I let her know how I felt, and she begged me to give her a second chance."

"Which you did?"

"Yes, but I shouldn't have, not after she began to behave strangely. Victoria's boyfriend left her in February, and after that, she changed. She couldn't concentrate, she missed appointments, and she stopped submitting reports. Sometime in April, she was fired from her job at Alameda Mall. I only hope it wasn't because of theft."

"Theft?" I said, suddenly alert.

"Of everything she did, that's what I couldn't forgive." Anna dropped her voice to a pain-filled low. "In March, money and goods were still coming in for the Herreras, and Victoria took a $10,000 diamond ring."

"You caught her?"

"No, but I'm sure she was responsible. When I asked her about the disappearance, she became very angry, and we haven't spoken since."

"Hm," I said softly, wondering if the missing ring might be the two-carat stunner Victoria wore on her right hand.

"What happened to the Herrera family after Pedro died?"

"They moved back to Mexico and are living in poverty."

"Where did the excess money in the trust fund go?"

Anna shuddered. "Because it was designated for Pedro's care, it's still tied up in litigation. No one can withdraw or refund it, and leaders in my community have demanded access to the records. How everything became so complicated . . . it's all upsetting."

"You shouldn't feel guilty."

She bit her lower lip. "The bitterness and finger-pointing made me lose some of my passion. I often think about the $315,000 that we could have saved by having the procedure performed in California, what that money could have done for other immigrant families in need. Victoria Farino wasn't the only one with dirty hands, not by any means, but she was the one I considered my friend."

"Are you still in touch with the Herreras or involved with the trust fund?"

Anna Cedra's eyes glistened. "Not anymore. Not since I was diagnosed with a bleeding ulcer."

•••

Obviously, after these revelations, I needed to reconsider Victoria Farino's involvement in the LoDo wilding case.

Where could I get more information?

From 11-up, the instigator Saul Eichelberg had identified at the scene.

When was Payday going to come through with that connection?

Soon, hopefully.

In the interim, I had two other leads connected to Victoria Farino: Bella Villa and Alameda Mall.

Bella Villa wasn't far from Cedra's, but at five o'clock on a Sunday, would I catch anyone in the marketing department who remembered Victoria Farino?

Highly unlikely.

I talked myself out of stopping at the shopping center and instead returned home, where I found the perfect spot for my newly acquired, handwoven, Nicaraguan basket. I placed it on the bathroom floor and filled it with rolls of toilet paper.

After that, I ate dinner (Raisin Bran and a leftover California roll) and watched football.

Perhaps not entirely recovered from my Friday night drinking binge with Roxanne Archuletta, I fell asleep on the couch in the middle of the Chiefs-Raiders game.

•••

Aside from my start from the couch, my Monday began like any other.

I got up. Wished I'd had more of a weekend. Dressed for work. Went to the office. Called real estate clients with obligatory weekly updates (I was monitoring six active listings, three of which I'd held for months). Composed written reports on all private investigation cases.

This week's P.I. inventory included the Dennis McBride arson case and the Roxanne Archuletta LoDo wilding investigation.

I wrote for hours, clarifying strands for my own benefit and the clients' benefits until a proposed midmorning run to Starbucks derailed my routine.

Climbing into the car, I noticed something stuck to the driver's side windshield wiper.

In no mood for solicitation, I slid out of the seat, snatched the scrap of paper, and began to crumple it when I noticed burn marks.

Turning over the white card, I saw my own name, address, and phone number.

Jesus Christ!

Someone had set fire to my business card and returned it to me.

CHAPTER 18

I sprinted into the office, locked the door, and fell on the couch.

I had to think straight.

Who had my card?

Pulling out a notepad and pen, I fought back panic and willed myself to concentrate.

I handed out stacks of business cards every month, but this had to relate to the arson investigation.

My breathing became more and more uneven as I worked my way back in time, through contacts I'd made in the nine days since I'd met Dennis McBride.

Yesterday. Anna Cedra and Victoria Farino.

Scratch that. I'd given each woman a card, but they had nothing to do with my arson case.

The day before Josh Mifflin.

He'd lost his job with McBride Homes, but he was too full of grief to plot revenge. Wasn't he?

Last week. Jerry Hess.

I'd exchanged cards with Dennis McBride's ex-partner, but he seemed levelheaded. This was the act of a lunatic, right?

Earlier in that day. Glenn Warner.

Had I given Dennis McBride's foreman a card? I couldn't remember, but passing out cards was second nature. I'd have to assume yes.

Think harder! Max Spiker.

I'd handed a card to the Metro Fire Bureau arson investigator when I bumped into him at the Southfield house. Could this be his idea of a practical joke? Not very funny.

Further back. Richard Leone.

The homeless man had one of my cards, but not the stamina to bike ten miles from Landry to my office. Or did he, after detaching the trailer?

My first contact. Daphne Cartwright.

I'd left a card with the lawsuit-happy mother, but her style was more confrontational. Less sneaky, right?

Think, think, think!

Whoever torched my card had to be among this group.

Did this mean I'd met the Landry and Southfield arsonist?

I shut off the overhead lights and returned to the couch, where in semi-darkness, I replayed every word, gesture, and nuance that I'd shared with the people who possessed one of my business cards.

Minute after minute dropped on the digital clock on my desk, until sometime between forty-six and forty-seven, my eyes almost popped out of their sockets.

There was someone else.

Dennis McBride.

•••

This fell into the category of, "You know you've lost it when . . . "

I desperately needed to make a call but couldn't find the cordless phone. I hit the page button on the cradle, only to discover the handset beeping in my hand.

I shook my head, tried to clear it, and rang up Rollie Austin.

She must have heard something in my voice as soon as I said her name. "What's wrong, sugar?"

"Remember the arson case I told you about?"

"The developer. Has something happened?"

"Someone set fire to my business card and left it on my Outback," I said, my voice wobbly.

"Your car's on fire?" Rollie hollered through static.

"No." I paused to wait for the reception to clear. "My business card. Someone burned it and put it on my windshield."

Rollie burst into a grating laugh. "Is that all, honey?"

"How is this funny?"

"Threats are part of the business. Haven't I taught you anything?"

"But what about—"

She cut me short, with a calming, "You should be tickled. Someone wants you to stop investigating. He—"

"Or she," I edited.

"Whichever, they may as well have shouted, 'You're about to solve the case.' I adore threats. They're like compliments."

"You carry a gun."

"We could outfit you."

"No . . . " I said, my voice trailing off. "I'll be fine."

"This is good, doll."

"It doesn't feel good."

"Threats never do. The first is the worst, but you'll get used to it. I'm on my way to Las Vegas this afternoon, but if you need anything, you call my cell. I'll get one of the boys to run over and look after you."

"How long will you be gone?" I squeaked.

"A week. The Ms. Senior America pageant is on Saturday. Wish me luck. The next time you see me, I might be crowned a winner."

"Good luck, and thanks for talking to me."

"Any time." She paused for an awkward moment. "Sorry I was such a stinker the other day."

"Me, too," I said swiftly.

"You've put in a lot of hard work, trying to find me a house."

"It wasn't just that."

"I know, sweetie, but I took what you said to heart. I've decided not to buy the coach. Keeping most of my stuff in storage all the time, that's no way to live."

"That's what made you change your mind?"

"The lack of a bathtub, too. I need my soaks."

"Should we keep looking?"

"When I get back. Until then, you take care of yourself."

"I will."

"I mean it, Lauren. Don't try to be a hero."

Rollie Austin must have meant it, because she never called me by my real name.

•••

For some reason, the news about the Grand Eaglebahn made me exceptionally happy.

I savored the feeling for all of seven minutes, until I remembered, with a start, that I had a two o'clock appointment with Eileen Whittington.

Three days earlier, I'd scheduled the get-together with the next person on Dennis McBride's directory of enemies.

Should I cancel? What did the unabridged list matter, anyway? I'd short-listed seven people. Why broaden the investigation? On the flip side, Eileen Whittington might be able to shed light on one of my remaining suspects, Dennis McBride.

I ended the debate by deciding to keep the engagement, and I headed to the Golden Opera House, which I found nestled between a curio shop and an ice cream parlor on the main drag of Golden, a foothills town west of Denver.

In the lobby of the three-story historic building, I met Eileen Whittington, and a few minutes into our conversation, her tone became more lilting. "I have every reason to believe that Mr. McBride will meet his contractual obligations to the opera. Many of our donors have fluid financial situations. At times, due to unfortunate reversals of fortune, they're unable to meet their philanthropic commitments."

"That's not the approach you took two weeks ago, when you screamed at Dennis over the phone."

Her attempt at a closemouthed smile netted only a straight line. President of the Golden Opera Foundation board, Eileen had white hair in loose curls, perfectly set and sprayed. She wore a royal blue dress that stretched from her chin to her knees, white stockings, a pink pearl necklace with matching clip-on earrings, and a brooch with a bud vase that held a single daisy. She reeked of old money, a birthright she'd undoubtedly preserved for almost a century.

"If I behaved in a high-spirited manner, it was only because this was not something I expected. Mr. McBride has been extremely generous in the past. The board is grateful for all that he's done."

"Three days ago, you sent a letter threatening legal action."

With force, Eileen produced another thin smile. "That was a mere formality, a standard letter that goes out to all of our patrons who fall behind. We politely remind them of their schedules and obligations, moral and legal."

"Isn't legal action a baseless threat? The promise of a gift isn't enforceable."

Eileen bristled. "It is, my dear, if we can show that we relied upon it. We've never initiated action against a donor, but I'm afraid Mr. McBride's egregious behavior may warrant recourse."

"Come on," I said patiently, "people must stiff you all the time."

"Not on this scale. Based on Mr. McBride's pledge, we ordered 530 new seats for the performance hall. For some time, we've promised subscribers a more comfortable experience. Most bring in their own cushions, but we try to discourage the practice. It diminishes the cultural experience to see gentlemen in tuxedos carrying pillows with sports logos."

"So the seats will have to wait?"

She wrung her hands. "As well as other projects. We've had to contact thirty opera apprentices from around the world and inform them that we won't be able to provide residencies next summer. We've suspended our urban outreach program and canceled a production of *Carmen.*"

As she spoke, Eileen shot a smoldering look at the subject of our discussion, or rather a likeness of him. Dennis McBride's portrait hung on the opposite wall, a gold plaque below it commemorating his significant contributions to the Golden Opera Foundation. In a black tailored suit, gray shirt, burgundy tie, and gold cuff links and watch, the builder looked straight ahead, unsmiling, arms folded, posture erect. I couldn't shake the feeling that he was eavesdropping as Eileen and I sat on the velvet benches in the lobby.

"Doesn't it irritate you that you named the grand tier of your performance hall after Dennis?"

Eileen Whittington's triangular eyebrows knitted together, but her voice remained tranquil. "The practice is customary. Our orchestra and dress circle are named after other renowned philanthropists. Mr. McBride isn't the first

147

benefactor to make misrepresentations. We've learned a valuable lesson. We can't allow our ambitions to get ahead of our cash flow."

"How much did Dennis fail to deliver?"

"A sizable sum."

I waited her out. I knew she was dying to tell me, and it didn't take long. "A million dollars."

My eyes bulged, and for a moment I was speechless.

"We have obligations, but we'll meet them. Neither care of our historic properties nor funding of our capital endowment is in jeopardy. We're one of the oldest opera companies in the nation. I can assure you, Mr. McBride's deceit will not stop the red curtain from rising."

I managed a weak reply. "I had no idea."

She was about to comment, when my cell phone rang.

Apologizing, I pulled it out of my purse, glanced at the screen, and saw the words "pay phone."

"If you'll excuse me, I need to take this."

Eileen clamped her mouth shut, but I persisted. "Hello."

"Well, hello there."

"Richard?"

"It is he, speaking," he said, the words slurred.

Not again. "I can't talk right now."

"Understood, but I'd be obliged if you'd listen. I wanted to thank you for the kindness—"

"Richard—"

"The blankets and comforters, the food. I can't begin to repay you. As we speak, I'm wearing the—"

"Richard, I'm in the middle of something—"

"I won't keep you. Do you still have a desire to talk to the boy?"

"Kevin Slyford? Absolutely."

"I know where he is. It's such a nice day today, isn't it?"

I cast a stealthy glance at Eileen Whittington and noted the red blemishes of indignation on her cheeks. "Could you call back and leave a message on my voice mail?"

"I would if I could, but I can't, so I shan't. I'm afraid I don't have any more change."

I drew in a sharp breath. "Okay, make it quick."

Richard took his time, filling the silence with coughs, snorts, and wheezes. "I just saw Kevin in Southfield, behind the parking garage on 23rd Avenue. I can't say how long he'll be there."

"Thanks. I owe you one."

"Don't mention it."

I put my phone in my purse and met Eileen's flinty gaze. "I'm sorry about that. Where were we?"

"We were discussing Mr. McBride and his refusal to honor commitments."

"Right," I said, packing my belongings.

"This may not have been entirely proper, but I tried to contact Mr. McBride's girlfriend, to see if she could persuade him to fulfill his pledges. I must say, I'm disappointed that she hasn't returned my calls."

"His wife," I corrected.

Eileen looked perplexed. "Goodness, they're married?"

"Just recently. Over Labor Day weekend."

"How marvelous," Eileen said, with pleasure. "Victoria succeeded in snaring him."

"Victoria?"

"She's such a treasure. A bit high-strung, but ever so passionate. No one appreciates a glorious musical score more than she."

"His wife's name is Marla."

"What ever do you mean?" she said, with increasing incomprehension. "What happened to Victoria?"

"Victoria?" I repeated numbly.

"She and Mr. McBride came to all our productions." Eileen Whittington sighed, in a consoling way. "Such a striking couple. Victoria Farino. Do you happen to know her?"

I stopped packing.

CHAPTER 19

Did I happen to know Victoria Farino?

I'd had breakfast with her the morning before.

She was Dennis McBride's ex-girlfriend, the one he wouldn't name? The same one Jerry Hess, his ex-partner, had implied he'd shafted?

Wow!

I knew Victoria had turned down a free bone-marrow transplant without consulting the dying child's family.

I also knew she'd stolen a diamond ring meant to pay for his care.

And I hoped I was well on my way to proving she'd had some involvement in the LoDo wilding.

Was it such a stretch to believe that she could have set two fires to retaliate against an ex-boyfriend?

She had my business card. I'd given it to her at the pastry shop. She could have burned it and left it on my Outback.

If somehow she'd heard that I was working for Dennis McBride, she must have freaked out when I confronted her with Roxanne Archuletta's accusation.

How torturous that must have been, sitting with me in Cherry Creek for two hours, without a mention of Dennis McBride.

This was too good to be true.

I could clear two cases with one felon.

How convenient was this? Too convenient.

I felt amped up, out of my mind with irrational, rapid thoughts.

Whoa!

I had to keep working the two cases separately, methodically and logically, as I always had.

I couldn't let the heat of the moment hijack my winning strategy.

I didn't know what to think, and maybe this wasn't the best time to think.

I needed to focus on driving as fast as I could, maneuvering my way through traffic. Down 6th Avenue to Quebec Street, north to 23rd Avenue, into Southfield, past the air traffic control tower, to the parking garage.

I had to get to Kevin Slyford before he faded back into the neighborhood.

As I pulled a U-turn to park on the north side of 23rd Avenue, I saw smoke rising from the field behind the parking garage.

Good Lord, what now?

•••

I slammed on the brakes, jumped out of the car, and sprinted in the direction of the plumes.

About a hundred yards into the run through waist-high weeds, I pulled up abruptly at the edge of a clearing, and in a depression in the ground, I saw a boy kneeling, his hands suspended above a small fire.

"What are you doing?" I shrieked, scrambling to douse the blaze with my feet.

He raised his head in protest. "Hey!"

"What are you doing?" I repeated, at the top of my voice.

"Nothing," he mumbled.

The boy's head was shaved except for a one-inch-wide strip of red hair coated with gel and spiked up. On the bald sections, black stubble protruded, contrasting sharply with a light fuzz on his face. He had big ears, crooked eyes, a peeling nose, and chapped lips.

"Are you Kevin Slyford?"

"Why?"

"Richard Leone told me I might find you here. I'm Lauren Vellequette."

He sat on his heels and stirred the ashes with a bent coat hanger. "How did you know it was me?"

"I'm a detective," I said, catching my breath.

"Huh."

I explained further, "Richard described you."

"No one likes Richard, except me. He used to live in that building over there," Kevin said, pointing to a ten-by-ten shed in the distance. "Now he lives in a ditch."

"Have you seen Richard's shelter?"

He shook his head. "It's too far away."

"Do you ever go to Landry?"

"Where?"

"Richard's neighborhood, south of here."

Kevin ran a hand along the top of his hair. "Huh-uh."

I sat in the dirt, next to the pit he'd excavated. "You shouldn't set fires, you know."

"I know." He looked down at his shoes, basketball sneakers that looked like they were four sizes too big for him.

I gestured at the lighter and scraps of newspaper. "Why do you do it?"

"Because it's fun."

"Don't you like to skateboard?"

His head jerked up. "Yeah, but my auntie took away my board."

"Why?"

"I lie too much," he said, reaching below baggy silk shorts that fell to midcalf and picking at a scab on his shin.

"What else do you do for fun?"

"Play video games and make weapons."

"What kind of weapons?"

"Swords. I carve them out of sticks." Kevin tugged a ring out of his shorts, on which he'd attached a house key, a stuffed bear, and a pocketknife. He held out the knife for my examination. "This used to be my dad's."

"It's nice," I said, admiring the mother-of-pearl inlay.

"I make forts, too," he said shyly.

From my purse, I pulled out a roll of Chewy Sprees. I popped a purple one into my mouth and handed Kevin an orange one. Wordlessly, he put the candy on his tongue and sucked.

"Richard told me you live around here."

153

Kevin nodded.

"About two weeks ago, did you see the fire on Visalia Street?"

He began to twitch excitedly. "That was so cool!"

"I'm working for the builder who owns the house, and he wants to know who started the fire. Do you have any ideas?"

The fervor went out of the boy's eyes, and he shook his head slightly.

"Did you do it?"

His head shaking became more animated.

"Richard thought you might know something."

"Richard wouldn't tell on me," he said resolutely. "He's my friend."

"Do the two of you hang out together?"

"Sometimes. He likes to tell stories."

"About what?"

Kevin moved his hands in a restless manner. "War. Fishing. Stuff like that."

"Did Richard watch the fire on Visalia with you?"

"He said he might come around that day, but he didn't. He would have liked it."

"Richard likes fires, too?"

"Yeah, but he has a girlfriend."

"Really?" I said, not bothering to mask my surprise.

"She picks him up in a silver car."

"Where do they go?"

He gave me a funny look. "Nowhere. They just park and sit there."

"You spy on them?"

Kevin lowered his head. "Maybe."

"Have you met her?"

He cast an apprehensive glance my way. "He won't let me."

"Maybe she's his sister."

"Huh-uh. He doesn't have any family."

I switched gears. "Did you ever build a fort in the house that caught fire?"

"I dunno."

My steady gaze unnerved him, and he amended his answer. "Once. Before it had walls."

"Not the day of the fire?"

He shook his head. "I wanted to, but all the doors were locked."

"You went to the house after school?"

"After dinner."

"Couldn't you climb in a window?"

His eyes wandered. "I was gonna, but some lady yelled at me to get away from the house."

My pulse quickened. "What lady?"

He shrugged.

"You didn't know her?"

He shook his head.

"Was she Richard's girlfriend?"

"I dunno. Maybe."

"What did she look like?"

He straightened up. "Like a mom."

"What's a mom look like?"

"She had a stroller."

"With a baby? How big was the baby?"

Kevin Slyford stared at me earnestly. "She didn't have a baby in the stroller."

•••

I left Kevin in the field, having stripped him of the lighter, and went looking for Richard Leone in Landry.

I found him— or rather, my yellow comforter—in his home away from home, the park at Trinidad Street and 12th Avenue.

I felt reasonably certain Richard was beneath the comforter, in the middle of a circle of evergreens, but I didn't want to take any chances.

This is where Rollie Austin would have drawn her 9 millimeter semiautomatic, but I settled for cautiously nudging the bulk with my toe, and to my relief, Pepper scampered out.

The dog greeted me warmly, with tail wagging, licking, and barking, none of which provoked Richard to stir.

I tentatively peeled back an edge of the cloth and discovered Richard curled up in the fetal position, eyes closed.

When I managed to rouse him with forceful shaking and repeated shouts, he tried to sit up but failed. Disoriented, he slid down again, onto his side.

"Richard!"

Inarticulate sounds came from the back of his throat.

"Richard! It's Lauren Vellequette."

He rubbed his nose with the palm of his hand, leaving more residue than he removed. "Do I know you?"

"Yes," I said, maddened. "We've met twice. And you called me an hour ago."

"Oh," he said lamely.

I relaxed on the grass, cross-legged. "You've been holding out on me."

"What?" he grunted.

Pepper climbed into my lap, and I rubbed the terrier's belly. "I hear you have a girlfriend."

He smiled crookedly. "A girlfriend? No, my nerves aren't stout enough for that."

I shot him an admonishing look. "Richard!"

"Too much rabbit in my feet."

"You get in her silver car and have long talks."

"Only in my dreams," he said, but he stiffened.

"Kevin Slyford saw you."

Richard became sedate again. "The boy makes up stories."

"Who is she?"

"An acquaintance." He shooed away an imaginary insect. "With mutual interests."

"Such as revenge on Dennis McBride?" I retrieved a tissue from my purse and cleaned gunk out of Pepper's eyes. With a comb, I began to untangle her mats. "Why didn't you tell me Dennis likes to throw rocks at you?"

"People have done worse."

"Or that he raided the outbuilding you lived in at Southfield?"

Richard began to rock. "It was time for a change."

"Are you and the woman in the silver car partners in crime?"

He covered his ears with the comforter.

"Is her name Daphne Cartwright?" I'd seen a jogging stroller on Daphne's porch and a silver Volvo S40 sedan in front of her house.

No response.

"Victoria Farino?" I couldn't visualize Victoria pushing a stroller and didn't know what she drove, but she was my favorite target for everything.

"What time is it?" With great effort, Richard moved his arm into a position that afforded him a view of his Mickey Mouse watch. Unfortunately, the face was upside down, which bewildered him.

"Four o'clock," I offered.

He pushed up to a slouched, sitting position. "I have some place I need to be. What's today?"

"Monday. Do you hate Dennis McBride?"

"I don't have enough get-up-and-go." Richard scratched his head, harder and harder. "Hatred requires get-up-and-go."

"You shouldn't have yelled that you would burn down his houses. Not in front of a witness."

He drained the last drop out of a can of Colt 45 and reached for the pack of Marlboros he'd tucked into the loose waistband of his jeans. "A witness?"

"A McBride Homes employee, Josh Mifflin, heard you make the threat."

Richard struggled to remove a cigarette and lighter from the mostly empty pack, and his hands shook so badly he couldn't work the disposable lighter. "It's the devil's wrath, not mine."

When I borrowed the lighter and held the flame for him, our eyes locked.

His displayed an emotion I couldn't categorize, and it was only after I'd left him and parked my car near the north entrance to Alameda Mall that it dawned on me what I'd just seen.

Fear.

•••

Once more using the pretext that I needed a reference for Victoria Farino, I met with Jan Schumacher, interim marketing director at Alameda

Mall, and before I could sit down, she'd enlightened me as to Victoria's true contributions to the mall.

According to Jan, trouble had brewed at Alameda Mall for years, in the form of unsupervised teenagers wandering the corridors with no money and nothing to do. As the teens became more of a nuisance, the shopping center responded by hiring parents to patrol the mall. When that didn't alleviate the situation, the mall set a 5 p.m. curfew for all unaccompanied youth under the age of seventeen. The bold move helped, and as loyal customers began to drift back to the mall, merchants reported a rise in sales.

In March, however, Victoria Farino killed all momentum, in one day, with one sentence, nearly canceling out $100 million worth of renovations.

During lease negotiations with one of the mall's temporary tenants, Pierre Boihem of Pierre's Wings & BBQ, Victoria informed the restaurateur that he would not be offered a permanent lease. She told him the mall was moving in a more "white-focused" direction, away from the "young, black customer."

Pierre Boihem, who'd secretly recorded the conversation, took the tape to a local news station, and backlash came quickly. From the city of Aurora, which had ponied up $15 million in tax incentives for the renovation, from the mayor of Aurora, and from leaders in the African-American community.

The day the story aired, Alameda Mall fired Victoria Farino.

Interesting.

That made it twice this year that Victoria had witnessed firsthand the power of the media, positive and negative.

She'd raised $425,000 for a dying child, the positive.

And she'd been fired from her job, the negative.

By the middle of the summer, when the merchants of LoDo interviewed her for a job that never materialized, who could blame her for recalling the dark powers of the media?

No one, but plenty of people could blame her for evoking them, including me.

If I had anything to contribute, Victoria Farino would pay for her bad judgment.

CHAPTER 20

Tuesday morning, I awoke with an acute sense of foreboding.
Whenever that happened, I automatically took stock of my life.
Let's see . . .

I was healthy, cancer-free for six years and less driven by death.

Sasha was healthy and safe.

Both P.I. cases were under control, more or less.

I had high hopes of wrapping up the LoDo wilding investigation in the near future. Once I connected Victoria Farino to 11-up, the tagger who had instigated the bedlam, voila! The day before, I'd apprised Roxanne Archuletta of the situation, and she seemed heartened by the update and the fact that business had picked up a notch over the weekend.

I had to admit, the arson case troubled me, but only slightly. According to Rollie, the burned business card left on my windshield represented progress, but I felt adrift.

I dreaded the next move, but couldn't divine an alternative.

I had to confront Dennis McBride.

•••

Dennis squeezed me in between a one o'clock haircut and three o'clock squash match, and acted as if I should thank him for the privilege.

As we greeted each other with a perfunctory handshake, my eyes darted to the personal items strewn about his office. "The new house isn't ready yet?"

"Movers come the day after tomorrow. Look, I'm backed up against it today," Dennis McBride said, folding his arms. "What do you need?"

I looked him in the eye and said genially, "I hear you like to harass the homeless."

He smirked. "Who told you that?"

"Several people."

"What am I supposed to do? Let them piss all over my property?"

"What's the harm in letting them use your Port-A-Let?"

"Why should I pay to have their shit hauled away?" he said heatedly. "If I let one of them camp out, before you know it, I'll have ten more lying around. Look at intersections around town. Panhandlers are stacked three deep. They could work, but they won't. They'd rather stand on a corner with a sign."

"No one would be on a corner if he had a choice."

Dennis leaned back luxuriously in his leather chair. "You don't know much about the real world, do you? I used to stop and offer those guys day jobs—paint, demolition, hauling, something they couldn't screw up. They don't want to work. They want someone to hand them money."

I shifted uncomfortably on the edge of the credenza. "What makes you so jaded?"

"Practice." He smoothed wrinkles from his putty chinos and black houndstooth shirt. "I know a minister who gave away one thousand free meal coupons. You know how many were redeemed? Sixteen. What's that tell you? The mayor wants to end homelessness in ten years. It's never going to happen. Remember his genius idea to convert vacant schools into shelters last winter? What would that do to property values? People don't want losers shuffling into their neighborhood after dark."

He continued calmly. "You know what happens when you put a bird feeder in your backyard? Pretty soon, your yard's overrun with birds. We may as well invite every bum in the country to join us for a free ride. If the mayor's handout goes through, the $122 million price tag will move into the billions. I'm sick of hearing their stories."

His tone changed to a mocking, whiny one. "We're victims. We can't work. Take care of us, so we won't have to take care of ourselves."

Dennis extracted a cigar from his side drawer and pointed it at me. "I'm not paying you to solve social ills. How does this relate to my houses burning down?"

I could scarcely endure this conversation, surrounded by the fragments of his wealth. A Calloway putter. A fishing rod. A Braun electric shaver. A set of twenty-pound barbells. A case of poker chips. A collection of beer steins.

I worked to control my temper. "Richard Leone used to live in a shed near your project in Southfield. Now he sleeps in a culvert in Landry."

Dennis lit the cigar. "Who?"

"Richard Leone. The man you threw rocks at."

"That slob with the bike and trailer?"

"Yes," I said, between clenched teeth.

He maintained a blank expression. "I never knew his name. What about him?"

"Richard knows the area, he has reason to hate you, and he threatened to set your houses on fire."

With a long draw on the cigar, Dennis expanded his chest, and for a split second, I wondered if he'd considered breast reduction surgery. "From what I've seen, that bum couldn't buy gas, light candles, and run away without killing himself."

I coughed. "How do you know gas and candles started the fire?"

"That's what Max Spiker, from Metro Fire, tells me about the Southfield fire. He called yesterday. Seven pools of gas, with candles at the edges. That's what did it."

"Has he released the crime scene?"

Dennis blew rings of smoke. "As of this morning."

"When were you going to tell me?"

"I'm telling you now. Forget the homeless guy. He's not capable."

"He could be when he's sober."

"I told you, no," Dennis said roughly, retrieving an ashtray from below a stack of CDs.

"Okay, then." I flashed a dangerous smile. "How about someone else with a gripe? Maybe someone at one of the arts organizations you stiffed?"

His face reddened. "What are you talking about?"

"Eileen Whittington told me—"

"I was upfront with you about her. She's on the list," he said, glibly talking over me.

"Yes, but you neglected to mention a few others." I dug into my purse and pulled out a handwritten accounting. "Aspen Wildflower Festival. $250,000. Had to cancel the eleventh annual event showcasing alpine meadows."

"That isn't—"

"Stanley Lake Theater. $150,000. Had to eliminate three plays and lay off an associate director. The worst blow in the summer stock's fifty-year history."

"I'm going to pay those people," he exploded. "Cut me some slack! Some of them have set collection goons on me. They're worse than the mob."

My voice lowered as his rose. "Dennis, there are fourteen groups on this list."

"What's the big deal? If the goddamn Air Force would give me my $2.7 million, they'd all get their money."

"Why didn't you stop making pledges when you couldn't deliver?"

"None of them questioned my character when I wrote fat checks."

"Why didn't you stop pledging?" I repeated quietly.

He let out a pained sigh. "The philanthropy thing was my ex-girlfriend's deal. They gave me awards and named projects after me. She served on the boards and received invitations to everything. It was a kick."

"Speaking of your ex-girlfriend," I said, at length, "I have to disclose that I met her recently."

Distrust covered his face. "How?"

"When I spoke to Eileen Whittington, she mentioned that you were involved with Victoria Farino. By chance, I'd just interviewed Victoria for a case I'm working in LoDo. She's the marketing director for an association in Cherry Creek, and I needed her input."

"What happened to her job at Alameda Mall?"

"Who knows?" I said evasively. "I have to ask again. Could Victoria have started the fires?"

"No way."

"What color car does she drive?"

"How should I know? I haven't seen her in months."

I counted to three. "What did she drive the last time you saw her?"

"A blue Maxima, but that doesn't mean anything. She leases a new car every summer."

"Was the split mutual?"

He shrugged.

After a discomfiting silence, I pressed. "I need details."

His upper lip curled. "Everything was a struggle with that woman. The sex was great, but get her out of bed, and she was a high-maintenance bitch."

"How long were you together?"

"Eight years."

I arched an eyebrow.

"Did you hear me?" Dennis said, defensively. "The sex was great. She's hot, edgy. We had some laughs."

"Did you intend to marry her?"

He pushed out the side of his cheek with his tongue. "I never thought about it."

"What about kids?"

"Victoria wanted them. I didn't. End of story."

"But you stayed together?"

Dennis laced his fingers behind his head. "Until February. She was putting the screws to me for a proposal by Valentine's Day. She should have known better than that," he said, his features hardening. "I took her to Strings and over crème brulee told her it wasn't going to happen. One thing led to another, and that was it."

"Your relationship ended on Valentine's Day?"

"Mine did. Hers didn't. She kept begging me to take her back, calling my office, cell, home. She drove by at all hours. I told her to get back on her meds."

"She's on antidepressants?"

"Damned if I know. It's just an expression."

"Has she stopped contacting you?"

His eyes flickered. "Stopped cold. On March 31."

"How do you remember the date?"

"Marla and I met on March 30. I called Victoria the next day, cut into her sob session and laid it on the line. I told her to move on, that I'd met someone else and fallen in love."

"The next day?" I said sharply. "Was that true?"

"Every bit of it." His voice softened. "I knew the instant I set eyes on

Marla. It all came together. One of life's strange twists—she told me this morning that she's pregnant."

"Congratulations," I said, the word sounding like an accusation.

He broke into a wide grin. "I can't believe it. Big changes."

"What happened to no kids, end of story?"

He spread his arms, turning up his hands. "What can I say? When it's right, it's right."

I stared at Dennis McBride in disbelief.

"I mean it," he said, with determination. "I'd take my last breath for her."

•••

I thought about Dennis McBride all the way back to my office.

Here's what I knew after eleven days.

He sold houses built on asbestos-laced dirt and double-crossed ranchers for their family land.

He stole tools from subcontractors and fired grieving employees.

He threw rocks at homeless people and backed out of commitments to girlfriends, partners, and nonprofit organizations.

Granted, he'd never win "Man of the Year," but had he torched his own houses?

I pondered the extent of my client's guilt until I walked into the office, where Sasha's appearance erased all other thoughts.

She'd outdone herself this time.

I almost laughed out loud at the outfit she'd worn to school: neon green aviator sunglasses, black hooded sweatshirt, and yellow hula skirt.

She handed me three message slips. "Somebody keeps calling and hanging up."

"What does Caller ID show?"

"Pay phone."

"That's probably Richard Leone. If he calls again, say his name before you say hello. Maybe that'll get him to talk." I fanned out the phone messages. "You haven't heard from Payday?"

"Oh, yeah. He said to tell you he's playing tagger tag with 11-up."

I sent her a pained look. "Which is?"

"It's like phone tag, but with symbols. Payday left a message on the utility box, 11-up left a message. Payday left another one, and now it's 11-up's turn."

I moved toward the watercooler, exhaling irritably. "There's no other way to contact this kid?"

Hand in chin, Sasha followed me with her eyes, never moving her head. "Payday says not."

"Shit."

"You shouldn't cuss."

"Lay off," I said gruffly. "It's my only vice."

She tucked her hair behind her ears. "You're not in a very good mood. I'd better ask you later."

"Ask me what?"

"Nothing."

My voice deepened. "Sasha!"

"All right, already." She flashed a loopy smile. "We want to work on a case."

"Who's we?"

"Me and Taylor."

I emptied the cup of water with one swallow. "What did you have in mind?"

"Taylor has a gym class with this girl, Bianca Johnson. We want to investigate her mom."

"For what?"

"Supposedly, she's this really cool mom," Sasha said, in a rush. "She throws parties for kids and buys them alcohol. Taylor heard she had sex with two of Bianca's friends."

"Boys or girls?"

"Boys."

"How old?"

Sasha covered her mouth with the cuff of her sweatshirt. "Sophomores."

"Which makes them sixteen." I sighed. "That's a crime. It's too serious for you and Taylor."

"But they're boys!"

"That doesn't make a difference."

165

She wrinkled her nose. "Maybe we could investigate the alcohol. All the kids pitch in, and Bianca's mom goes to the liquor store. She buys everyone beer, vodka, rum, anything they want."

"No!"

"Couldn't we tail Mrs. Johnson, just for practice?"

I practically imploded. "No, no, no!"

"I knew you'd say that. You're no fun." Sasha shrugged carelessly. "I'm caught up on my work, so I'm going to Taylor's to play with the ducks."

"Okay," I said tentatively.

Sasha responded to my puzzlement. "Taylor's babysitting three baby ducks. Mr. Fuzzles, Uggy-Pants, and Myla."

"Where did Taylor get ducks, and how do you play with them?"

"From her mom's friend. We put water in the tub, but just a little, so they can walk and swim. Why don't you have a pet, Lauren?"

I shook my head vigorously. "I need to save my energy for a human relationship."

"You're weird." She grabbed her backpack. "See you later."

"Sasha, wait. What's the name of Bianca's mom?"

"Brigid Johnson. Why?" she said, suspicious.

"I'll call the principal and talk to her."

Her face lost color. "Don't tell her I told you."

"I won't."

"And don't use your real name, or she'll know it was me."

"I'll take care of it," I said, in my most soothing voice. "And I'll keep you out of it.

"Okay." Sasha waved good-bye over her shoulder and exited blithely, content to play with ducks, not at all concerned that she'd just dropped this mini-bomb on me.

•••

I shouldn't have complained.

A bigger bomb fell eight hours later.

At eleven o'clock, my cell phone rang, sending my heart racing.

On the other end of the line, Dennis McBride calmly informed me that his Carnival house was on fire.

CHAPTER 21

I dressed quickly, trading Nick and Nora flannels for a sweatshirt and jeans, and dashed out the door.

Forty-five minutes later, I arrived at Smoky Hill Road and E-470, where I turned south and drove on a frontage road parallel to the highway. In a few blocks, I found County Line Road, the divider between Douglas and Elbert counties, and headed east.

Along the darkened landscape, only a smattering of lights was visible, some from mini-mansions that had sprouted in a recent building boom, others from farmhouses and outbuildings that had withstood decades on the plains.

On the paved road that seemingly led to nowhere, I continued for three more miles, when suddenly an orange-red light appeared across the horizon, as bright as the rising sun.

My God . . . were all five Carnival homes engulfed?

At mile eight, the asphalt gave way to dirt, forcing me to slow down from ninety to thirty, and at mile ten, I crossed through the stone entrance to Prairie Acres at a crawl.

I followed flashing lights to a dead-end street, where I saw an ambulance, three police cars, and nine fire trucks. Four news copters circled overhead, no doubt collecting footage for morning reports.

In haste, I parked at the opening of the cul-de-sac, jumped out of the car, and shivered at the wave of radiant heat. I left my jacket on the backseat and searched for Dennis McBride, who stood near his silver Audi sedan, looking on grimly. I gave him a hug, a glancing, self-conscious embrace. "When did it start?"

His shoulders heaved. "Sometime around 10:15. A neighbor heard explosions and saw a bright light. She called 911, and firefighters arrived at 10:30."

I wiped sweat from my eyebrows. "When did you get here?"

"Thirty minutes ago."

"Can they save it?"

He pointed helplessly at the inferno. "It's gone."

I touched his sleeve. "I'm sure they did all they could."

"What does it matter?"

"Maybe the wind will die down."

"It's always windy out here," Dennis said, his face pale but composed.

A firefighter approached. "A word, Mr. McBride?"

His reply was lifeless. "Sure."

The fireman stared at me pointedly, and I took the hint.

I wandered off, climbed a nearby hill, and found a bare spot on the ground, clear of yuccas, sunflowers, brush, tumbleweeds, and cacti. From a safe distance, I had an unobstructed view of the fire and the four other Carnival homes. Two- and three-story monstrosities on one-acre lots, they were similar in scope to Dennis McBride's French Chateau, and aside from a Colorado Lodge interloper, the block was all European. An English Manor, Tuscan Villa, and Spanish Mediterranean stood in various stages of completion, and as the McBride home disappeared, firefighters worked to protect the other structures with defensive walls of water.

I watched as dozens of men fought the primary burn. Organized and efficient, their practiced movements were devoid of panic or rush. Teams of two knelt in the yard and aimed hoses at the lower level of the main house, challenging the flames with arcing showers, while other pairs perched on the edges of extension ladders and attacked the fire from above with powerful sprays.

At one point, I caught sight of a vaguely familiar face across the street, and we exchanged waves, but I couldn't place him. Not in darkness, from a hundred yards away.

I kept trying to tear myself away from the fire, but I couldn't.

There was something spectacular about it, almost spiritual.

Over the next hour, the battle raged, and as soon as it seemed as if firefighters had won, the fire would rear up again in ferocious waves, sending one-hundred-foot flames and black smoke spiraling into the air, shooting embers across the sky. The crackle and smell reminded me of campfires in my youth, but that's where the similarities ended.

This conflagration was on a scale almost impossible to absorb.

At its height, the blaze seemed as if it would spread and consume acres, but firefighters eventually wrestled control, and by two o'clock, they had the flames extinguished and had begun to rewind their snaking hoses.

Hypnotized by a skeleton crew tending to the last smoldering bits, I barely heard the shout from Dennis McBride.

When I turned, he glared at me. "Meet me in my office at eight o'clock. You're getting a partner."

With that, he strode toward his car, leaving me in shock.

Partner.

I did not like the sound of that word.

•••

On the drive home from Prairie Acres, I ruminated about Dennis McBride's dictate, and back at my apartment, I lay on top of the bed covers, too wired to attempt sleep.

What was I supposed to do now? Disobey him? Bad idea.

Fire him before he fired me? That was a thought.

I tossed and turned until dawn's break, tormented by the anxiety he'd planted in me with one loaded word.

Partner. Damnit!

By seven-thirty, I was so rattled, I bypassed my office and Starbucks and headed straight to the Denver Tech Center.

Wrong move, skipping the coffee.

I could have used the caffeine to bolster my coping skills, which evaporated the second I shuffled into Dennis McBride's office.

My client didn't budge from his chair. "There she is. Lauren, this is—"

"We've met," I said curtly, tucking my hands in my pockets.

From across the room, my new partner snorted. "She poached my crime scene at Southfield."

"Good. We can skip the introductions," Dennis said, equally brusque. "Now that—"

Max Spiker interrupted and shot me a stony look. "Have you led any arson investigations?"

"One," I exaggerated. "Have you led any real estate fraud investigations?"

"No," he replied, his stern expression never wavering behind rimless glasses.

I flashed a phony smile. "Then we should get along just fine."

He put his hands on his hips. "How do you begin an arson investigation?"

"You start outside and work your way in. You look at the exterior, the interior, the room of origin, and finally the point of origin. Biggest picture to smallest element."

My interrogator's face reddened. "What's a V pattern?"

"The mark left behind by flames and gases as they travel. The narrow point of the V, where the two lines meet, is the point of ignition. The shape of the V tells you the pacing and severity of the fire and how it moved. A skinny V indicates an intense, rapid burn, whereas a broad V signifies a slower burn."

Max Spiker's tone hardened. "Will a fire spread faster if it's set at the center of the room or up against a wall?"

"The wall."

He sniffled and picked at his nose. "Lucky guess."

"Against a wall, less cool air flows into the plume, and there are longer flames, higher gas temperatures at the ceiling, and faster flashover."

"How many arson cases have you worked?" he said, his voice full of tightly controlled emotion.

"This would be my second."

Max Spiker's lips turned downward, his eyebrows moved upward, and he nodded grudgingly. Tall, barrel-chested, and in his late fifties, he had rutted skin, a light brown handlebar mustache, and no sideburns. A short haircut and frontal balding added unattractive inches to an already oversized forehead.

I forced an amiable tone. "If a husband and wife own a house together, but only the husband's name is on the mortgage, can he refinance without her permission?"

"Don't know, don't care."

"No," I answered in a sing-song voice. "That would be fraud. If two sisters own land as tenants-in-common and one dies, what happens to her interest in the property?"

"Passes on to the other sister."

"Wrong! That would be accurate if they were joint tenants. As tenants-in-common, the dead woman's interest transfers to her estate." I gained steam. "A house that's under contract, but unfinished, burns and is declared a total loss. What obligation does the builder have to the buyer?"

"Depends."

"Lucky guess. On what?"

Max Spiker didn't hesitate. "The cycle of the moon."

"On the performance clause in their original contract," I corrected, without rancor.

Max moved around restlessly. "I fought a fire at a gas plant in Commerce City. Fireballs the size of houses hanging a hundred feet up in the air, heat you could feel a half-mile away, noxious fumes, and seventy-eight thousand square feet of propane at risk. Had to wait four hours before we could get in close enough to put water on it. You ever done anything like that?"

I studied him wordlessly. After he blinked first, I spoke quietly. "I sat through a twelve-hour closing for a house in Harvard Gulch. Problems with the buyer, seller, title, and financing. No air conditioning, no lunch break, restroom three floors down. A closing agent wearing Giorgio perfume and two hundred pages of documents. You ever done anything like that?"

We shared a glare, which Dennis broke. "Are you two finished?"

"I suppose she might be of some use," Max said.

"Likewise."

After Max shoved piles of Dennis's possessions off the couch and cleared space for both of us, I sat, careful not to touch him.

"We've got to stop this torch before he does something really dumb," Max said.

Dennis gurgled with contempt. "You don't consider burning three of my houses dumb?"

Max shrugged. "You can rebuild houses. You can't rebuild bodies. Skin grafting is trickier than drywall repair."

"Will you rebuild?" I interjected.

"Who knows?" Dennis said, his face slack. "The Carnival opens in 210 days. My phone hasn't stopped ringing this morning. Builders, subcontractors, tradesmen I haven't heard from in years, all wanting to help, but I can't think straight."

"The good news is, you were only at framing," Max said, chipper. "The bad news is, you didn't have sheetrock up, and there was nothing to slow down the fire."

"I have a $120,000 stairway on order," Dennis said, with a start. "What will I do with that?"

"Could you cancel?" I suggested.

"Not an option," he replied bleakly. "The carpenter started working on it in his shop six months ago, and he has a three-year backlog of custom projects. His staircases are works of art."

"You're still in shock," Max said easily. "It happens. Settle down, get your bearings, wait a few days to make a good decision."

"Who's doing this to me? Lauren, what have you found out?"

"I can't connect anyone directly to the fires," I said, hedging.

Dennis popped the cap off a bottle of Budweiser. "I need answers."

Max declined his offer of a warm one from the six-pack on the desk and turned to me. "C'mon, give us the benefit of your female intuition."

Dennis didn't offer me a beverage, and I fought to overlook the slight. "I'd rather not say."

Max leaned back in the folds of the couch. "We won't hold you to it."

Dennis burped, and his voice rose with emotion. "I want to know who destroyed my houses at Landry and Southfield!"

"Richard Leone—" I began reluctantly.

"Forget him!" Dennis bawled.

"A background check turned up nothing. Absolutely nothing, which is extremely unusual, even if—"

"Leave it. Next subject."

Fighting the urge to cower, I began again. "Victoria Farino—"

Dennis banged his fist on the desk, and shouted, "Goddamn it! Drop it! Do you understand?"

Max looked at him with interest, and back at me, but didn't say a word.

"There's a twelve-year-old boy who lives in Southfield," I stammered. "Kevin Slyford. He could have walked or biked to Landry. The two sites are about three miles apart. He lives with his aunt, who works all the time, and he likes to set fires. The day before yesterday, I caught him with a small one in a field near his house."

Max's forehead wrinkled. "What did you do?"

"Put it out."

Max shook his head in remonstration. "You should have called the fire department. There's no such thing as a free pass. Next thing you know, someone calls 911, the house goes up in flames before we get there, and one of the siblings is dead."

"I needed to get Kevin to trust me—"

Max tugged on his mustache. "I used to go into schools, as part of my job, and teach kids about the dangers of fire. You think they'd listen? I brought in graphic photographs, introduced burn victims, anything to scare the shit out of them."

"It didn't work?"

"With 99.9 percent, sure. But with that one kid in every thousand, I could see him get off on the power of the burn."

"Always boys?" Dennis asked.

"Just about."

I tried to snap out of my pout. "Do they outgrow it?"

"Some don't. They develop a taste for fire and need to see bigger ones. That turns them into criminals. Or firefighters," Max added.

I unfolded my arms. "Do most arsonists watch the fires they set?"

"Depends. Thrill seekers and pyromaniacs wouldn't miss it. They're on the perimeter with the rubberneckers, drooling. Professional torches and revenge seekers, they're long gone. They have a mission, accomplish it, no reason to hang around."

"What have you turned up so far?" Dennis asked Max. "Start with Landry."

"Landry, there's not much to tell. That was the first fire, and we ruled it accidental. Wet rags, soaked with stain and tossed in a bag of sawdust, spontaneously combusted. Sure as hell, though, a candle could have started it. I'd love to go back and take another shot at the scene, knowing what I know now."

"But it's been bulldozed and hauled away," I said merrily.

"I've still got Southfield," Max replied stubbornly.

"Have you ruled the cause of it as suspicious?" I asked.

"Suspicious is a term misused by inexperienced investigators. It's not a recognized cause."

"Excuse me," I said testily.

"You're excused. Let's call the fire cause undetermined, until we can prove it's incendiary. Southfield, I'm thinking our perp entered through the bathroom window on the main floor. The screen was set to the side, up against the house."

"You can pop out these new screens in seconds," Dennis offered. "They're designed for convenience."

"I'm guessing he opened the unlocked window and climbed in. As soon as he made his way inside, he could have come and gone through the interior garage door."

"From now on, we'll install keyed deadbolts on all the doors and bars on the windows."

Max ignored Dennis's sarcasm. "The lab confirmed gasoline as the accelerant. Whoever did this poured pools and came back, laid candles at the edges, and carefully lit each wick. He started on the second floor and worked his way down. Seven spots in all, every one in the corner of a room."

I cocked one eyebrow. "You're sure the igniter was a candle?"

"Candles are the most popular timing devices. For flash-and-run jobs, I've seen lighters, matches, flares, and propane torches, but those would have killed him at Southfield, with all the gas he poured."

"How long would the candle have burned?"

"Rule of thumb, one hour for a 7/8-inch model. A teacup candle would have given him about forty-five minutes, which fits the timeframe. The last construction worker left the site at six, and our 911 call came in at 7:35."

Dennis broke in. "What about my Carnival home? What happened there?"

"Too soon to tell. As we speak, guys are sifting through the rubble, searching for hot spots, hitting them with water."

Dennis took another swallow of beer and pointed at me with the neck of the bottle. "How could this kid have made it from Southfield to Prairie Acres?"

"Nineteen miles one way," Max said obligingly. "I clocked it last night. That would be about four or five hours round-trip by bike, fifteen or sixteen by foot."

My eyes narrowed. "You asked about Landry and Southfield. Obviously, the Carnival fire doesn't fit for Kevin Slyford."

Max tilted toward me. "Anyone else on your radar?"

"Daphne Cartwright."

"Who's she?"

Dennis answered. "A housewife with too much time on her hands."

"She was one of the first people to buy a McBride home in Landry," I explained. "Six months after her family moved in, the Landry Redevelopment Authority discovered asbestos in her yard."

"She's a nutcase."

"What made you single her out?" Max asked.

"She's obsessed with the asbestos fight, here and across the country, commercially produced asbestos and naturally occurring veins. She's also consumed with military base cleanups. She doesn't believe bases should be converted for civilian use. She thinks it's impossible to make them safe for residential or commercial development. She's convinced that Dennis knew about the asbestos contamination before he sold her the house."

"I didn't," Dennis said bluntly.

"Daphne Cartwright believes she's fighting for the health of families everywhere. She might be trying to make an example of McBride Homes. She intends to sue Dennis and the Air Force, and she has some experience. My background check turned up nine civil cases in which she's been a plaintiff or defendant in the past five years."

Max addressed his next question to Dennis. "She have any beefs with Southfield?"

Dennis shrugged, unconcerned.

I enlightened them. "Yes. Millions of gallons of fuel and de-icing fluid settled into the ground when Southfield was used as an airport. Also, a TCE plume has migrated from Landry to Southfield."

"TCE?"

"Trichloroethylene. It's a cleaning solvent that takes grease off metal," Dennis said distractedly.

"A zealot," Max commented. "That's motive. How about means and opportunity?"

"She could have set the Landry fire," I said, not very persuasively. "She lives a few blocks away. And at Southfield, Kevin Slyford saw a woman pushing an empty stroller past the house on Visalia Street shortly before the fire. Daphne Cartwright owns a jogging stroller, and she could have used it to transport the gas and candles."

"Maybe the stroller still smells like fuel," Max said, with relish. "Check that out!"

Dennis joined his laughter, before Max turned somber. "Kidding aside, boys and girls, we need to get cracking and find this torch before he sets another fire."

"You'd better do it before I lose another house!"

"Screw property," Max said matter-of-factly. "I'm going after this perp before he kills someone."

Dennis guffawed. "Isn't that a little dramatic?"

Max stared at Dennis fixedly. "Every arsonist is a potential mass murderer."

CHAPTER 22

"Why did you do that?" I said to Dennis McBride, as soon as the door closed behind Max Spiker.

All of a sudden, papers on his desk required his undivided attention. "Do what?"

"Bring him into my investigation."

He raised his head in a flash of anger. "Because you're not cutting it."

"I can't stand him."

"My purpose wasn't to find you a buddy or a boyfriend," Dennis said, in a loud whisper that grew into a shout. "I want my goddamn houses to stop burning to the ground. Is that too much to ask?"

"No," I said diffidently.

"Then get out there and find out who's doing this to me."

"Does his boss at the Metro Fire Bureau know about our partnership?"

"Spike's no longer employed there."

"Spike?" I said, butchering the word.

"Max Spiker, the guy you're trying to cut loose."

"Since when?"

"Last Friday."

"What happened?"

Dennis motioned dismissively. "Something about a public relations mix-up."

I frowned until my forehead hurt. "What kind of a mix-up?"

"Ask him, Lauren. I don't really care. I'm not in the market for a choirboy. I want to combine his expertise with your expertise, and I want this sicko caught." His eyes, full of hostility, met mine. "Is that clear?"

I answered by leaving.

•••

"What happened to my office?" I cried, an hour later, and I mean cried. A tear rolled out of my left eye.

"It's nice, huh?" Sasha said, with a proud smile.

"Everything's been moved," I croaked.

"Taylor and I did it last night. We gave you a feng shui makeover. Do you like it?"

"Why do the walls have splotches on them?"

Sasha adopted an authoritative tone. "In the Far East, white symbolizes mourning and death. White rooms need to be dotted with red or green to break the color's negative force."

"Dotted!" I screeched. "With furniture or wall hangings, not random clumps of paint."

She cocked her head. "I never thought of that. Anyway, red represents happiness, fire, and power. Green represents tranquility, better health, and growth."

"I feel better already." I had to lean against the wall for balance. "Taller somehow."

"Lauren!" she said, hurt.

I cast a suspicious eye. "Why aren't you in school?"

"Teacher planning day, remember? I told you about it yesterday."

"Yeah, yeah," I said, meekly waving my hand. "Why didn't you just feng shui your own office? Why did you have to screw up mine?"

Her face fell further. "We started there, but your chi was blocking mine."

"Do you even know what feng shui is?"

"I knew you'd ask me that. I do! I do!" she said, jumping up and down. "Wait, wait, wait!"

Sasha left the room, and I stood alone in the center of my office, hands on my head, on the verge of sobs. The office never had been a showroom—I'd furnished it in mid-1980s office liquidation motif—but this, I wasn't ready for this.

I felt a mild stroke coming on.

When Sasha returned, she read from a piece of parchment paper. "Feng shui is a Chinese art and science that was developed six thousand years ago. The practice uses elements of astrology, geology, physics, mathematics, philosophy, and intuition to study buildings, environments, time, and people. Feng shui is based on the principles of yin and yang and the five elemental energies and how they react." She used her fingers to count. "Fire, wood, earth, metal, water."

I stared at her blankly. "Come again?"

"Don't ask me," she said, flustered. "I'm just using tips the instructor gave us. Taylor and I took a class at the rec center. I wanted to surprise you."

"This is a surprise," I said dully. "How do the fish fit in?"

Sasha beamed at the aquarium on the credenza next to my desk, home to seven gold and two black fish. "Nine is an auspicious number. They'll help us increase business."

"We can't keep up as it is, and where's the copier?"

"On the table in the hallway."

"I hate fish."

"The two black fish will die," she said, with a trace of melancholy. "That's their job. They absorb the negative energy."

My eyes contracted. "I hope they weren't expensive."

"Taylor gave us the aquarium, and I took money out of petty cash for the fish." Before I could react, she added longingly, "I wish we had marble floors. They help generate traffic."

"We don't need anymore traffic," I said desperately, thankful for the stained gray carpet beneath my feet.

"Maybe in our next office. We need to harmonize with nature."

"We're on the busiest boulevard in Denver, steps away from I-25."

Sasha shook her head regretfully. "We shouldn't live or work across from a highway, construction site, or cemetery."

"Or under power lines," I muttered.

"How did you know?" she said, awed.

I let out the breath that threatened to detonate inside me. "It's common sense."

"Feng shui's more than that," Sasha said insistently. "There's so much energy to pick up, but most people don't know how. Your environment is supposed to be comfortable. Totally. Not too stagnant or too lively."

"Which was mine?"

She crinkled her nose. "Stagnant. That's why I had to purge."

"Purge!"

She touched my arm and said, in a soothing voice, "It's okay, Lauren. You have to surround yourself with things you absolutely love, that reflect who you are. Let go of everything else."

I felt a panic rising. "Where's the photo of my parents on their fortieth wedding anniversary?"

"It was bothering you," Sasha tossed off. "They were never happy together."

"You threw it away?"

"Chill, Lauren. It's in the closet with your real estate plaques."

I spun around to face the wall where my awards had hung. "Those meant something to me."

"But you hate real estate," she said, deepening her voice. "They drained your self-esteem."

"My old MLS books, from the early 1990s, where are they?" I blared.

Sasha stretched out her arms, hands open, palms up. "Gone."

"Where's my bike?"

"It had a flat tire, and you never rode it."

"Did it occur to you that I didn't ride it because it had a flat?"

"Whatever. You never fixed it. I traded it to Taylor for the aquarium."

My $5,500 triathlon bike. The one I had custom built from the Kuota Kalibur frame up. S-Bend extension bars, Shimano Dura Ace components, carbon HED.3 race wheels, Keo Ti clipless pedals. I felt faint. I sat in my leather swivel chair—at least I still had that—and grabbed the desk for support.

"Your desk was in the right spot," Sasha said cheerfully. "Diagonal to the door. That's where it's supposed to be, so you can maintain control of your space."

I said tightly, "I've never had a problem with control."

"That's because of your desk. The universe is mysterious, isn't it?"

"Extremely." I sniffed. "Did you burn incense?"

"No."

"Sasha!" I said accusingly.

"No, Lauren. I swear." She wiggled a finger at the other side of the room. "You haven't said anything about the wellspring. Clear, running water represents money."

I'd tried to ignore the three-tiered, ceramic fountain on the floor, because it made me want to pee, but I couldn't say that. I'd spread enough negative energy for one day, and I didn't want to kill the black fish. "It's lovely."

"Aren't you glad that I'm growing up, claiming my own space?"

As well as mine. "I appreciate the thought."

"Did we do good with the makeover? Now that I've explained it, do you like it?" she said, excitedly.

I couldn't help but return her smile. "I'll give it a try."

She hugged me in a rush, but let go when I said, "I do have one request."

"What? You hate it, don't you?"

"No, not hate," I said feebly.

"You look like you're going to cry."

"I've had a wretched morning."

"I'm sorry," she said, in a tiny voice.

"Could we please take down the crystals?"

She made a face. "They're supposed to redirect the chi in a positive motion."

"What's the matter with the chi over there?" I said, inclining my head toward the corner of the room where three crystals dangled from the ceiling.

She tried to suppress a guilty look, but I caught it. "What?"

"Taylor and I couldn't remember the part about chi from class, so we hung the crystals wherever," she said, bursting into a fit of laughter.

"I knew it!" I sprang up to yank them down.

When Sasha stopped laughing, I handed her the stones and said, without a hint of sarcasm, "Doesn't it feel more harmonious?"

By the look she imparted, I could tell she thought I was being facetious, but I wasn't.

I felt much better without the crystals.

Next up for elimination: the fish, the red and green spatters of paint, the mirrors, and the prayer book.

•••

"How goes it?"

I didn't bother to look up. "Fine."

"Never pegged you as a fish person."

"I'm not."

"What do you think of our new partnership?"

"Not much."

"Shit happens," Max Spiker said playfully, tapping on the side of the aquarium. "Hey, I saw you last night."

I did a double take. "That was you across the street?"

"The one and only. You loved it, didn't you?"

"Loved what?"

"The fire."

"How could anyone love that?" I said, closing the McBride file.

"You felt the heat, didn't you?"

I flushed crimson. "I don't know what you're talking about."

"C'mon, I saw it in the way you watched," he said, his grin widening. "It's better than sex, isn't it?"

My chest pounded. "Different."

"But similar, am I right? It never gets old." He came around to the side of my desk and sat on the edge. "I'm in the mood for a house tour. How about you?"

"Not particularly."

He leaned forward, close enough for me to smell lemon on his breath. "Not just any home. A Carnival home. Care to join me?"

I eyed him warily. "Are we supposed to do that?"

"Nope, but let's. We'll meet at Prairie Acres at, say, six o'clock?"

"Tonight?"

"Yes, indeed."

"I have two appointments this afternoon. Depending on traffic, I might not make it by six."

"Not a problem. I'll start, and when you get there, we'll use up what's left of the daylight, then grope around in the dark. Should be fun."

My face bunched up. "It has to be tonight?"

"Sooner, the better."

"Isn't it against the law to breach a crime scene?"

He chuckled. "I've got nothing to lose. How about you?"

I hesitated. "I guess not."

"Good. Now what else have you got?"

"What do you mean?" I said innocently.

"Cut the bullshit. You have a prime suspect." He headed toward the fountain, crouched, and felt the temperature of the water.

"Maybe."

"I have a theory myself. We could trade. Ladies first."

I spoke after a considered pause. "When we met, I gave you one of my business cards. Do you still have it?"

"I might."

"I need it back."

His head snapped around. "For what? You ran out and are too cheap to reprint?"

I didn't smile. "Where is it?"

"Probably in my truck. According to my ex-wife, I never throw anything away."

"Could you please get it?"

He straightened up and gazed at me thoughtfully. "Are you always this hormonal?"

"I'm not working with you until I see my card."

He sauntered out, returned five minutes later, and tossed a card in my lap. "Satisfied?"

I turned over the business card and read his handwriting. September 11. Met at arson scene, 3022 Visalia. Good looking.

I passed the card back to him without comment, and he unwrapped a candy and popped it into his mouth. "What's with you? You on the rag or something?"

"Or something." I pulled the singed card out of my desk and handed it to him. "Someone left this on my windshield Monday morning."

"Bummer," he said, removing his glasses to scrutinize the business card. "Wasn't me. Can we share now?"

I faltered for a moment before replying. "My prime suspect is Richard

183

Leone, a homeless man who lives in a culvert in Landry. He's had several nasty run-ins with Dennis."

Max raised his eyes. "Does he have transportation?"

"Just a one-speed bike, but he's familiar with Landry and Southfield, and he's always out and about."

"Makes him invisible." Max replaced his glasses and nodded approvingly. "If he did set the Carnival fire, someone must have given him a ride. Victoria Farino?"

I looked at him keenly. "You know her?"

He sucked noisily. "Never heard the name until this morning. Why did McBride cut you off?"

"She's his ex-girlfriend."

"My, oh my, this is getting better and better," Max said, rubbing his hands together. "What's her connection to Leone?"

"I haven't made one yet, but Kevin Slyford saw Richard talking to a woman in a silver car. I'm trying to catch Richard when he's drunk enough to slip up but coherent enough to make sense, which is harder than it sounds. Let me ask you . . . could the three fires have been set by different people?"

"The methods are different, but I'm doubting different perps is the answer." Max scratched his neck, deep in thought. "Isn't this better? Sharing."

"It's somewhat one-sided."

He bit down on the candy. "Fair is fair. I have my own prime suspect in mind."

"Who?"

"Our boss."

My jaw dropped. "Dennis McBride?"

Max's smile came and went in a split second. "None other."

CHAPTER 23

I lowered my head to within inches of the water and anxiously examined the two black fish.

Was it my imagination, or did one of them look a little skinnier?

I crossed the room to the office supply closet, returned with a magnifying glass, and studied the lean one as he floated past.

Was he on the verge of death?

I looked at my watch and registered the time as five o'clock.

Could negative energy have caught up with him that quickly?

I left for Prairie Acres before I killed the scrawny fish.

After wending through rush hour traffic on I-25 and E-470, I exited at Smoky Hill Road, and from there, I drove and drove.

And drove some more.

Adrenaline and high speed must have shortened the journey the night before, because this time it seemed endless.

Everything I'd missed in the dark came to life, most of all the ticky-tacky subdivisions. One included hundreds of houses with every shade of white siding. Another featured narrow three-story homes with faux rock exteriors that extended three-quarters of the way up the sides. Many of the structures looked as if a stiff northeasterly wind could blow them down.

As I continued east, the size of lots grew, from fractions of an acre, to one acre, to five acres, and the tradeoff was conspicuous. More commuting bought more land, but not necessarily more privacy. In the barren region, most neighbors could see and hear each other across vast expanses. They could distinguish airplanes, too. Twenty-five miles south and east of Denver International Airport, remarkably, the roar of jets dominated.

Rolling prairies covered in scrub eventually gave way to a majestic sight: stands of black forest ponderosas and rows of cottonwoods that followed a gulch.

The trees denoted the boundary of Prairie Acres, and I slowed down, drove through the stone entryway, turned into the cul-de-sac, and let out a gasp.

What had looked divine in the middle of the night now presented as an ugly mess.

Gray sky added a gloomy backdrop to the charred remains of Dennis McBride's Carnival home, a husk with collapsed walls and no roof. Blackened shards stood, separated by openings for windows and doors, and around the perimeter of the house, tentacles of scaffolding prevailed, climbing at twisted angles.

I parked next to the lake in the middle of the street, a low-lying area where runoff from firefighters' water had gathered, and as soon as I opened the car door, a gust caught my hair, whipping it into an unattractive tangle.

While I fought to remedy the style faux pas, Max Spiker came around the side of the house. "Right on time."

Geared up and ready to go, he reached into the cab of his truck and deposited into my outstretched arms a disposable face mask, coveralls, black goggles, leather gloves, and steel-toe boots.

After I suited up, we approached the yellow tape, and Max ducked under it like a pro. Attempting to step over a strand, I became temporarily ensnared, but luckily he didn't notice.

We trudged through the swamp in the front yard, and I said nervously, "I know Dennis owns the property, but should we be here?"

"Technically, no. But why quibble over minutia? The arson boys won't rush to give up their scene. Once they release a site, they can't get back in without the owner's consent or a warrant. That means they'll hold out as long as possible, and we can't wait. With this wind, we're losing evidence by the minute."

"Are you sure it's safe?"

"Safe enough. The guys haven't put water on it in hours."

I shot Max a reproving look. "How do you know?"

"I was here earlier, checking out the scene."

"They let you come around?"

"Sure, the brotherhood of firemen and all. I saw them pull apart the building, and they didn't find any deep-seated fire. Heavy smoldering's ended, and enough air came through to dissipate carbon monoxide and any other gases."

"I don't know about this," I said, halting.

"Quit busting my chops! After thirty-one years, you think I can't spot structural fatigue? What we have here is a concrete foundation with no basement. You won't fall into anything, and nothing will fall on you."

"Then why am I wearing a hard hat?"

"Precautionary measure. You need a hand up?" Max said, his long legs easily closing the distance between the ground and the front door threshold.

"I'm fine," I said, stumbling and falling to my knees. I rose and brushed off. "What was the response time of the firefighters?"

"Eleven minutes. Damn good, considering how far they came, but they couldn't have saved it from across the street. This baby was a wide-open shell of fuel. You saw. It burned hot and bright. Let's get going. I need to make a rough diagram of the scene, and I've got you down for still photographs. Think you can handle that?"

I nodded, and my hat fell forward.

"Follow me. We'll start with a visual inspection, get a feel for the flow pattern. We want to push the fire back to its point of origin."

I tightened my chin strap. "What are we looking for?"

"V patterns, plants, trailers, accelerants."

"Translation on the middle two, please."

"Plants are boosters, say a pool of liquid accelerant or a pile of combustibles. Trailers are streamers, paths that convey the fire from one location to another, maybe a trail of liquid or a line of gas-soaked cloths or newspapers. Got it?"

"Got it."

I followed Max in a slow zigzag through the main floor of the house.

Primarily, I saw wet, black chaos. Occasionally, I could discern items such as nails, ladders, air compressors, tools, and portable generators, but I couldn't competently evaluate the scene.

Fortunately, Max Spiker had a more trained eye.

Using a lightweight metal poker, he jabbed at piles and shifted debris. Muttering under his breath, he took notes on a small spiral pad, and in less than five minutes called out, "Bingo!"

He used technical terms—splatter, spalling, puddling, secondary burning, shields, shadows, beveling, areas of demarcation, depth of char, oxidation, and alligatoring—to explain his conclusions, but as my eyes glazed over, he rephrased.

"Our torch piled something, probably newspapers, cardboard, wood shavings, or cloth in a pyramid at the center of the great room. The perfect spot, middle of a room with a three-story vaulted ceiling. He soaked it all with gasoline. It could have been alcohol or turpentine, but I'll lay money on gas. He kept pouring until he reached the front door, a nice wide trail of accelerant. Then he doubled back and created another path to the bonfire. Smart. In case one track petered out, he had his fallback. Both trails came together about a foot short of the threshold. He lit a wick, maybe. You can buy those at any hobby store. Or he could have tucked a lit cigarette into a book of matches. That'd buy him ten minutes. Or maybe he tossed in something, a Molotov cocktail. Doesn't matter. He left himself enough time to jump in his car and drive away."

"You're good!"

I saw the smile in his eyes, but it quickly faded. "I won't miss this. Coming up with a theory about the origin and cause of a fire, that revs my engine, but the bullshit takes it out of me. Every time I make a move, I have to look over my shoulder for defense attorneys. If I don't collect evidence properly, it isn't admissible in court. I spend days taking samples and comparative samples, weighing and measuring, putting evidence in, hell, you name it. Envelopes, vials, pillboxes, bags, jars, plastic containers, metal cans. I have to identify, tag, catalog, and register every scrap into the logbook. If I don't preserve and document chain of custody, I risk losing the case. I transport everything with care, watching out for cross-contamination. I can't let any fragile or brittle items break or disintegrate. You know how many rough sketches and final sketches I've drawn? At midnight, I'm typing notes, labeling photographs, slides, and disks. That's not what wore me out, though. Heat from prosecutors and horseshit from departmental chain of command did me in. Thank those pricks for my return to the private sector."

His voice faded with weariness. "I don't know how I lasted as long as I did. Scenes change by the hour, no rewinding, one chance to get it right. I'm beyond fried."

"Couldn't we skip the documentation?" I said hopefully, the ruins beginning to agitate me.

"No, ma'am. I'm still a professional, and we're just beginning." Max headed toward the front door, where he'd deposited a shovel, rake, broom, and pry bar. He reached into a toolbox the size of a toy chest and handed me a 35 mm digital camera.

I began to snap random shots to get a feel for the features of the Nikon.

"Hold on, hold on," Max said, in a friendly way. "You're not a tourist jumping off the bus at Niagara Falls. Get the exterior first. Give me street views, wide-angle exteriors, and close-ups of all doors and windows. Inside, bring me rooms, halls, stairways, closets, walls, floors, and ceilings."

I gestured with both hands at the cavernous shell.

"Sorry. Standard operating procedure," he said, preoccupied with arranging supplies. He extracted a clipboard, graph paper, colored pencils, and two tape measures, one steel, the other optical. "Start outside and work your way in."

"Maybe I should reverse the order. The lighting is terrible in here, and it'll get worse when the sun goes down."

"Stick to the plan. I've got floodlights in the truck."

"Yes, sir," I said, secretly relieved to exit the house.

I spent twenty minutes shooting outdoor scenes before returning to the front door, where Max's bark stopped me midstride.

"Don't come over here!"

"What?"

"God! Damn! It!"

"What is it?"

Max Spiker shook his head in disgust. "We've got ourselves a body."

189

CHAPTER 24

"I've seen dead bodies before," I said, my voice splintering. Mostly in funeral homes, carefully prepared, but why call attention to the distinction?

Max waved me over. "Suit yourself."

On second thought, I didn't need any more disquieting images carved into my brain. "Is it the arsonist?"

"Not this far from the origin. Not unless he set the timing device and curled up to take a nap."

"Who is it?"

"Hard to tell."

"Male? Female? Age? Race? Height?"

His lips tightened. "All unknown."

"Nothing's left?"

"Plenty's left. You don't know much about burning bodies, do you?"

"Of course not," I snapped.

"Commercial cremation takes two hours at two thousand degrees Fahrenheit," Max said nonchalantly. "You want the thumbnail analysis of how a body burns outside a crematorium?"

"No."

"In ten minutes, arms are charred. At fourteen, legs, too. In fifteen, face and arm bones show. At twenty, ribs and the skull appear. Takes twenty-five for a shin bone, and at thirty-five, every leg bone is exposed."

"Too much information." I added meekly, "How many minutes did this body burn?"

"I'd say twenty. You don't want to see this."

"No, I don't," I said, tempted to peek.

"The skin is sloughing. There it goes, separating from tissue. We have serious rips here."

"Have some respect," I admonished. "If this person didn't start the fire, was he killed before it? Could someone have moved the body into the house?"

"Neither of the above. This one's an Ali."

"A what?"

"Pugilistic attitude, a natural phenomenon of fire. The victim looks like he's in a defensive boxing position or fetal position. Intense heat makes the leg and arm muscles contract. Sometimes the hands cup into claws. This one wasn't moved. Otherwise, rigor mortis would have set in, and we wouldn't have pugilistic attitude. Also, he's face down, which tells me he rolled over or staggered or crawled through smoke. Don't take my word for it, though. The coroner will make the final determination."

"How?"

"He'll come in and check the underside of the body and the surface it's lying on, root around in debris surrounding the victim, take samples, note any obvious wounds or injuries. Back at the morgue, he'll analyze lividity, soot, skin, hair, and extremities. Damn it all to hell!" Max said miserably. "This is a death investigation scene, and we've been trampling on it like a herd of cows."

"Speak for yourself," I said lightly. "How did you find the body?"

"I was sifting through large debris with the pry bar, like the goddamn investigator should have done this afternoon. What a moron!"

Max let out a streak of curses, before he calmed down and said in an eerily quiet voice, "C'mon, we've got to get out of here. Try not to touch anything."

Before turning to leave, I stole a parting glance at the dead body and immediately wished I could give it back.

Feeling nauseous, I ran outside as fast I could.

That would be the last time I ate a black bean burrito with corn salsa.

In the front yard of the Tuscan Villa, I covered the remnants of my dinner with dirt and glanced back once more at the carcass of Dennis McBride's Carnival dream.

•••

I remember little of the drive home.

Evidently, I was in shock.

Back at my apartment, I responded to a note Sasha had left on my door by knocking on hers.

She cracked open the door and dragged me in by the arm, whispering conspiratorially, "Payday texted me. The meeting's on for this Saturday."

"With 11-up?"

Sasha bobbed her head affirmatively, in slow-motion, coarse movements. "At four o'clock."

"Where?"

"Somewhere downtown. Payday said that 11-up will leave instructions on the utility box the night before."

I rolled my eyes. "I assume Payday will interpret the tagger marks and convey them to you?"

She smiled. "Yep. Then I'll call you on your cell. Cool, huh?"

I closed my eyes for a moment and struggled to reopen them. "It'll have to do."

"Payday told me not to tell you this, but he almost went along with them."

I cocked my head. "The wilding kids?"

Sasha nodded. "They needed Latino kids, and they asked him to come. He wanted to go, but he had a project due for art school."

"Rioting doesn't sound like something Payday would do," I said, puzzled. "With or without a prior commitment."

"He wants to buy a color laser printer. One with all these cool features that will let him—"

"Sasha!" I interrupted.

She looked hurt. "Don't you want to know how much the printer costs?"

A sigh leaked out. "Sure."

"Almost $700."

"How does this relate to the LoDo wilding?"

"Every kid could make $200, that's what 11-up said."

My eyes widened. "Someone paid them? Who?"

"Payday doesn't know. He said to ask 11-up."

"I'll do that," I said, suddenly revitalized.

•••

For the second night in a row, I fretted more than I slept.

My mind ping-ponged between thoughts of the LoDo wilding and the Carnival fire. At three o'clock, I gave up on the prospect of rest and sat up in bed with a notepad.

What a lovely couple, Dennis McBride and Victoria Farino.

Max had him down for arson, and I had her suspected of . . . what? Paying kids to behave like jerks in LoDo? After my meeting with 11-up, if my hunches proved correct, I'd have one transgression in the bag, but what else could I pin on Victoria Farino? Driving a silver car and meeting with Richard Leone? I had proof of neither.

I needed to broaden my thinking.

For both cases, I spent a good portion of the night constructing timelines and flowcharts and doodling on the sides of a legal pad, willing the disparate parts to coalesce into logical solutions.

Fat chance.

By seven, the best I could do was cover the bags under my eyes with concealer and stumble toward the office.

The trek took longer than usual, due to a sleep-deprived delirium and two emergency stops at Starbucks, and before nine, I set four empty coffee cups to the side and lay my head on the desk, unable to resist a five-minute siesta.

Two hours later, a call interrupted my deep sleep.

Max Spiker offered to buy me lunch, and I agreed readily, not realizing I'd have to serve myself.

We met at Farmhouse Buffet at noon, where we stood in line for ten minutes waiting to pay, before joining the mad scramble for food. I weighed the choices and deemed most too risky, but Max had no reservations.

He came back to our two-top with plates up to his elbow, which prompted our shift to a four-top.

He'd loaded one platter with fried chicken, prime rib, ham, turkey, sausage, and fish sticks. On another, he'd created a food pyramid, but not the model most nutritionists recommend. He had a slew of side dishes balanced precariously, and I cringed at the amalgam of Jell-O, green beans, spaghetti, rice, coleslaw, jalapeno poppers, peas, and salsa. On another full-size plate, he'd spread butterscotch pudding, carrot cake, brownies, and vanilla soft-serve.

I'd kept it simple. Four ounces of mac and cheese, iceberg lettuce with ranch dressing, and cherry cobbler, all of which I sampled in cautious bites.

Max molested the plates with salt and pepper and shoveled in food, chewing with his mouth open. "We need to divide up the tasks and move quickly," he said, making noises like a horse.

I picked at my food. "I still think we should tell Dennis about the dead body."

"He'll find out soon enough, when a homicide investigator drops by for a chat."

"Shouldn't we warn him?"

"Innocent men don't need warnings, and guilty men don't deserve them. Let's make a list," Max declared, meaning me. He had no room on his side of the table for stenographer duties.

I pulled a pen and pad from my purse. "What do you want me to do?"

"Me first. Here's how we'll work this." He paused to swallow and clear morsels of fried chicken batter from his mustache. "Write this down. I'll identify the 911 caller from fire tapes and interview her. I'll check for previous reports of police activity or vandalism in the area. I'll talk to the first-responding firefighters."

"What do they know?"

"They're our best witnesses. They're trained to save lives, put out fires, and observe and preserve the scene, in that order. The guys'll tell me weather conditions, the extent of fire and smoke on arrival, the color of flames and plumes, and the rapidity of spread. They know what section of the house caught fire first. If they heard explosions, they'll know whether they sounded like thunder or whip cracks," Max said, continuing to eat with gusto. "They might have smelled a peculiar odor. Maybe they came across a pocket of extreme heat. They'll have noticed the condition of the hydrant—was the cap missing? They'll know if sprinklers or alarms were disabled, a moot point in this case, but valuable information otherwise. They might have seen suspicious parties leaving or arriving."

I made notes. "What else?"

"On my end, I'll hunt down what was in the house that shouldn't have been. Flammable materials, combustibles, the like. Who stored what, where, and how. Anything that seems out of place for a construction site, I'll flag. I also have to get back in and examine the structure. It's a slow, dirty job, layer by layer, content sifting."

"We know this was arson. Why do you have to—"

"That doesn't mean squat. I have to eliminate accidental causes, even if I see gasoline spread everywhere and an empty can. The District Attorney won't press charges unless I've checked out electric motors, outlets, switches, and junction boxes and disqualified them as alternative causes."

"Electrical wasn't in yet."

"You're right. Cross that off my list."

"And we're not building a case for the D.A.," I said reasonably.

"The hell we're not."

I looked at him in amazement. "You want your job back!"

"I want the option," Max retorted, pride injured.

I pointed to my side of the page, which was noticeably blank. "I thought we were going to divide up the tasks."

"We've got plenty for you to do. You can figure out who owns the building and profits from the fire. Look into the financial positions of everyone involved in this deal. McBride, subcontractors, investors."

"Dennis McBride is the sole owner of the house."

"Says who?"

"Dennis."

Max finished off his second chocolate milk and reached for his first Coke. "Don't take his word for anything. Start with the insurance company. We need the lowdown on primary and secondary policies, amounts of coverage, history of payments, recent changes, previous claims. Find out if the house was appraised recently. If so, why and what did the value come in at."

"Slow down," I implored.

Max carried on in rapid-fire sentences. "Interview McBride's workers and the crews at the other Carnival homes. Ask about comings and goings the week before the fire. Don't rule out anyone. We'll need to know what tools, equipment, or other valuables were in the house at the time of the fire. Who's going to file a claim? I want to know what was present and what's missing. What's going to show up on an insurance form that may or may not have been destroyed in the fire?"

"I can't write this fast."

"Find out from independent sources if McBride's current on payments to subs. How about his construction loan? Has he had any health, sanitation, zoning, or building violations at the Carnival house? Has OSHA or Workers' Comp paid a visit lately? Any liens or judgments against the property, outside of lenders and subs? We need McBride's bank records, personal and corporate."

"I'm not really comfortable doing all this behind Dennis's back."

Max Spiker's gaze narrowed into a fierce beam. "This isn't playtime anymore, Lauren. Someone died in that fire. You gotta do what you gotta do, or else get out of the way and let me do it."

"I know we've been over this, but I don't see how Dennis gains from losing properties."

"Why does anyone do anything? Why does some rich celebrity shoplift? Sure as hell not because they can't afford whatever they're trying to steal. Are you listening to me?"

"No," I said, pensive. In fact, I'd been remembering a troubling incident in Dennis McBride's past. Who told me he'd stolen tools from a job site, for no apparent reason? Jerry Hess, his ex-partner.

Max continued, unabated. "Check with area gas stations, the ones closest to Prairie Acres. Our torch probably filled up nearby."

"I didn't see any stations after I passed through the retail sprawl at Smoky Hill Road and E-470."

"Me neither. That's probably your best bet. Maybe a clerk noticed someone filling containers. With pay-at-the-pump, it's a long shot, but you never know. Do you have access to license plate traces?"

I shook my head.

"Me neither. Not anymore. Too bad. I'd love to compare the list of owners for plate numbers at Southfield and Prairie Acres."

"You have lists?"

"Meticulous. I took down numbers on all vehicles that weren't fire, police, EMT, or press. Part of the routine canvass, but that's about all I have. Usually, I catch someone at the scene who makes an accusatory statement. In front of a blaze, people will tell me things they won't say later. I love trauma."

"You're cruel."

"What can I say?" Max used his knife to balance peas on his fork. "My job is to take advantage of shock and anguish. While you drooled over the Carnival fire, I studied the crowd."

"For what?"

The peas fell off before a single one reached Max's mouth. "Anyone who tried to leave when I approached or who tried to stare me down."

"Did anyone meet that criteria at Landry, Southfield, or Prairie Acres?"

"I wasn't on-call for Landry. At Southfield, everyone seemed kosher, but that fire was a cluster. I must have counted fifty rubberneckers. At Prairie Acres, the only distressed observer was the owner of the lodge home next door. He was terrified the flames would lick the side of his house. I took a statement from him, but he's not our torch."

I flicked my left cheek to indicate he had something attached to his. "You worked the Carnival fire, even though you'd been fired?"

"I had a job. Not with Metro, but I was collecting a paycheck from Dennis McBride."

My jaw went slack. "Dennis hired you before the Carnival fire? When? Why?"

"The day before. He thought you could use some assistance."

"That bastard."

Max chuckled slyly. "You on board now?"

"Completely," I said, seething. "What else can I do?"

He let out a loud belch. "That's a good start. We'll meet Saturday for lunch and compare notes."

"You really believe Dennis McBride is a legitimate suspect?"

"If this were a horse race, I'd have him a furlong ahead, coming around the final bend." Max smacked his head. "That reminds me. Put on my list to call the IT guy. He never got back to me about the expanded database search. Let's hope he hasn't heard I was canned."

"Database? What were you looking for?"

"McBride got away with one when we closed out the Landry fire as accidental. But two fires, forget coincidence. After Southfield, I ordered a preliminary database search. When that turned up a tantalizing tidbit, I ordered an expanded search."

"What's the difference between preliminary and expanded?"

"Preliminary's done on computers, goes back five years. Civilian volunteers perform an expanded, poring through old databases, microfiche, and boxes of records, looking for a match. I wanted to know if anything else Dennis McBride owned had ever burned."

"And . . . ?"

"That was the tantalizing part," Max said, with a wide smile. "Four years ago, Dennis McBride was a shareholder in Sherman Enterprises, a limited liability corporation. Its only asset was a three-story office building at 6th Avenue and Sherman Street."

"Let me guess. The building caught fire."

"You got it." He crushed his napkin. "The insurance company declared it a total loss. Funny thing, the rundown building had no tenants in it at the time, and after Sherman Enterprises received a check from Liberty Mutual for full rebuild at replacement cost, they flipped the lot to a developer who put up a condo tower."

"Perfect timing," I whispered.

Max grunted, "Too perfect, that son of a bitch!"

•••

My cell phone rang before dawn the next morning.

Max Spiker again.

This partnership deal was beginning to wear thin.

He barely acknowledged my hello. "It helps to have friends in the coroner's office. I have a copy of the report on our body. You in the mood for gore?"

"No, but give me the abbreviated version."

"Our male victim died of acute alcoholism, plus carbon monoxide asphyxiation."

"He was drunk and died from smoke inhalation?"

"You catch on quick. All par for the course. CO asphyxia is the most common cause of death in fires. To continue, John Doe had a fractured skull."

"He was killed before the fire?" I said, confused.

"No, ma'am. It was an explosive fracture, not implosive."

"Meaning?"

"How can I put this delicately? The fluids in and around his brain boiled and expanded until the pressure fractured the skull. According to the coroner's report, the fracture followed the natural suture lines, as expected."

"Did they identify him?"

"Not yet, but they came up with a few distinguishing characteristics. Let me see . . . most of his teeth were chipped or missing. Also, at some point, he broke his right hip and had it set with pins."

"That's it?"

"For personal effects, they list one article. A watch, and it wasn't a Timex. It took a licking, but didn't keep on ticking. Mickey perished in the fire," Max said, with mock grief.

I felt as if someone had kicked me in the stomach. "Our victim had a Mickey Mouse watch?"

"Yes, ma'am. Worn on his right arm."

I couldn't speak.

After a long pause, Max broke the silence. "You still there?"

"That's Richard Leone," I said, as soon as my breathing returned to normal.

CHAPTER 25

"Come again?" Max Spiker said.

My voice shook. "Did they find a dog's body near Richard?"

"No mention of that in the coroner's report," Max said, in an easygoing manner. "But what does—"

"I've got to go."

I disconnected, dressed frantically, flew out the door, and arrived in Landry just as the sky was changing from gray to blue and the sun was beginning its spread across the horizon.

The first time I met Richard Leone, he'd mentioned that he lived in a culvert off 11ᵗʰ Avenue. Between Landry's west and east boundaries, Quebec Street to Havana Street, that meant I had thirty blocks to search for his shelter. As I drove down 11ᵗʰ Avenue, scanning connecting streets to the north and south, I hatched two scenarios.

In one, I theorized that Richard and a coconspirator had set the Carnival fire, and probably the Landry and Southfield ones as well. More than likely, the cohort had purchased the accelerant and incendiary devices and driven the getaway car. Depending on the degree of malice, he or she could have innocently misjudged the ferocity of the flames at the Carnival home and left Richard behind to die or preplanned his death and intentionally killed him with liquor and smoke.

In another line of conjecture, I cast Richard as the victim through and through. Suppose someone, Dennis McBride for instance, had lured him to the Carnival house for the express purpose of murdering him. Dennis could have deflected suspicion by burning two other houses in advance of the killing. After the Landry fire, he'd suffered little inconvenience, moving the original buyer to another property and rebuilding the home with insurance money. The Southfield fire had come along almost as a bonus, allowing him to void his contract with Fritz Jubera and line up a more amenable buyer. The Carnival home, interestingly, had burned during a phase of construction when maximum fuel load was present, yet minimal hours and materials had been invested. Dennis still might make the deadline for the spring start of the Carnival of Homes. He'd said it himself.

But I was jumping too far ahead.

Richard Leone might still be alive.

After all, nothing more than a Mickey Mouse watch implied his death.

At 11th Avenue and Yosemite Street, I entered a rotary, shot out the other side, and came to a stop a few blocks to the east where the asphalt ended. A hundred yards away, I saw the gleam of a drainpipe in a dry ditch that dropped ten feet below the road. Not a bad location for a shelter. About a quarter-mile from the nearest house, quiet and private, surrounded by fields, with a sweeping view of the mountains.

Taking care not to twist an ankle, I picked my way down the slope, at the bottom of which I saw the edge of a sleeping bag dangling from the lip of a corrugated pipe.

I poked in my head, half expecting Richard to extend a slurred greeting, and my heart raced when a shadowy figure squatted into a defensive position.

After my eyes adjusted to the light, I called out, "It's Lauren Vellequette."

"Oh," came the small reply from Kevin Slyford.

I breathed fully for the first time since I'd left my apartment. "Hi, Pepper."

The terrier moved forward tentatively, on wobbly legs.

"It's okay," I said softly, addressing the dog and Kevin.

Kevin sniffled. "Richard's not coming back."

"How do you know?" I crawled into the pipe and sat facing him, which invited Pepper to burrow into my lap. I rubbed her with both hands to quell the shivering.

"I saw him on Wednesday, and he told me he had an important mission. 'For the betterment of all of mankind,'" Kevin quoted stiffly, tucking his head into his knees. "He's gone to war."

"I think he might have died Wednesday night," I said gently. "In a fire."

The boy's face lost all color. "Where?"

"About twenty miles away, in a new house that's being built. Now's the time to tell me—did you know Richard had been setting fires?"

"Maybe," he said, eyes downcast.

"Did he set the fire on Trinidad Street?"

"I dunno."

"How about the one near your house, on Visalia Street?"

No response.

"Richard can't get in trouble anymore, Kevin, and neither can you."

"It wasn't his idea," he protested.

"Someone helped him?"

"She made him do it," he said venomously.

"She?"

"His girlfriend. That lady in the silver car. I know she did."

"Is that what Richard told you?"

"No, but I know."

"Would you mind showing me what's in the bag?" I said, referring to the small sack he clutched tightly.

"It's just stuff," he said defensively. "Richard told me I could have it if anything happened to him."

"I have to notify his family, and—"

"He didn't have any family."

"Everyone has someone. They'll want to know what happened to him, and they might want something that belonged to him. Could I take a look?" I coaxed.

He pushed the plastic bag toward me, and I emptied its contents onto a purple rectangle of carpet.

"I'd better keep these," I said, setting aside a dozen votive candles, two Sterno cans, a Marlboro lighter, and a pack of cigarettes.

Kevin shrugged listlessly.

I sorted through the remaining items, which included a scratched magnifying glass folded into a worn leather case, three issues of Playboy, a roll of quarters, and a small metal lockbox.

I reached for the box. "May I?"

Kevin pried it open with his pocketknife, and I rifled through the contents. I skimmed a summons for public intoxication, a checkout form from an overnight detox facility, a list of homeless shelters and addiction recovery programs, paperwork from a three-day hospital stay for treatment of hypothermia and pneumonia, and home care instructions for regaining strength and mobility after hip surgery.

"Could I copy this?" I said, extracting a card from the papers.

"You can have it."

"Thanks." I pocketed the business card of someone named Kim Reed. "Did you happen to find my business card?"

"Huh-uh."

"Could you help me look for it?"

Kevin nodded, and we spent twenty minutes searching the remainder of Richard Leone's estate, a disconcerting collection of items that included a large pot with food particles and a rusted cookie sheet. Cans of beets, corned beef hash, and dog and cat foot. Unwashed clothing and a gallon jug of water. A camping stove and mismatched silverware. Empty half-gallon jugs of cheap wine and sleeves for wrapping coins. Stained blankets and coats. A plastic razor and a toothbrush with frayed bristles. A sliver of soap and a tube of Preparation H. A kerosene lantern and bag of moldy bread. Stacks of branches and twigs and couch cushions. A metal waste bucket and stubs of candles. Empty vodka bottles and a chipped ceramic dish with two mice sitting on a piece of Swiss cheese. A battered suitcase that wouldn't close and a lamp with no cord, shade, or bulb. A ten-inch pipe filled with concrete and a bible covered in plastic wrap.

No Lauren Vellequette business card.

Apparently, Richard Leone had burned my card and left it on the windshield of my Outback.

I felt more depressed than ever when Kevin let out a cheer.

"I've got it!" he said, extracting a card from the lining of Richard's sleeping bag.

I was overcome with emotion when he handed it to me. I hadn't wanted to believe the worst in my relationship with Richard, and yet this brought me to wit's end.

If I held the card I'd given him, I was back to my original list, minus

Max. I scrolled through the names: Dennis McBride, my client; Daphne Cartwright, angry mother at Landry; Glenn Warner, McBride Homes foreman; Jerry Hess, ex-partner; Josh Mifflin, ex-employee; and of course, Victoria Farino, ex-girlfriend.

The possibilities hurt my head.

Desperate to return to the light, I climbed out of the culvert, with Kevin and Pepper in tow.

"If Richard's dead, someone needs to take Pepper. Would your aunt let you keep her?"

He shook his head.

"Couldn't you ask?"

Again with the negative head motion.

I ran a hand across my mouth as the dog looked at me expectantly, tail wagging. "I'll take her to the pound," I said decisively. "She's cute and friendly. Someone will adopt her."

Kevin looked away, disinterested.

"If I bought you another magnifying glass, could I have Richard's? Someone from his family might want it."

He handed it to me. "You don't have to give me anything."

I caressed the childish scrawl branded into the leather, Ricky P. Leone, and couldn't imagine what had happened between the engraving and now for his life to end like this.

Kevin broke into my thoughts. "You could get me one of those Mercedes things."

"An emblem, from the hood of the car?"

He nodded. "Richard used to have one, but his enemy stole it."

"Who's that?"

"The man who threw rocks at him."

I sized up Kevin. "Dennis McBride?"

He shrugged.

After I described Dennis, down to the birthmark on his right cheek, Kevin exclaimed, "That's him! He steals stuff all the time."

"Richard told you that?"

"No, but I've seen him."

•••

After Kevin and I parted, I could have sworn I saw a silver car pull a U-turn on the dead-end asphalt, but I was looking directly into the sun, and it might have been wishful thinking.

I didn't have time for that.

I had to deal in hard-core realities, and I considered my next move as I drove to the office.

Someone needed to identify Richard Leone's remains, but locating next of kin could prove challenging.

Nothing connected him to other people, except for Kim Reed's business card. According to the card, she worked for Urban Transitions, a nonprofit organization that served the homeless. Other than that and the contents of the metal box, I had nothing else. No wallet, address book, cell phone, employment history, or last known address.

Richard Leone had lived invisibly, but I was determined he wouldn't die that way.

I knew a bit about him from our first conversation, assuming that what he'd shared wasn't fantasy or fabrication. He was forty-eight, had grown up in Conifer, attended Evergreen High School, and graduated from the Open School.

That was a start.

However, if I were to believe the version of his life he'd shared with Josh Mifflin, Richard had served in the Persian Gulf War and killed the son of a sheik.

To make inroads, I'd have to separate fact from fiction, but I'd had training in such matters.

Rollie Austin's firm had an open-ended contract with the Denver coroner's office. When its seven in-house investigators fell behind processing the county's five thousand deaths per year and notifying next of kin, they called Rollie, and she called me. Typically, we assisted with the deaths in which the person died without an attending physician or an obvious tie to family, friends, or coworkers.

On my first day on the job with Rollie, I'd learned that everyone in the United States leaves a paper trail recording life's journey.

It's impossible to avoid.

We all begin with birth certificates and end with death certificates, even if our documented paths in between diverge radically.

Some passages are joyous and full, marked by drivers' licenses, voter registrations, telephone listings, property deeds, wedding licenses, utility records, and awards or accomplishments. Others are more troubled, as evidenced by divorces, hospitalizations, military discharges, rap sheets, and trial records.

On this day, though, I didn't have to dig deep for a connection to Richard Leone.

Back at the office, I simply went online and obtained a listing in Conifer for Robert and Mary Leone.

•••

Before I could make the call, Sasha came into my office and dropped onto my couch.

At the sound of company, Pepper came out from under the desk and nudged Sasha's legs.

"Ohhhh," Sasha burbled. "You're so cute!" She swept up the dog in her arms, and they nuzzled.

"Don't get attached. I'm taking her to the animal shelter."

Her face fell. "When?"

"Soon. I meant to do it earlier."

"What's her name?"

"She doesn't have a name."

"Can't we keep her?" Sasha said, as Pepper licked her face. "Please, please, pretty please. We could call her Lala."

With more of a wince than a smile, I said, "Her name's Pepper."

"She's thirsty," Sasha murmured, in response to Pepper's panting and drooling. "Did you give her anything to drink?"

"Not much." Only a few sips of Frappuccino.

"I'll get her some water. Dogs need lots of water. We used to have one, when I was little." Sasha carefully placed Pepper on the floor and stood.

As she passed the window, she said casually. "What's that smoke?" She

207

paused to peer out and added, in a hysterical tone, "Lauren, your car's on fire."

"Very funny."

Sasha ran out of the room, shouting over her shoulder, "I'm serious. I see flames."

CHAPTER 26

This was becoming tedious.

Sasha had been stuck in a practical joke phase for weeks.

She'd planted plastic cockroaches in the office kitchen and accidentally startled herself. She'd ordered a stripper for "Bosses Day" and tipped her the entire petty cash fund, $300. She'd hidden my purse too many times to count and had once forgotten its location.

I was ready for this obnoxious period to be over, and I refused to play along.

From her desk, Sasha called 911 to report the fire.

Clever touch.

Her voice held just the right amount of fright, but I knew she'd never dialed.

She continued the charade by dashing out of the building, in an exquisite imitation of someone in crisis.

I had to give it to her—her skills were improving.

I stepped into the outer office, in search of a dog bowl, and wondered absentmindedly when Sasha would give up the ruse and return.

Two minutes later, I heard sirens.

I smiled.

Masterful . . . and impossible!

I looked out the window in panic.

Through a thick cloud of smoke, I saw flames spilling out of my Subaru Outback.

By the time I made it down two flights of stairs and went crashing through the door—literally, I fell to my knees, tripped up by the rumpled plastic runner—the first firetruck had arrived.

Using water from the pumper, firefighters doused the blaze in minutes.

How many?

I couldn't say.

Time stood still, losing all relevance, as shock set in.

I sat on a nearby curb, Sasha at my side. With one arm draped loosely around my shoulder, she used her free hand and one of her socks to dab at my knees, which bled profusely.

I spent the next hour in a fog.

For the first few minutes, I could do little more than stare ahead blankly, unable to comprehend what had happened, much less the meaning of it.

Sasha used my cell phone to call the insurance company, and when I became more coherent, I answered questions from a police officer and an arson investigator.

I used Max Spiker's name as a reference, but either they didn't know him or didn't respect him. In either case, they treated me like a criminal, and I felt as if I'd been violated twice: by the arsonist and by the men charged with solving the crime.

From the nature of the questions fired at me, I gathered the gist of what happened.

Someone had gained access to my car and doused the seats and cargo area with gasoline. For extra measure, the arsonist poured a river of accelerant around and under the car. From a distance, the torch tossed an incendiary device, possibly a Molotov cocktail, and fled the scene.

I always parked at the far end of the lot, a longstanding habit from when the car had been showroom new and I feared dings.

Dings.

This was one monumental ding.

I shook with grief every time I looked at the blackened frame of the car, blistering cream paint, disfigured bumpers, sagging roof, and melted glass.

The car was a total loss.

If the arsonist's intent had been to scare me off the hunt, the assault had the opposite effect. I felt galvanized, determined to catch this creep.

Too bad my bravado wore off before day's end.

I fell asleep that night quivering.

•••

The next day brought a host of problems, not the least of which was transportation.

Sasha came up with a temporary solution by lending me her car, and I viewed the offer as generous, until I tried to drive the Ford Tempo. The engine wouldn't turn over until the fourth crank, and the ride was anything but smooth. On the three-mile commute from my apartment to the office, the car stalled twice, and every time I accelerated, there was a distinct hesitation, followed by a lurch and more faltering, as the automatic transmission shifted between second and third. Top it off with a hole in the muffler, and I should have driven straight to the junkyard.

When I pulled up to the office, I became enraged all over again at the sight of my mutilated Outback, covered in dew.

However, I set aside my feelings and spent the morning tending to items on the list Max Spiker and I had designed, and at noon I met him at Le Central, a casual French restaurant on Broadway. My choice.

We pulled into the parking lot at the same time, and he grinned crookedly.

"Fancy wheels," he said, rubbing the hood of Sasha's car.

After Sasha's grandmother had given her the Ford Tempo, Sasha had promptly painted it in light blue, with hundreds of Frisbee-size polka dots in rainbow colors.

"Max, I'm not in the mood."

"Me neither, but with a bottle of wine . . . "

"Cut it out."

"No sense of humor? All righty then. Straight to lunch."

"Could we skip the meal?" I said faintly. "I'm not hungry."

"Your call." He opened the door to his Chevy pickup. "Step into my office."

He cleared piles off the front seat, gave me a boost, and scooted around to the driver's side. "What's up on your end? You look like hell."

"Didn't you get my message?"

"On the home phone?" he said, slightly out of breath.

"On your cell."

"Nah. That voice mail's been acting up for days. Six calls to Verizon, and it still doesn't work right."

"Someone set fire to my Outback yesterday."

"You're shitting me."

I pressed my index fingers against my temples. "Do I look like I'm kidding?"

"Where was it parked? What time of day? Anyone hurt? Anything else catch fire?"

"At my office, around three o'clock in the afternoon. No and no."

He rubbed his chin. "Someone wants you out of the picture."

"Fine with me," I said, sullen.

"You're ready to give up so easily?"

"I loved that car!"

He clapped me on the shoulder. "The new Outback looks good. I saw a commercial for it last night."

"It's not just the car. I lost real estate files, too. Nothing on clients, but information I'd compiled over the years. I had three plastic containers in the back, filled."

"Be glad it wasn't your house," he said seriously. "Plus, I thought you were retiring from real estate."

"Not today. Not because an arsonist decided this was a good time to destroy my life. I'll quit when I'm ready."

"Where's the car now?"

"In the parking lot. I can't have it towed until the insurance company sends an adjuster."

"When's that supposed to happen?"

"Sometime next week. I hate looking at it, and I hate driving Sasha's car," I said, on the verge of tears.

Max touched my arm lightly. "You want to trade?"

"Lives?"

"Vehicles."

"I can't drive this truck," I said, gesturing at the giant steering wheel and stick shift. "And you wouldn't survive an hour in that polka dot car without flipping someone off."

"You're right about that."

"Why did they have to treat me that way?"

"Who?"

"The police officer and arson investigator. Like I did something to cause the fire."

"That's their job," he said, twisting the ends of his mustache. "Their questions might have been prickly, but that should be the end of it. If no one was hurt, Metro Fire Bureau doesn't put a lot of resources into vehicular fires. Other jurisdictions do, but not ours. Not unless death's involved. Tell you what, I'll take a look at the car and make a few calls. Who caught the case?"

"Jim Neelen."

"I trained him. Leave it to me."

"Thank you."

"Everything else okay?"

"Dennis called this morning and threatened to fire me."

"What set him off?"

"He probably heard about the background checks I've been conducting. Did he say anything to you?"

"Not a word. Must mean I still have job security. How did you leave it with him?"

"I told him the truth—that I'm not trying to frame him, that I'm following the evidence wherever it leads. If he's innocent, then what I uncover should help him stage a defense."

"Tactful response. Doesn't let him know we're on to him."

"We're not on to him, are we?"

"I sure as hell am."

"This might rein in your rush to judgment. The fire in the office building on Sherman Street doesn't incriminate Dennis. He only owned four percent of the limited liability corporation, and he claims the insurance company settled for less than fair market value."

"He's lying," Max said heatedly. "I called the investigator who worked that fire. The building was full of lead paint and mold."

I shrugged. "I'm just telling you what Dennis said. He wants to see me in his office Monday at one o'clock. Are you coming?"

"I haven't been invited. You need me there?"

"Not necessarily," I said, before reacting to his furrowed brow. "You don't think I'll be in danger?"

"You will be if McBride's the one who torched your car."

"I don't know," I said vaguely. "What have you found out?"

Max removed his glasses and wiped them with the inside of his fleece jacket. "Not much. I contacted the 911 caller, an elderly lady who lives on a horse property on the county road, right about where it turns from pavement to dirt. You might have noticed her house, the one with big iron cutouts of buffaloes and bears near the drive."

"I missed that."

"The night of the Carnival fire, she saw a silver car speeding down the road."

"Hmm." I felt a surge of optimism. "Could she identify the make or model?"

"Neither," Max said, exasperated. "But I'll go back and show her a photo of the Audi that McBride drives. I'm curious to see if it rings any bells. Her ID could go a long way toward making our case. She noticed the car about an hour before she saw flames. That means our torch used a time-delayed ignition device."

"Which you suspected all along."

He folded his arms and nodded. "Everything I theorized has been on the nose. I got ahold of a guy who worked the Carnival fire and bought him a beer. His impressions of the scene matched my initial scenario. Ditto with my return visits to the site. The fire started at the front door and followed two rapid paths into the great room, where it hit the planted fuel load and exploded."

"Can you tell if Richard started the fire?"

"Could have been him or his accomplice. That's about it for me. How about you?"

"The gas stations were a bust. I checked with attendants at the three stations closest to Prairie Acres, and they didn't see anything. Then again, someone could have filled a tanker, and they wouldn't have noticed."

"That's typical."

"Which is why you assigned me the time-wasting task?"

"Had to pull seniority," he said affably.

I rolled my eyes. "McBride Homes, Inc., owns the Carnival house, and Dennis McBride owns 100 percent of the corporation. He's disputing an invoice from a concrete company and has withheld payment. Otherwise, he's current on construction loans and disbursements to subcontractors. I'm still researching OSHA, workers' comp, and possible code violations, but I did find out that he recently bumped insurance coverage on the house—"

"Got him!" Max said, cutting me short.

I put up a hand to slow him down. "The amount of coverage matched the rising value of the building as construction progressed. There was at least $180,000 in lumber in the house when it caught fire."

Max grimaced. "Stymied!"

"I, too, came across a silver car. Two, in fact. The week of the fire, a roofing crew on the Tuscan Villa reported seeing Dennis on the cul-de-sac every night. He usually came right before dark as workers finished up for the day."

"Clank!" Max said cheerily. "The sound of the jailhouse door slamming."

"Not necessarily. Lots of builders come to a job site at least once a day. They pay for work, and they want to make sure they receive full value. The more frequently they visit, the better the work."

"Huh," he said, unmoved.

"The other car was a silver BMW. Construction workers at the Spanish-style house told me they'd seen one drive by the day of the fire. Who should own a silver BMW but . . . "

He grinned appreciatively. "Give it to me."

"Virginia Farino."

"Ah, the ex-girlfriend."

"I went by her office yesterday and saw the car. She parks in a lot behind the Cherry Creek North Restaurant and Bar Association building, in a reserved space. The BMW had dust on its underside, maybe from the dirt roads in Prairie Acres."

Max snorted. "With the wind we've had lately, everyone's driving a dirty car. I can beat that. What would you think if I told you McBride had another arson in his past?"

"Your expanded database research came through?"

"Early this morning," he said happily. "Six years ago, McBride sold a 1968 Mustang Shelby GT500 convertible to the insurance company."

Responding to my puzzled look, he added, "That's an industry expression. Say you own something valuable, no one wants to buy it, but you need the money. What do you do? You sell your prized possession to the insurance company through theft, loss, or destruction. You'd be amazed at how many people get away with it."

"What was the car worth?"

"In mint condition, with an original factory engine and transmission, try $200,000."

I felt dizzy. "Two hundred grand?"

"You heard right. There are less than two hundred in the world. Many a man would kill for that Mustang. McBride's was candy apple red, in case you're interested."

"Six years ago?"

"You got it."

"Fascinating."

Max leaned in urgently. "What?"

"That matches the time frame of Dennis buying the land at Prairie Acres. His ex-partner, Jerry Hess, told me he kept postponing the closing because he was waiting on funds."

"Which he found sitting in his garage! Presto!"

"He could have used the check from the insurance company to exercise his option on the land. On the other hand," I said pensively, "Victoria Farino could have burned the car. The perfect comeback in a lover's quarrel."

He curled his upper lip. "You're stuck on her."

"I am," I said bluntly.

"You're wrong. Landry, Southfield, Prairie Acres, your Outback. This arsonist can't be a woman. Trust me."

"What about my burned business card?"

Max released a grudging smile. "That sounds like a woman."

CHAPTER 27

Max drove me to the nearest Avis outlet, where I left behind Sasha's car in favor of a Toyota Camry.

Taking advantage of a beautiful engine that didn't stall, I sped down Broadway Street, turned on Hampden Avenue, and followed it west as it switched to Highway 285.

Entering the mountains, I had a heavy heart.

Contrary to Richard's lies about the disappearance of his parents as revenge for a Middle Eastern assassination, Robert and Mary Leone were alive, living in Conifer, in the cabin where they'd raised Richard.

They took the news of his death as well as could be expected, as if it were expected.

Their grief wasn't raw, more a resigned replay of emotions experienced one too many times.

I asked them to contact the Denver coroner's office, outlining steps in the process, and I clarified that they wouldn't have to view the body. They would, however, need to provide Richard's childhood dental records, but I spared them Max Spiker's lesson in identifying fire victims.

Teeth were almost indestructible, able to withstand more heat than any other part of the body. A forensic odontologist would take X-rays of Richard Leone and remove his upper and lower jaws for charting purposes. The specialist would compare these to charts, X-rays, and orthodontic models provided by Richard's dentist and study the number and position of teeth, sinus cavities, nerve paths, root canals, and dental work (implants, crowns, bridges, and shape and position of fillings).

Once Richard's identity was confirmed, I explained to the Leones, the coroner would release their son's body, and they could make funeral arrangements.

They confided that they couldn't afford a service or burial, but insisted Richard would have wanted a Catholic mass and entombment, with all the trappings.

In a moment of impulse, I agreed to fulfill his wishes.

On my way out the door, I gave them the magnifying glass Kevin Slyford had found in Richard's culvert, and as they stoically passed it back and forth, they thanked me for coming.

I drove as fast as I could from Conifer back to the city, stopping only at a funeral home in southwest Denver that had served as the last stop for my parents. Blocking out the music playing quietly in the background, I made a numbing amount of decisions on Richard Leone's behalf. I picked out a midpriced silver coffin, a towering flower arrangement, and a simple Mass card. I tentatively planned a visitation and rosary at the mortuary's chapel by selecting hours, music, and deacon. I designated readings, an organist, a vocalist, and a priest for a funeral Mass. I coordinated interment at Mt. Olivet, with a funeral procession that included a coach, a limousine for the Leone family, and a two-motorcycle escort.

Mourners would never miss what was missing, I reasoned, as I declined a full choir, simultaneous webcast, memorial website, and countless other options that could have honored my "loved one."

I walked out of the mortuary with a staggering price quote, blurred vision from a splitting headache, and three urgent messages on voice mail from Sasha.

I returned her call on the spot and obtained the designated location for my long-awaited meeting with 11-up.

•••

At four o'clock, I came face-to-face with the graffiti artist Saul Eichelberg had seen participating in the LoDo wilding incident.

We met at the Spoken Word, a coffee shop and performance space on East Colfax Avenue, and twenty minutes into our first pot of tea, I hadn't recovered from the shock.

No one had bothered to tell me that 11-up was a teenage girl named Tanza Lloyd.

The fact was at once obvious despite her height and build and shiny, hairless head. She had dark skin, thick eyebrows, a dazzling smile, and vibrant eyes. She wore a nose ring on the side of one nostril, hoop earrings the size of saucers, and a tie-dyed button-down shirt and full-length white skirt.

Her mellifluous voice justified the headliner gig she'd landed for the upcoming rap poetry night. "They drive their Beemers and Benzes in from safe land to live it up large one night a week, all ghetto. To bend and grind and show their di-versity and tol-erance, and we put the fear into them. It was hi-larious. Better stay in your gated communities, where we can't get to you. You can come down to our urban den, but we won't be going back to your hood. Not in without a police escort out. You can take our hip-hop culture and man-ipulate it. We'll sell it to you, but we can't afford to buy it back. Where, oh Lord, is the justice in that? On Market Street, on one hot August night, I made a social state-ment."

"Which was?"

"Folks are racist. Deep in their bones, stem cell to marrow. You know who was in LoDope that night? Me and my homeboys. Two blacks, two Latinos, two Asians, and four Caucasians. Affirmative action, I say, but what did the blind people see? Young black men out of control. They sighted people of color and said gangs and gunplay. Perception colored everything, changing brown and white to black. What's that say about race in this city, all that flack?"

I pushed back my chair and crossed my legs. "Nothing positive."

"We're chillin' at 7-Eleven, on the street corner, in the park, we scare people. The thirteen- to eighteen-year-old children of color, we're people's worst fear because of our skin, a reason no other. White boys and girls, you see them, they're football players, boy scouts, missionaries, and cheerleaders. Us, you click on drug dealers, crackheads, gangbangers, and whores."

"Who led the wilding?"

"That be me," she said proudly. "It was street theater, an extension of my hustle. Me and ten homies messin' it up in peace. 11-up we branded ourselves, after my tag."

"What's your tag mean?"

She cocked her head and paused. "Nothing, but ain't it pimp? I feel it."

"Did you have any idea the wilding would get out of control?"

Her eyes narrowed into threatening slits. "It did not. That's what's suspicious. We were ballin' with our rehearsed moves. Kinky's the karate king with a black belt, and he showed us how to pull up punches and kicks. No one was supposed to get hurt. We were grabbing at each other, pushing, yelling, cursing, playing it up like a Kung Fu movie. We had it taken care of until Rambo came along."

"The man who was injured?"

Tanza laughed scornfully. "Stinky's elbow caught his nose, and that cat falls to the ground, blood gushing."

"Joseph Verre claims someone grabbed his arm, twisted it, and caused a spiral fracture."

She shrugged and smiled engagingly. "High props for the man's lies, but he ran up on the wrong one, that's all. Wet dreams look good to his girl, maybe. An injury in combat, all that shit, but he tripped and fell. Crash, boom, bang, ow-ie, mama make it better. He probably got some extra lovin' that night."

"The supposed victims in the car weren't victims. They were part of 11-up?"

Her smile widened. "Co-rrect. Little Man's brother fixes cars, and he parted with a beater Riviera for a Ben Franklin. Cruiser and Nasty peel up in the beater, and the rest of us break out back windows, stomp the hood and trunk, harmless funk. Cruiser leans on the horn and revs the engine. We're kids foolin' around, but it becomes an al-tercation, now a racial thang. How's that? Po-lice behave badly, media gets video, take stills out of context, and now who has the light shinin' on 'em? Not me, nope! It was dope."

"You seem pretty pleased with yourself," I said placidly.

Tanza threw up her hands in celebration. "It's all about the race. Supremacist websites across the U.S. of A. are using this in their crusade against people of color. Isn't that con-venient? 11-up had four white kids in it, but they don't see them. Lit-er-ally, they don't see them. Some ex-cop in Iowa called for a hate-crimes investigation. Hate crimes against whites, ain't that just not right, when Cruiser and Nasty, the so-called vic-tims, are my black brothers? Mouths on talk radio blame it on hip-hop, and I laugh,

laugh my ass off. We shook it up for one night, and the masters of the estate have to fuss about how to set it right. Payday told me bar owners hired you because they don't like cops trampling their playground. Live a day in my spinning, grinning world. Do you know why the po-lice haven't arrested anyone in 11-up?"

I shook my head.

"They have pictures, and they can't ident-i-fy us, because no one has a record or street cred. Not one soldier in 11-up. We're all clean," she said, slicing an index finger through the air. "This was a demonstration, an act of un-civil disobedience. I knew our rights cold to frozen if they cuffed us. Public fighting, deferred judgment, plead guilty, stay out of trouble for a year, record wiped clean. Spielberg had film rolling, and he made the tape as proof. The cops ill-egally confiscated the camera and tape. They know what went down, but look at what they play to the masses. Truth sliced into lies, shame on their asses."

"Too bad you don't have a copy of the tape."

"Pre-cisely," she said mournfully, hanging her head. "Measure it up frame-by-frame to a flash mob. You know it, that's what I was gonna do."

"Flash mobs? The ones that organize over the Internet and meet for pranks?"

"Pranks, you say." Tanza became more animated. "When they're milk-colored from the middle classes, everyone gives them passes. They meet at a supermarket and stare at fruit for two minutes, then dis-band. They meet at a park and wave their arms and act like Super-man. They meet on top of a parking garage and throw origami birds to the street below. Do you be-lieve anyone charges them with trespassing, littering, or causing a public disturb-ance?"

She paused, leaned across the table, and shook her upper body. "Do you? If one of the paper birds had distracted a pedestrian, and he fell off the sidewalk and broke his arm, would the po-lice show up in riot gear at every lunch hour to prevent a re-occurr-ence? Would the media portray the epi-sode as an epi-demic? You know not. We live in a racist society, born in and perpetuated by the media. Admit it, one and all, I came up with a way for others to take the fall."

I looked at Tanza Lloyd keenly and wondered how many years had passed since I'd felt that much passion, about anything. I raised my eyebrows and said with a sigh, "I can understand why Saul Eichelberg didn't turn you in to the police."

"Saul wouldn't do me that way," she said, grinning. "He supports the move-ment."

I returned the smile. "As long as you don't tag his alley."

She didn't blink. "I'm into other things now."

"With someone else's backing," I said pointedly. "Do you have other projects planned with your patron?"

Tanza dropped my gaze. "LoDo was a one-up. Time next for hiber-nation."

"Whoever paid you to stage the wilding incident isn't your partner anymore?"

"Never was, cuz," she said, a five-second intermission between words. "We were going in the same direction and caught a ride."

"How much were you paid?"

She glared. "A tainted token, but that takes no stripes off of me. I had to pass out bills for the car and videocam and my brother conspirators. Some would have joined for the sake of the revo-lution, but not all. They had free will, their call. I came to the game with a track on my crack."

I frowned in confusion. "What are you talking about?"

"My pa-tron, as you call her, caught me taggin' a building in CC. She told me I could do her bidding and go on about my business, or she'd start me a rap sheet. Ain't that sweet?"

My heart skipped a beat. "You're telling me a woman in Cherry Creek forced you to do this?"

Tanza's voice deepened. "Forcibly per-suaded."

"What's her name?"

"PR-ho. She's all up in that, pros-ti-tut-ing herself for titans."

"I need a name."

"Find out for yourself. Every gangsta got her day, but that's not my way."

I wanted to put my hands down Tanza's throat and pull out the words. "A name!"

She looked away, as if the subject had ceased to interest her.

I gazed at Tanza steadily, and she jutted her chin aggressively.

"Farino. Victoria," she said eventually. "But ya'll don't be wantin' none of her."

CHAPTER 28

"I'll take it from here," Roxanne Archuletta said an hour later, as I straddled a bar stool at Sports Fanatics.

"What will you do?"

"First off, call the cops on the girl, 11-up or whatever her name is."

I shook my head. "Tanza Lloyd, and that might not be such a good idea."

She cast a sideways glance as she filled three glasses with Coors. "Give me one good reason why."

"I'll give you several," I said, shelling peanuts and lining them up in a row. "I'm not sure we have enough to convict Tanza of anything. Maybe aiding, abetting, or encouraging a riot, but she has valid points about race and what constitutes a riot. You don't want to get in the middle of a debate you can't win, especially if it's played out in the media. Business is picking up, isn't it?"

"Look around," she said, motioning toward the thick crowd. "This is the first normal Saturday I've had in a month."

"Don't jeopardize that."

She set the beers on a tray. "You want me to pretend this girl didn't do anything?"

I ate ten peanuts, in one swallow, and washed them down with a sip of Heineken. "How would you feel about a mural?"

"Come again?"

"Tanza's a talented artist, and the north side of your building could use some sprucing up."

She threw her head back and laughed. "Oh, you think, do you?"

I smiled impishly. "Maybe she could paint something, as a form of restitution. One for you and every other business owner affected by the wilding."

"She's talented?"

"The best."

Roxanne shrugged, wiped the counter next to me, and threw the towel over her shoulder. "I'll think about it."

"What about Victoria Farino? What do you want to do about her?"

"Don't get me started." Her face darkened. "For one, I'll get her fired. A call to the cock-and-rob should take care of that. Two, I'll make sure she never works in Denver again. Three, I'll talk to the owners in LoDo Business Interests and find out if they want to sue her for everything she's got. Four'll come to me after that."

"If I could ask a favor . . . "

"What?" she said, with an acquiescent smile. "Not leniency again?"

"No, but could you hold off until the end of the week?"

She took my hands in hers and bent forward. "The owners are counting on me. I need something."

I squeezed back. "Seven days. That's all I ask."

"This has something to do with the other angle you're working, the one you can't talk about?"

"It does."

Our eyes met, and she sighed heavily. "I'm such a sucker."

Before I could reply, she'd excused herself to serve two regulars who'd squeezed through the throng.

Watching Roxanne Archuletta expertly mix margaritas, my mind took a dangerous turn, and I thought about sleeping with her.

I wondered if she snored.

God, how long had it been since I'd had sex?

I didn't care about body shape, technique, or stamina—only a quiet night's sleep afterward.

Something was wrong with me.

•••

I slept by myself that night, deeply and satisfyingly, failing to rise until close to noon.

I ate a late breakfast of hot oatmeal and cold sesame noodles and puttered around my apartment for hours.

When I'd run out of distractions and had to face my next task, I shuffled out the door to Urban Transitions, the homeless shelter run by Kim Reed, the woman whose business card I'd found in Richard Leone's shelter.

I drove to the industrial, one-story building near 6th Avenue and I-25 and cut through a queue of men waiting for the doors to open at five. A few stood independently, but most needed the structure for support and were sitting or lying against the side of the building.

Kim Reed answered my buzz, escorted me through the facility, and invited me to join her team in evening preparations.

I agreed, with decided reluctance.

Was I the only one who could smell urine, ammonia, and chicken fried steak commingling?

I adapted by taking small, infrequent inhales through my mouth, hoping the smell wouldn't cling to my throat. This was a slight improvement from earlier, when I'd held my breath to make it past the tang of vomit at the entrance.

While a swarm of volunteers cooked dinner, finished up the day's laundry, and restocked a first aid station, Kim and I toiled at cot duty. In a large open room—with exposed rafters, concrete floors, and massive steam radiators—cots were lined up in rows, barracks style, each with a wooden locker at its foot. As we made up the cots, an elderly man hobbled behind us and placed a folded towel and rag on each pillow.

"Six hundred to nine hundred people sleep on the streets each night, some in life-threatening cold," Kim said, snapping open a bedsheet. "Forty percent are homeless for the first time. Our programs are designed to restore independence, not create dependence."

"By providing food and shelter?"

"Fundamentally, but we also have general health services, mental health programs, substance abuse counseling, job training, life skills workshops, parenting classes. Contrary to public opinion, people in this predicament aren't all drug addicts or alcoholics. Many suffer from mental illness, medical conditions, or disabilities."

I helped Kim spread a white cotton sheet, and we tucked in the corners. "When did you meet Richard Leone?"

"About a year ago. I knew he was respected within the homeless community, and I asked him to serve on a committee the mayor formed. Richard's attendance was sporadic, but he offered interesting perspectives. Many of his ideas were visionary."

We moved in tandem to the next cot. "Was Richard sober at the meetings?"

She pushed a smile. "Sometimes. At the first meeting, he floated the idea of a tent city next to the South Platte River. I helped him draft a proposal, which city officials rejected, but it sparked the mayor to push for an initiative to end homelessness in ten years."

I looked at her skeptically. "Is that possible?"

"I don't see why not," she said, tossing back her head. Her black hair, long and parted in the middle, resembled a witch's wig, without the shine, and a pasty complexion, black lipstick, and deep-set dark eyes added to the sorcerer's look. In her forties, she had a short, bulky body, stubby fingers, and distressed skin. She wore brown slacks that were too short, an orange knit top that had gone out of style, and black zip-up ankle boots that needed polishing.

"How could you eliminate homelessness in ten years?"

"By redirecting money from programs already funded. Every cent the mayor intends to spend, we spend already, on triage. We house the homeless in jail, we pay emergency medical bills at Denver Health, we place children with the state, we pay for overnight detox visits. The ten-year plan is a more commonsense, proactive approach. It creates 3,200 transitional housing units and 1,500 extra beds in emergency shelters. Housing has to come first, before we can begin to address underlying problems."

"Wouldn't the program encourage homeless people from outside the area to seek services in Denver?"

"What else can we do?" Kim retorted. "Ignore the problem? In 1988, an estimated two thousand homeless lived in the metro area. Today, we have eleven thousand."

Ten cots down, ninety to go. "Do you know what led to Richard living on the streets?"

She shook her head. "He never said, and I never asked. Some want out of the life, but he didn't."

"Did he stay here often?"

"From time to time he would come by for Sunday dinner, but that was the limit of the charity he'd accept, as he phrased it," she said, with a reminiscent smile.

I slid a case on a one-inch-thick pillow. "What were some of Richard's ideas?"

"Last winter, he proposed opening public buildings as emergency shelters. He spoke in front of Denver City Council on the issue. Whenever the temperature dropped below zero, Richard wanted to let the homeless come inside, into vacant schools and government buildings. The Council refused to approve the necessary zoning changes."

"Why?"

"You'd have to ask them, but let them spend one night under a viaduct and justify how they can lock the doors of heated buildings. Let them spend one day without a meal and explain how they can refuse to feed hungry people with food they'd rather throw away."

I rubbed my back, sore from bending. "I don't see how—"

"The Catholic shelter holds a lottery every morning for one room. One family wins and is allowed to stay indoors. The rest, most with young children, ride the bus until the shelter reopens at 5 p.m. That's the best we can do, as individuals and a community, in the twenty-first century? It's reprehensible."

"But what would—"

Kim spoke with her hands, as if signing for the hearing impaired. "Tonight, when the citizens of Denver snuggle into their beds with bellies that are too full, they should realize something. Only a thin line separates them from the clients we serve who eat out of and sleep in Dumpsters. One illness, one death, one job loss—some people rebound, others don't. Should we discard those who can't? We couldn't if we tried. What are we meant to do with individuals who have layers of chronic problems? We have a duty to help them merge back into society. I learned that from Richard. Most homeless people want to reconnect, in a meaningful way, not separate."

"Richard must have challenged people's perceptions."

"He did," Kim said passionately. "His latest project was an outdoor slumber party to promote awareness of the issue. He imagined people from all economic backgrounds gathering on the west steps of the Capitol to spend one night outdoors. He got support from churches, from shelters, and from men and women in the homeless community."

"A winter night?"

She nodded. "December 21, the longest night of the year. I'm hoping we can follow through with the event, perhaps in his memory. Months ago, I put him in touch with a board member who specializes in publicity. They met here once a week to brainstorm." Kim Reed drew in a sharp breath. "I'll have to call Victoria to tell her Richard passed away."

I felt like clapping. "Victoria?"

"Victoria Farino."

"Richard Leone knew Victoria Farino?"

"They were inseparable," Kim Reed said sadly, having missed the exultation in my voice.

CHAPTER 29

Monday morning, I spent hours creating a timeline for Victoria Farino, Dennis McBride, Richard Leone, and the fires at Landry, Southfield, and Prairie Acres.

The intersection of lives and crimes was intriguing, and when I inserted the burned business card left on my windshield and the obliteration of my Outback, telling patterns began to emerge.

I couldn't wait for my one o'clock appointment with Dennis McBride, but apparently he didn't feel the same.

He kept me waiting for fifteen minutes outside his office before greeting me with bluster. "I want to know where you are with this case. What the—"

I spoke over him. "Did you know that your ex-girlfriend, Victoria Farino, was friends with Richard Leone?"

"Who?" he blasted.

"The homeless man you liked to badger. Remember him? He was about five-eight, one hundred pounds. He rode around on a bike with a trailer, and you threw rocks at him. What did you do with the bike?"

Dennis glowered. "Glenn tossed it in the trash, where it belongs."

I eyed Dennis carefully. "You don't think Richard will be needing it?"

"From the grave, no. The son of a bitch died in my Carnival house. A detective interrogated me about it for two hours yesterday."

"With your attorney present?"

"No, but I'll damn well bring him to the next conversation. The cop had a bright idea that I hired a vagrant to burn down my houses in Landry and Southfield. Supposedly, we had a falling out, and I drove him to my Carnival home, liquored him up, and set the house on fire. Why would I do that when

231

I'm rebuilding all three properties? I gain nothing. Besides which, can you see me partnering with a derelict who slept in a storm drain?"

"No," I said frankly.

"I have to clean out that human dump." Dennis took a comb out of his top desk drawer and ran it through his hair. "I was there yesterday. What a sty. He lived like a stray dog."

"Is the culvert on your property?"

"It belongs to the Landry Redevelopment Authority, but it's dragging down all of our property values."

"Yesterday's visit wasn't your first to Richard's shelter, was it?"

Dennis measured me. "I'd been there a few times, to make sure the bum wasn't stealing anything from my job sites."

"Was he?"

His mouth turned downward. "Not that I could prove."

"Then I'll take this," I said, reaching for the Mercedes emblem on the bookshelf behind me, the one Kevin Slyford coveted.

Blood rushed to Dennis McBride's face, but he didn't protest.

"Did the police ask about your past arsons?"

"We've been over this," he said crossly. "I owned 4 percent of the partnership on Sherman Street—"

"But 100 percent of a classic convertible Shelby that burned in a fire of undetermined origin. Who set that blaze six years ago?"

He stared me down. "You tell me. I cried when I lost that car, and I didn't cry when my father died."

"If you didn't do it, then your ex-girlfriend must have. Did something prompt Victoria to destroy the Mustang?"

Dennis became expressionless. "Like what?"

"An argument, jealousy."

His eyes flashed. "I had so many knock-down, drag-out fights with that woman, I can't remember them all. Nothing came easy with her. The night we hooked up, she made me swear if she died first, I'd turn her cremated remains into a diamond. How's that for crazy?"

Before I could comment, he spoke again, loudly. "She wouldn't sign a prenuptial, she harped on me about kids, she accused me of having problems with intimacy, she dragged me to a couples counselor. That was the story for eight years. She was thirty-nine going on nine when I met her and forty-seven going on seven when I left her. The drama never ended."

"I need to verify several dates," I said, pulling out a pocket-size appointment book. "When did you ask Marla to marry you?"

"June 1, but what's that got to do with anything?"

"Did you have an engagement party?"

"A small get-together."

"When?"

"Hell if I know," he said loudly. "Sometime in June. So what!"

I managed an uptight smile. "Could you look in your calendar?"

Dennis reached for his Blackberry. "Saturday, June 10. Satisfied?"

"The day before the Landry fire," I said lightly. "Was Victoria at the party?"

"Did I lose my mind and invite her? No."

Despite the meanness in his tone, I kept mine neutral. "Could she have heard about it?"

He balanced his elbow on the arm of his chair, rested one cheek against his hand, and shrugged. "We have mutual friends. Someone may have told her."

"How about your wedding? Wasn't that Saturday, September 3?"

He sat up straight. "Where are you going with this?"

I didn't flinch. "And on Wednesday, September 7, the Southfield house burned."

"Victoria wasn't invited to the wedding," he said condescendingly.

I cocked an eyebrow. "How many people were there?"

Dennis clenched his jaw. "Three hundred and fifty, but she didn't necessarily know about it."

I groaned. "She knew."

"Forget this," he said blandly.

"I can't. I believe Victoria set the fires, with Richard Leone's help."

His voice faded. "I've told you before, move on!"

"You hired me to get to the bottom of this," I said, with little emotion. "I'm down to two suspects: you and Victoria. I need to turn one of you over to the police. Any preference?"

Dennis McBride's face twisted violently. "I'll fix this. Be at my house tonight at six."

"Should I call Max and tell him to meet us there?"

"Come alone."

•••

"It's him," Max Spiker said convivially a few hours later.

"It's her."

"Never pegged you as a dog person."

"I'm not," I said, rubbing Pepper's belly with my foot as she lay on her back, all four paws in the air. "I rescued her from Richard Leone's culvert. Sasha wants to keep her, but I'm taking her to the pound. They'll find her a good home."

He tapped on the glass of the aquarium. "Mind if I feed the fish?"

"Feel free. Do you see two black ones?"

"Yep."

"Alive?"

"Yes, ma'am. Swimming at a good clip." He took a pinch of food and spread it across the tank. "I've got Dennis McBride dead to rights."

"Listen to me! It's Victoria Farino."

"What's her motive?"

"Revenge. What's his?"

Max moved to the couch, where he lounged in a narrow beam of midafternoon sun. "Aberrant behavior."

"What kind of answer is that?"

"You want simple, easy-to-understand words? He screws his partner. He screws his girlfriend. He screws his employees. He screws his buyers. He screws his subs. He screws charities, for Chrissake! He steals for kicks. He's tied to five arsons. The building on Sherman Street, the Shelby, Landry, Southfield, and Prairie Acres. Most people don't have any experience with arson. He's had more than his share."

"Granted," I said begrudgingly, "but that's because of his character flaws. He attracts calamity. Maybe he set fire to the office building and car, but not the three houses. I know Victoria Farino did this."

"What makes you so smart?"

"The timeline explains it all," I said excitedly, handing him an Excel spreadsheet Sasha had created to help me sort it all out. "Dennis McBride dumps Victoria Farino on Valentine's Day. In March, her friend Anna Cedra confronts her about a diamond ring she stole from donations for Pedro Herrera, the boy who needed the transplant."

"Very Freudian."

"Right around that time, she's fired from Alameda Mall for making racist remarks, and Dennis informs her that he's met someone and fallen in love."

Max wiggled his eyebrows. "The start of the meltdown."

"Victoria's life worsens over the summer, just as she meets Richard Leone. In June, she finds out that Dennis is engaged. She responds by burning his house in Landry or having Richard do it. I'm not certain on the particulars. Maybe they both participated." I waved my hands impatiently. "In July, bar owners in LoDo mislead her with the possibility of a job that never materializes. In August, she retaliates by getting 11-up and her followers to stage a wilding incident."

"You can prove that?"

"The wilding, yes." I took a hurried breath and continued. "Labor Day weekend, Victoria's boyfriend of eight years marries the love of his life, and it's not her. Four days later, Victoria torches his Southfield house."

Max pinched his lower lip with his front teeth. "Makes sense, but I've been doing this a long time. I'm going with my gut."

"You're wrong," I said touchily.

His eyes contracted. "Care to place a wager on which one of our suspects is charged with first-degree arson and first-degree murder: Dennis McBride or Victoria Farino?"

"Not especially."

"It's him."

"It's her."

•••

Throughout the afternoon, I felt nervous about my upcoming appointment with Dennis McBride, and I even debated canceling it or asking Max Spiker to join me.

In the end, though, intent on catching a killer (and maintaining my independence), I arrived at Dennis McBride's house a few minutes before six, alone.

My anxiety jumped up another notch when I spotted the silver BMW stationed at the end of the circle drive.

CHAPTER 30

I had a sickening feeling as I walked up to the side of Victoria Farino's car and tapped on the glass.

When she rolled down the passenger window, we exchanged pleasantries, and she invited me to join her in the car.

With my heart pounding, I climbed in next to her.

Desperate to ignore what lay in the backseat, I coped by absorbing other meaningless details. I observed Victoria's hollow cheeks and vacant eyes. The long, blonde mane, blown out and curled. The white lace bustier, pink suede jacket, tight black jeans, and silver stilettos. The tiny velvet purse with a fuchsia smiley face.

"How are you?" I said gingerly.

"Feeling stressed. You?"

I swallowed hard. "I've had better days."

"I've been naughty," she said flirtatiously.

"I can see that."

Victoria raised her eyes languidly. "I lied to you."

I put my hands to my head and forced a breath. "Really?"

"I did cause the mischief in LoDo." She studied the flawless manicure on her right hand, then began to drum her nails on the steering wheel. "I had to teach that LoDo group a lesson, that they needed me and they'd be sorry without me," she said, no inflection in her voice. "In my interview, I told them they were one crisis away from losing everything. When they didn't believe me, I showed them. I had no other choice."

"You didn't stage the wildings to push business to Cherry Creek North?"

She smiled shyly. "Maybe just a teeny bit."

My throat felt dry. "You also set three fires, didn't you? At Landry, Southfield, and Prairie Acres."

"Only one of those. I delegated the others."

"Richard Leone started the Landry and Southfield fires," I said, more a statement than a question. "How did you become partners?"

"Fate brought us together at Urban Transitions," she said sweetly. "Richard attended one of our board meetings and informed us about the way certain people treated the homeless. He never named anyone, but I knew he was speaking about Dennis. I'd heard the stories before, from my boyfriend who used to brag about what he did to trespassers, and I realized that Richard was one of the poor men he'd bullied. At the end of the meeting, I approached Richard and told him we were both victims of Dennis McBride."

"Whose idea was it to set fire to McBride houses?"

"Richard said he wished Dennis knew what it felt like to lose everything, and I suggested we teach him a lesson. I can't recall specifics, but somehow, we went from there. After Richard heard everyone thought Landry was an accident, we had to send Dennis the message again. What else could we do?"

"By burning his house in Southfield?"

Victoria nodded blissfully. "Richard and I made a good team. I bought the supplies and pushed him to do the work. He tended to forget things, silly man."

"And both of you were at the Carnival fire?"

"Of course! That was a wonderful experience, wasn't it?"

My shoulders tightened. "You watched?"

She dropped her head and looked at me sideways. "I wouldn't have missed it for the world. I drove down the road and parked near an abandoned farmhouse. What a sight, all the emergency vehicles racing to the fire with flashing lights and sirens. If only I could have stayed on the cul-de-sac," she said wistfully. "I saw you drive by. What was it like up close?"

"Destructive."

"There's something cleansing about fire, wouldn't you agree?"

"Not necessarily," I said flatly.

She unleashed a withering look. "It signifies rebirth. Look at forest fires, the most perfect example in nature. Lightning strikes, trees burn, ashes settle, seeds sprout, and saplings grow."

"Fire didn't do much for my Outback," I said resentfully.

Victoria laughed mirthlessly. "Can you forgive me? I was a bad girl. I needed to buy time after I saw you rummaging through Richard's camp."

"Why did you kill Richard in the Carnival fire?"

She met my stare. "He wanted to die."

"I doubt that."

"Look at how he lived, he was killing himself. That night, we had a few drinks and laughs, and he passed out. As I was leaving, I lit candles for him," she said indifferently. "His death was painless, much more peaceful than his life."

"Had he threatened to expose you?"

She tossed back her hair. "Richard wouldn't have done that. He had the cutest crush on me. He'd do anything I asked."

"Was he on the verge of confiding in me?" I persisted. "The day of the Carnival fire, someone called from a pay phone and hung up three times. It was Richard, wanting to confess, hoping I'd intervene, wasn't it?"

"You are precious," Victoria said, with a high giggle. "That was Richard following my explicit instructions. At ten o'clock, noon, and two, if I'm not mistaken."

"Something like that," I said tersely.

"When he was sober, he was very obedient. How did you like the gift he left on your windshield?"

"My own card, burned? Richard didn't do that. After he died, I found the card in his shelter."

"That was the card you gave me," she said affectionately. "He burned his and left it as a warning, which you shouldn't have ignored. I gave him the other card so he'd have your phone number for his little ring-and-run prank."

I shook my head furiously. "Why are you here, Victoria?"

She lowered her voice to a seductive level. "Take a guess."

CHAPTER 31

I remained mute, refusing to give her the satisfaction of an answer.

Victoria Farino gazed ahead dreamily. "By the way, do you like my boyfriend's new house?"

I glanced at the modern-day stone castle, complete with three-story turret and four chimneys. "It's too big."

"But it feels cozy inside."

Goosebumps formed on my arms. "How do you know?"

"I'm imagining," she said lightly. "Dennis described it to me. Did you know it's 16,000 square feet and sits on two acres? It went on the market three years ago for $14 million. Guess what he paid?"

"Less than that," I said lamely. How would I know? I'd never helped anyone buy or sell a home in the Polo Grounds, the most prestigious neighborhood in Denver.

"It's been under contract twice, but the buyers couldn't get financing. That's the only clue I'll give. Now guess," she said meanly.

My throat constricted. "I don't want to do this."

"The first time we met, you told me you had twenty years' experience in real estate. Isn't this what you like to do?"

"Not anymore." I paused. "Maybe $11.5 million."

"Too high. Only $8 million," Victoria said childishly. "Can you believe it? You couldn't build this house for less than $12 million. Dennis is quite proud of himself for the acquisition. The craftsmanship inside is supposed to be superb. If it matches the gorgeous exterior . . . goodness! I'm dying to see the inside, aren't you?"

"Not particularly."

Her eyes had a wild look. "Let's go ring the bell. Dennis will show us his six garage bays, one with a lubrication pit. That's his favorite feature, other than the screened-in summer cottage at the back of the lot. He's assured me that I'll drool over the mountain views, the swimming pool with infinity edge, and the five-room wine cellar. The kitchen's equipped to serve two hundred, although I'll need catering help. It has Euro cabinets and a fireplace. One of nine fireplaces in the house. Sixteen bathrooms, too. Not to mention a movie theater and bowling alley. Let's help ourselves, shall we?"

This was beyond torturous. "You know we can't do that," I said despairingly.

Victoria let out an acidic laugh. "Oh, but we most certainly may. Dennis invited me for cocktails. He didn't say anything about bringing a friend, but I'm sure he won't mind. He wants me to meet his new bride. If I give her a chance, he knows I'll like her. Everyone does."

I looked at Victoria with loathing.

"If you don't believe me, ask him," she said, handing me her cell phone. "Press two."

I complied, and after three rings, Dennis came on the line. "Victoria?"

"Dennis, it's Lauren Vellequette." My voice sounded strangled. "Are you home?"

"Where else would I be? We have a meeting at six. How did you get Victoria's phone?"

"Hi, Denny," Victoria called out brightly.

"We're here together."

"Where?"

"At the end of your driveway," I said, with difficulty.

He sounded confused. "You came together?"

"No, but we are now. Did you invite Victoria to stop by for a drink?"

"Yes, but—"

"Why did you invite me at the same time?"

"So you could see that we're both innocent—"

I interrupted. "Where's Marla?"

"At the doctor's. I expect her any minute."

Victoria whispered something to me.

I focused on Dennis again. "Where are you in the house?"

"Upstairs. In my study."

"Can you come down to the living room and stand by the picture window? Victoria wants to wave to you."

"What's going on?"

"I need you to listen to me," I said urgently. "When you come downstairs, you'll see me and Victoria in her car. What you won't be able to make out is that she's filled the backseat with one- and two-gallon containers, which, I'm assuming from the vapors, are full of gasoline."

Victoria nodded in delight. "The trunk, too."

"I'm coming out there!"

I remained calm. "I wouldn't do that, if I were you."

Dennis appeared in front of the bay window and stood still.

Utterly still.

Victoria waved at him, a baby wave, but he didn't wave back.

"What does she want?" he muttered to me, as if lowering his voice would help.

"What did he say?"

My breathing became shallow. "He wants to know what you want."

"I want to be friends," she said, with a joyful sigh. "He wants me to be happy for him, and I am. He told me this afternoon that he hoped I could find happiness, too. Well, I have. At long last. Eternal."

As she spoke, she reached into the driver's side cup holder and retrieved a sixteen-ounce water bottle. "Care for a sip?"

"No, thanks," I said nervously, noting the darkish yellow color of liquid.

She began to squirt the contents on herself, and I almost passed out from the fumes.

"We said we'd be together forever, and we will be."

Dennis spoke again, loudly. "What's going on out there?"

"Get out of the house," I implored.

"I'm not going anywhere."

Sweat trickled below my ears. "Leave, Dennis. Go now."

He didn't shift position. Not an inch. "Tell Victoria I can't help it. I fell in love."

I shook my head in disgust.

"She'll find someone," he continued, in an avuncular tone.

Victoria flashed me a saccharine smile. "You'd better get out of the car."

My hands and feet went numb. "I'm staying."

She aimed the bottle at me menacingly, and a dribble hit my pants. "I'd rather you didn't. I don't want to be a stickler, but you didn't bring a gift. Dennis deserves a housewarming present."

"To go along with his engagement and wedding presents, the Landry and Southfield fires?"

Something flickered in her eyes. "I couldn't let such special occasions slip by unnoticed."

"Victoria, please—" I begged, hoarse with emotion.

She sprayed me with gasoline, and I scrambled out of the car.

As she started the engine, I thrust my head through the window. "Don't do this!"

I heard sirens in the background.

Thank God! Dennis must have called 911 from a landline.

In seconds, the nightmare would end. Help would arrive. Police officers with training in hostage situations. Firefighters with lifesaving water.

"I'm going to drive up and say 'hi.' Dennis won't mind if I'm a few minutes early," Victoria said, revving the engine.

"Victoria, please, he's not worth it."

"I'm worth it," she said resolutely, but her words barely registered.

Out of the corner of my eye, I saw something that filled me with terror.

On the street behind us, a silver Audi A8 approached at slow speed.

In seconds, Marla McBride would be pulling into the driveway.

I looked toward the picture window and saw that Dennis had realized the same thing.

He began to shout into the phone, his voice catching. "Marla's pregnant, Victoria. I'm going to be a dad! You always told me I'd make a good father."

Victoria Farino heard every word.

Letting loose a full-body shudder, she put the car into drive, and with me clinging to the frame of the door, she pressed the accelerator.

I let go when the car lurched forward, and she continued at full speed.

Up the drive.

Across the lawn.

Into the house.

244

•••

My memories of what happened next became tangled fragments that I've tried at once to remember and forget.

Marla McBride, staggering out of her car, running toward the house. Me, tackling her on the grass, her body collapsing into a ball. Horror disfiguring her face, tears pouring out in streams.

Black smoke spiraling in the air. A wall of red flames growing. Intense heat searing my skin. Balls of fire shooting in the sky. Debris flying everywhere.

Whenever I replayed the images, they showed up in slow motion, out of sequence, without sound.

I could imagine, but never heard, the boom of the explosion, the scream of the sirens, the wails of grief.

Firefighters told me I should be proud I saved the life of Marla McBride and her unborn child, but I couldn't help feeling I should have saved three more.

Richard Leone.

Dennis McBride.

Victoria Farino.

JENNIFER L. JORDAN

CHAPTER 32

Two weeks have passed since the day I almost died.

It seems like longer.

Thankfully, each day brings another shred of normalcy.

Within hours of Victoria Farino's murder-suicide, I stopped by Sports Fanatics, and Roxanne Archuletta and I began what has now been a fourteen-night stand. And counting.

I'm planning to train for a triathlon . . . starting someday soon. I gave Taylor $200 for the aquarium, and she returned my bike. I haven't repaired the flat, but I will eventually.

Max Spiker alleges he wants to get into shape, too, and he'll start running with me. For the moment, though, he's busy applying for reinstatement with the Metro Fire Bureau. He calls or stops by every few days to see how I'm doing . . . and to check on the fish.

Both black fish are still alive, but that might change soon. Rollie Austin's supposed to come over this afternoon, and she's in a foul mood, a lingering side effect of the Ms. Senior America pageant. She came in second and has been calling herself the "first loser" ever since.

As suspected, the remains found in Dennis McBride's Carnival home were positively identified as Richard Leone. The state of Colorado paid for a simple burial at Mt. Olivet, and I wrote a check for the obscene amount on the mortuary quote but instead gave it to Kim Reed to establish a program in Richard's name.

That's about it.

Oh, I almost forgot.

I decided to keep Pepper.

She comes to work with me every day, and Sasha and I divide custody at night, shuttling her between apartments.

She's gained a little weight, but it looks good on her.

Must be those java chip Frappuccinos.

About the Author

Jennifer L. Jordan is the author of the Lauren Vellequette Mystery Series and the Kristin Ashe Mystery Series.

She is a Golden Crown Literary Society (GCLS) Finalist as well as a two-time Lambda Literary Award Finalist. In 2008, she was awarded the Alice B. Readers Appreciation Award for her contributions to lesbian fiction.

Self-employed since the age of twenty-one, Jennifer has taught thousands of people how to start and run their own small businesses. She currently owns a marketing and consulting firm that specializes in search engine optimization (SEO).

As a teenager, Jennifer developed an interest in real estate, and over the years, she's participated in dozens of successful real estate investments and transactions.

Jennifer enjoys snowboarding, cross-country skiing, hiking, golfing, and collecting watches. She divides her time between homes in Winter Park and Denver, Colorado.

For more information or to read excerpts from her books,
visit http://www.jenniferljordan.com.

Clover Valley Press
publishes quality books written by women.

CLOVER
VALLEY
PRESS

For more information about our books, go to
http://clovervalleypress.com